METAL HEADS

METAL HEADS

A NOVEL

Tom Maremaa

CLEARWATER I FL I USA

For information, contact Kunati Inc., Book Publishers in Canada.
USA: 13575 58th Street North, Suite 200, Clearwater, FL 33760-3721 USA
Canada: 75 First Street, Suite 128, Orangeville, ON L9W 5B6 CANADA.
E-mail: info@kunati.com.

FIRST EDITION

Designed by Kam Wai Yu
Persona Corp. | www.personaco.com

ISBN 978-1-60164-170-0   EAN 9781601641700
Fiction

Published by Kunati Inc. (USA) and Kunati Inc. (Canada).
Provocative. Bold. Controversial.™

http://www.kunati.com

TM—Kunati and Kunati Trailer are trademarks owned by Kunati Inc.
Persona is a trademark owned by Persona Corp.
All other trademarks are the property of their respective owners.

Library of Congress Cataloging-in-Publication Data

Maremaa, Tom.
Metal heads : a novel / Tom Maremaa. -- 1st ed.
    p. cm.
Summary: "A surreal story of the Iraq war, told by a young American
veteran being treated for traumatic brain injury in a California hospital
where the patients are treated as objects for experimentation in the
creation of a new super-soldier"--Provided by publisher.
ISBN 978-1-60164-170-0
1. Iraq War, 2003---Veterans--Fiction. I. Title.
PS3563.A646M48 2009
813'.54--dc22
                    2009002311

In memory of my brother,

a warrior to the end

Then our troops began fanning out and becoming custodians of law and order. It was then that the defeated enemy—or, rather, an enemy that had vanished or melted away but had not felt itself defeated—waiting and watching in the shadows, decided to strike, decided that we werc killable. Why were we killable? Because they were able to observe us at close hand and see that we operated without the logic of a superpower that knew what it wanted to do. We did not have mastery of the terrain, the language, the culture; there was an open debate about what we wanted. We were attackable.

• Jon Lee Anderson, *The New Yorker*

What does God want? Does God want goodness or the choice of goodness? Is a man who chooses the bad perhaps in some way better than a man who has the good imposed upon him?

• Anthony Burgess, *A Clockwork Orange*

Chill out, life is better in orange.

• Soldier talk

Part I

The orange sky melts away.

Shadows fall and twist in the wind. I'm on patrol with three of my buds, there to retrieve the body of a fallen comrade, Bill's body, we're told. They got him, used him, then dumped his body in a ditch and said, "Hey, he's yours now. Go get him." No Marine is ever left behind. Ever. Ramadi is a hornets' nest for the asking and we're feeling all the pain of a million bites, a million stings. The triggers of hate are all around us.

Out of the shadows we're greeted by a pair of private contractors, men who got word of Bill's release, men working security for one of the internationals. The taller of the two steps forward and I'm overwhelmed by his dominating presence: he stands six feet six at least, a big, mean-looking beast of a man with scars and tattoos and a smear of black stubble covering his cheeks and jaw. He's wearing his full battle rattle, flak vest and Kevlar helmet. Over one shoulder he's got weaponry, an M-16 and a Mossberg 12 gauge shotgun, good for clearing out insurgent houses, both loaded and ready to pop; over the other a samurai sword, gleaming in the twilight.

"Name's Travis," he extends a cold hand. "Protection's my game. What's yours?"

We introduce ourselves, me, Lance Corporal Witherspoon, and my buds, one of whom is blunt: "What're you protecting, sir, if I may be so rude to ask?"

"Why gold, of course," he snarls. "Black gold."

We nod knowingly, cracking smiles as we walk toward the

ditch where Bill's body is lying in wait, eyes behind our heads. The enemy is out there, lurking in the dark narrow passageways between buildings, ever vigilant, always ready to pounce and light up—open fire. A quiver of fear snakes down my spine, then coils around in the pit of my stomach. Are we in a kill zone, or what? We start to cough, our throats parched and dry to the bone from breathing razor-sharp particles of sand blown across the desert by a summer wind, a northwesterly they call the *shamal*. The stench of death, foul and unforgiving, fills the night air.

"That's pretty skanky, Mr. Travis," I blurt out stupidly.

"You have a problem with that, soldier?"

The man's face turns beet red, his eyeballs glazed. He must be high on something. He looks as if he's going to waste anybody and anything that stands in his way. I feel his anger rising to a boil, turning into a fierce, unstoppable rage. He can't contain himself, a contractor gone mesmerotic.

I back off and pull away. The moon's first light appears as we haul Bill's body out. Bill's badly mutilated, chopped up. My bud says, "Bill was, dammit, a football player, a linebacker with a future, president of his class, a brave man. He didn't deserve this. An angel. It's not right what happened."

"Know who did it," interjects Travis. "We know. We'll exact revenge. Privately. You with me, soldier?"

We nod again. Knowingly.

🌱

THEY CALL ME SPOON. My name's Jeremy Witherspoon, actually. And I've got a story to tell, one you might find hard to believe, but believe me, all of it's true. I swear it is. You've got my word on that, as Dad used to say with a wink and a smile when I was growing up. My gulliver wounds got me here, in recovery, chilling out from the war. Taking it one day at a time, hanging on by the skin of my zoobies, I'm waiting to go home so I can put the memories of my unspeakable actions, unthinkable deeds behind me and move on. That's before Skank shows up, before Kamal and his daughter Leila come into the picture and before I can figure out what's really going down in the Body and Repair Labs at St. Richard's.

Speaking of the war, I did some pretty baddiwad things over there; I mean, things I don't really want to talk about right now. There's a lot about the war nobody, but *nobody* wants to bring up, or should know about. I'll tell you if you promise to keep what I did a secret, at least until I'm ready to come clean myself. Fair enough?

I'm one of the TBIs, one of the metalheads on the ward, Lance Corporal Witherspoon with a steel plate attached to his skull, sir. That's me, all right. Just in case you don't know what I'm talking about, bear with me while I explain. I've got what they call medically, according to the docs, a Traumatic Brain Injury. Can you dig it, mon? That's what happens when your gulliver gets jarred and all shaken up by an explosion from a roadside bomb.

Inside your skull there's all that gray matter, billions of neurons and synapses connecting nerve cells, the dance of life, the docs tell us, and when you get hit by one of those improvised devices, it may blow off your hand as it did mine outside a Baghdad café, but worst of all, it'll rattle your brain, move what's inside your gulliver from side to side. A violent, uncontrollable shaking, the docs call it. Your gulliver feels like it's had scrambled eggs with a side order of burnt toast for breakfast. Hey, I'm not joking. The explosion creates a lot of pressure, pounds and pounds of it like a steam engine, and sometimes your skull swells up until it's bigger than a watermelon. That's when the docs have to perform surgery and cut a swath of your skull open to relieve the unbearable, mounting pressure. After they've cut it open and let the insides breathe, for God's sake, they'll patch it up with a metal cover, a plate, held tight with metal screws twisted into your skull. You won't feel it because there's no feeling when they work on your gray matter. But you'll feel the cutting of the skull and the drilling for the screws.

One doc here even cut a chunk of skull out of Major Pink's gulliver about the size of a sliced cantaloupe, replaced it with a metal cover, and then performed surgery on the dude's abdomen, where he found a cavity below the ribcage where he could store the chunk, so the body could nourish it until the swelling went down in his gulliver and the chunk could be put back in its place. Meantime Major Pink, good man that he is, soldier of the night in Fallujah, is walking around with this big metal plate on the exposed part of his gulliver. That's the way it is for me too, why we're all metalheads here, although my chunk of skull was blown away. You could say I've got a big hole in my gulliver, though my senses and cognition seem to be okay, at least they were before Private Contractor Skank made his appearance known and changed it all. I'll get to that part of the story soon enough.

If you do the arithmetic, you'll viddy our numbers keep mounting and counting up: each day a new shipment of TBIs arrives at dawn in the house of pain, most of them with serious body parts missing, all feeling the angst, knowing something's not right in their gullivers. Welcome to the club; pleased to meet you, returning soldier. There's some *healing* to be done and we can do it. Be *patient*. Your turn will come. That's the mantra, anyway.

❧

THE DOCS ARE AMAZING, REALLY AMAZING, I'm telling you. They're miracle workers. I wouldn't be alive if it weren't for them. I got hit really baddiwad. I'm in that crowded café when I run outside and that bomb, some roadside contraption made of nails and crap, blows up. Kamal, our interpreter, a great man, an Arabic scholar and teacher and devoted father, comes sprinting to my rescue. He risks his own life for me, and nobody's ever done that except my dad. Kamal's got reflexes like I've never seen. The man can deal with disaster, with grief and suffering, as if it's in his bones, which it is. I'm on the ground, splattered in blood orange. I'm looking around stupidly and viddy my hand on the other side of the road, with my arm below the elbow gushing red like the fountain of youth in some gory Hollywood B-movie. M'kay, so I lost my hand, I'm thinking to myself, big deal, and I'm blind in one eye, no big deal—at least I'm alive. Or am I? Before I know it, the medics have got me out of there, evacuation, stretchers, hospitals in the Green Zone, then Germany, then days later all the way to Kahleefornia, in a recovery program with nurses and docs running around to take care of me, even though I committed more than my fair share of crimes in war. You'd be

METAL HEADS ■ 11

hard pressed, even if you tried, to find anything good about me. I can't be your friend as much I'd like to.

Some things you ought to know if you want to grok my story. The ringing in my gulliver won't stop, not ever, or never. "It goes with the territory," John Hart, Captain and National Guardsman, told me that, and he knows because he's got the same problem. John Hart started the garden in the open field we called St. Richard's Annex, after Kamal came one day for a visit carrying a bag of seeds, along with rootstock vines from the city of Shiraz where wine was made thousands of years ago, and changed everything. I mean, nothing was ever the same after that. Before long, the open field next to the hospital compound, where we'd been growing the most amazing crop of fruits and vegetables, herbs and grapevines in the world, had to go. Security and the higher ups couldn't take it; everybody paid the price.

And then there's the bit about Private Contractor Skank I promised to tell you. He's the renegade soldier of fortune, employed by a private security firm, who did all those baddiwad things in Ramadi. I witnessed what he did and I did nothing; I hid the truth and he came back to haunt me with it. I'm an accomplice to Skank's crimes of war, crimes against the innocent, because I stood there alongside him, speechless, numbed by the brutality of it, and did nothing. Not until he showed up here one day a while back.

❦

IT'S NOT CLEAR WHO RUNS St. Richard's, which is named after the founders, Dr. Richard and Elizabeth Richards, saints, both of them, for putting up the deng needed to establish this facility for wounded vets, brave soldiers and private contractors from the endless war. In the lobby up front there's a big plaque listing all the contributors to the medical center and right at the top of the list are their names, etched in white marble. Right there in the lobby too, you can't miss it if you try, is a big statue of an Indian chief made of solid bronze. It stands a good six feet eight inches tall, life-size, gleaming in the morning light, with the chief's head cocked to one side, his huge body leaning on the butt handle of a long broom.

Thing is, when I got here I couldn't figure how or why this yahoo rated a bronze statue. What had he *done*, anyway?

One day I'm in the lobby, poking around. There's a plaque underneath the statue with fancy lettering engraved on it, but I can't really see what it says, shards of glass in my eye giving me trouble, causing my vision to blur. I move a few steps closer. First line on the plaque reads: I used to be big, but not no more. USED TO BE BIG, BUT NOT NO MORE. The words have a ring to them, don't they? My throat gets tight, I'm choking up a bit. And why do they sound familiar?

I viddy the face again. Is this that Indian from the movie, the one with Jack Nicholson and all those looney guys romping around in the bin? Chief Broom, right? I think it is, must be.

Suddenly, I know why they put a statue of him here in St. Richard's. It comes to me in a flash. But there's something that bothers me about that movie. Why'd they think he was *deaf*? I can almost hear the growl of his voice as I read the next line on the plaque: It wasn't me that started acting deaf. It was people that first started acting like I was too dumb to see or hear or say anything at all.

Not him. Not Chief Bromden, son of Chief Tee Ah Millatoona, meaning, The Pine That Stands Tallest on the Mountain, and a white woman, Mary Louise Bromden.

And then, what happened happened without anybody expecting it. All he did, the Indian who was once big and would be big again, was to lift up that huge fountain, the one nobody could move, and throw it with all his might right through the bars. And then get the hell out of there.

The glass in my eye isn't all that causes the blur. I can't help but nod. I'm nodding fast, I'm thinking to myself, If he can do it, I can do it too. Or can I?

So, come on, who's *really* running the show, you might ask, as I did when I got here a while back. Some say it's Major General Heddie Smith, Four Stars and Counting, as we say, who runs the joint, along with the heads of the six families that run the country, two of them living right here in the land of milk and honey, in Kahleefornia. That's what Ricki says, at any rate. She tells me, "Who says it's a democracy, who says?" I have no answer.

Nobody's seen or heard from Major General Smith in years; the dude's a phantom figure, like my phantom limb, the left hand that was blown away, even though my gulliver, all those neurons that won't stop firing, keeps telling me to look and feel for it, because it's convinced that it's still there. At any rate, if Four Stars and Counting Major General Smith runs the place, he's doing it by remote control, he's outsourcing the management, playing games with us, little pawns that we are in the chessboard of life, soldiers to be mechanized into better fighting machines. So maybe the general is one of us, after all; I'm told he's got wires coming out of his gulliver and is of short stature, with a titanium right arm controlled by electrical impulses from the brain.

I'm a little over six feet tall myself, with a shaved gulliver that once had dark curly hair, and I've got blue eyes, or at least one blue eye, while the empty socket is waiting to be filled with a glass ball. My shoulders and legs are still strong, after my training in boot camp as a Marine, but I can feel them weakening with lack of use and all the sitting around we do every day in Group, in the Large Assembly, or in Therapy.

We're metalheads, all of us here, as I was saying, some worse than others. Loud music is a killer, so nobody's allowed to play hardcore rock on their stereos, and drugs are plentiful. I've got more meds on my tray at dinner than gumballs in a candy store. I'm told if I don't take them I'll die. I've seen too much death already to want to join the parade. The metalheads are a cool bunch, and I've picked up on their stories, assembling the pieces in my gulliver because, for some reason, my memory's better than ever since coming back from the war. I certainly won't forget what Skank did in Ramadi, how he brutalized that poor young Iraqi girl while the rest of us stood by without lifting a finger or saying a word to the contrary. I told you we're baddiwad and we carry the guilt around with us, like hundred-pound weights strapped to our backs, until our bones crack and we're bent in half.

❦

ONE THING'S FOR SURE: you don't want to rattle Ricki's cage, no sir, if you know what's good for you. She's the leader of the pack, a woman warrior, former colonel in charge of

Special Forces in Afghanistan. She's the alpha male and the alpha female at the same time. I've got a whole long riff on Ricki, and I promise you, if you stick around, you won't be disappointed.

On good days I dream of when I was just a kid, hanging out in the City, riding my skateboard on the steps of the Plaza, raising a bit of hell for the tourists; of chasing Latina girls, bitchin' beautiful, in the back alleys of the Mission; of sneaking onto BART trains without paying a nickel; of pinching an item or two from a clueless street vendor, no harm done, sir; of just hanging out with my good droogs from skolliwoll and riding the airwaves of my favorite hard metal bands (I won't bore you with their names).

Most of the time, not all but most, I dream other people's dreams, and I'm pretty good at it because I don't sleep much. Dreams keep me awake, wide awake. I dream of the great times John Hart once had with Mary and his son and daughter. I dream of John Hart going home to his wife and kids, all patched up, a new man, healed by the miracles of modern medicine, but it's an empty dream. John Hart asked the docs one day, "Tell me, will you, plain and simple, up front, unequivocally, when, when, and when again, can I go home?"

And they told him. I was there, hiding behind a door, ears glued to the exchange, because, if you want to know the truth, I'm something of an earjacker: "Don't even think about it. Just don't."

He took a deep breath, exhaling from the bottom of his gut and said, "You mean it's *unacceptable* to think?"

"You could say that."

"So, if I've got this figured right, it's unthinkable," replied

John Hart, dropping his jaw as he comes out of the room, his eyes watering, his lips tasting the salt from his tears, his body enveloped in a shroud of grief.

"Your words, not mine," was the answer.

❧

JOHN HART WANTS TO LEAVE, but if he leaves on his own, somehow breaking free, he won't get far. That's for sure. He'll be out on the streets, with no direction home, like a complete unknown, like a rolling stone, as Bob Dylan sings, or as my dad, who grew up with Dylan, tells me, and he won't have his meds around to kill the ringing in his gulliver, or halt the weird gyrations of his body. John Hart's a little spastic, but good-hearted. That's why he's got the name John Hart, I guess. Besides, John Hart's done too much good for everybody, so they like to have him around. Not me, I'm waiting for the day when I get my artificial hand, so all the neurons in my gulliver can come to terms with my phantom limb. And then I might take my chances on the outside, or at least that's what I thought until Skank appeared and things turned ugly.

Enter John Wu, another warrior among us, six feet ten inches tall, like the legendary Chief Broom, really tall for a soldier and a man of Asian descent. He says nothing, hasn't spoken for a couple of years now. You can prod him all you like but he won't speak. The docs are saying he's got Cotard's Syndrome, which is this bizarre disorder where you walk around thinking you're dead. I mean it, you claim to be a dead man and even if there's concrete evidence to the contrary, like a pin prick on your finger and you bleed, you still cling to the assertion. You just say, "I didn't know dead people could bleed." I'm not sure if the docs have got it right. Cotard's Syndrome, according to Nurse Judy, is all about being disconnected from the emotional parts of your gulliver, of not having anything hooked up to your senses. You don't feel a thing, but that's not the John Wu I know. He's got deeper and more powerful feelings than anybody on the ward; he just keeps it all inside, maybe as a protest against the war.

Now here comes Ricki O' Brien. She's the one I was telling you about and she's talking up a storm. Man, can she talk. She wants to mobilize the troops and make us head outside, even if we're not allowed, and she's promised to call up her Afghan buddy, a guy named Masood, who drives a cab, one of those big airport vans, and lives over in Fremont, where they've got the biggest Afghan community in the country right now. She says he'll take us on a secret mission downtown one night next week. We've got to get involved in civic affairs, she says, and there's a Town Hall meeting, a public event, open to all, where the powers that be are going to decide the fate of St. Richard's Annex. There's a movement afoot, she says, to convert the land into high-rise condos. We've got to oppose it, she insists. How? She wants Masood to load up the van with a dozen members of our crew, in the stealth of night, without permission from the hospital staff, and get a bunch of placards made up to save the Annex, this magical field of dreams where John Hart started all the planting and growing. She wants us to wear T-shirts with peace symbols emblazoned on our chests. The Lone Ranger, another private contractor, and his buddy Tonto got a big laugh out of this, particularly the bit about T-shirts. The Lone Ranger's got this thing when it comes to T-shirts; like, *soldiers don't wear T-shirts*. "First thing you do, if you want to change things, is collect all the goddam T-shirts in the world," he tells Ricki, "and then, you skvat a box of matches, light up, and have this big, booming bonfire. You get it?"

"The biggest bonfire in the world?" Ricki smiles at the Lone Ranger.

"That right, Keemosabee," says Tonto.

Enter and exit the Brass. They don't come often for visits and when they do, it's only for purposes of military inspection. We line up at attention in the Large Assembly, holding onto crutches and metal canes and whatever else we've got to keep us erect for five or ten minutes while the Brass, usually a couple of Two Stars, check us out. Behind the Two Stars and a Baby G, there's always a retinue of clowns dressed in black business suits; they're civilians, architects of the war, chickenhawks who've never gone to war but are happy to send others. Major Pink calls them the Max and Moritz clowns and gets a laugh out of viddying them in suits and starched white shirts and crummy ties. I doubt they'd like the idea of us heading out to some Town Hall meeting and raising a stink in public. To their mind, everything must look and behave normal around here, all of us sedated to mush, like mooshlovely, us soldiers with wounds that never heal, pliable and easily controlled. But there's been talk, whispers in the corridors among them of cutting off funds for work in the hospital, where they've got an advanced Body and Repair Shop, and tossing us all out on the street to fend for ourselves, homeless men and women, like after the last big war. I'm not looking forward to that, though I figure I can survive as well as the next guy on the street.

RICKI'S THE WOMAN WARRIOR I most admire in our platoon, officially Colonel Louise 'Ricki' O'Brien. When she got here (I can't remember if it was before or after me), she turned the place on its gulliver. Every nurse and doc was up in arms, trying to calm her down. I got angry about the way they treated her and tried to come to her rescue, but one of the docs kicked me hard in the yarbles. I mean, you've never seen such pandemonium break out when that happened. Ricki's a fighter, though shy and a bit withholding once you get to know her, and she had the place in an uproar. Talk about rage, bitchin' rage against the dying of the light, and all that Dylan Thomas stuff. She had it.

Thing is, it came about even though she'd been hurt bad, really bad, in the war. I mean, she'd lost her left leg from the knee down, and the right side of her face was all twisted and torn up. She had fingers missing, like we all did. Rather than being resigned to her fate, she worked up an anger I'd never seen in any woman before. She threw things at the docs and refused to take her meds. On crutches, she hurled epithets in their faces, even if they weren't to blame for her wounds from that roadside bomb that blew up her Humvee in Al Anbar province, outside Baghdad, and killed a couple of fellow soldiers in the process. When you viddy a wounded warrior like Ricki on a tirade, you learn to step out of her way.

Did I? You bet. But I also learned to keep cool, run silent, run deep. Okay, most of us here are like me, wounded and a bit crazy. John Hart told me, "Spoon, you've got to come clean. Fess up to your part in the actions you took. You won't be able to live with yourself until you do." How he figured me out, reading the buried thoughts in my gulliver, discerning my guilt, demanding I confess to the Brass, I'll never know, but he did. I mean, I lost my left hand, and only have partial sight in my right eye, which is all blurry and full of broken glass, and my gulliver's not the same; probably never will be. But my secret's safe. Only John Hart knows and he can't prove it without evidence or an eyewitness account from another soldier on that patrol. That's why I'm riveted to the Intake room, screening for any familiar faces who might recognize me, despite my rotten condition, and turn state's evidence. I'd get court-martialed for sure, then tossed into the slammer for the rest of my days. What's the good of that? I want to tell John Hart, but I know he won't listen. He's made up his rassoodock about me.

Docs don't seem to know what's wrong, which is good, far as I'm concerned, so they've got me pretty heavily medicated to kill the pain. Probably it's my own fault, all of it, the way I joined the Marines and betrayed my oath of honor. I was looking to kill in the name of answering the call to duty in Baghdad without really being prepared. I mean, I knew nothing about Iraq. I'd been kicked out of high skolliwoll a couple of times in my native state of Kahleefornia, and was lucky to get in. Not that they were taking just anybody, warm bodies off the street, to serve our country in the mess that's become Iraq. I had to pass a couple of tests and persuade the recruiters of my good intentions, my commitment to God and Country, and all the rest of it. Hey, it worked, but I did wrong, unlike John Hart.

He worked in a computer company in Silicon Valley, doing sales, making field trips, while serving as a National Guardsman on weekends to bring in some extra for his family, after having already served in the First Gulf War. He told me all that. "Spoon, I was doing my part to support Mary and my two kids, Jake and Josh, nine and twelve, respectively, if you're interested in knowing. Job kept me and my family going until I had to report for duty and deployment in Iraq. Do I sound rational? Am I making any sense?"

"Of course you are, John Hart," I told him. "You're an honorable man, unlike me. I'm the worst of the worst."

"You believe in God?"

"Yes. Who doesn't"

"Spoon, stop lying. You never spent a day of your life in church and you did some bad things over there. But you can be redeemed."

"Me? Redeemed? What are you talking about, man? There's no redemption for my kind. None. Nobody can ever forgive me for what I've done."

"I can. And if I can, so can others. Others like me. Ever heard of Truth and Reconciliation? They did it in South Africa, after suffering under apartheid for a century and a half, if not longer. They came together and told each other what happened, and asked for forgiveness. It can happen to you, to us, to everybody."

"Man, you are one amazing piece of work, John Hart. Not me."

"Watch. You'll see. Things change in mysterious ways, always have, always will."

I started laughing and couldn't stop for at least an hour. I mean, John Hart would never turn me in, now would he? He's too busy being an idealist, a savior of humanity, a high priest of goodness, and all that crap.

♥❦

IN THE INTAKE ROOM, I watch the new TBIs roll in, study their faces to viddy if there's anybody coming here I recognize, who might've witnessed my crimes of war in Ramadi. That's what draws me there to the periphery of the room, to the outer edge. I linger by the doorway leading to the main entrance, keeping a low profile. It paid off when one day Skank himself, the infamous Skank, his body covered in tattoos, his eyes glassy and bulging from heavy doses of drugs, his lips breathing fire and anger—when Skank showed up and, like he did over there, began tearing things apart, going on a rampage. And again, with nobody to stop him. That's part of my story.

The day John Hart came in, things also changed around here. I mean, they were never the same, if that makes any sense. John Hart's a rainmaker, all right, best of breed. A former National Guardsman, firefighter, soldier, he's the man, as I was saying, or *was* the man until what happened happened.

♥❦

MY OLD GIRLFRIEND FROM HIGH SKOLLIWOLL SHOWS UP one morning, without notice, at the hospital. You'll want to know about it. She's down there, in Reception, waiting to viddy me, I'm told by one of the nurses. Man, I am not up for this. Tell you that right away. How she even found out I was here is a mystery to me; word must travel fast. In Iraq, I wrote her a bunch of letters but she never wrote back, or at least I never got any letters from her. I even tried e-mailing her after one of my buddies was able to shake loose her e-mail address from one of *his* buddies who happened to know her. Now she's here, chomping at the bit to viddy me, according to the nurse. "She's hot, Spoon," Major Pink whispers in my ear. "Spotted this girl—isn't she kind of young? I mean, she's a babe and all, but man, you must like 'em young—in Reception, being questioned by the admins and filling out this form, and when I asked which metalhead she was here to see, they told me it was you. You, *dude*. And I'm thinking, hey, Spoon, you are one lucky dude. Nobody's come to see me in months and you've got this dolled up babe waiting to get her hands on you."

If it were only true, Major Pink, I resisted saying. Then I winked at Pink and said, "Hey, if you can believe it *she's older than me*. Makeup does wonders to keep you young, doesn't it? Maybe I should start wearing some, too." That got Pink laughing.

One of the nurses took me down to Visitors after I'd slapped some cold water on my face and gulliver. Meds have been making me groggy and tired lately; can't seem to focus on anything, can't get it up to viddy Brianna, and we went out a lot in high skolliwoll. What's she doing here? What's she want? I drag myself down the long corridor to the elevator, climb inside and ride down to the first floor. Sunlight's breaking across the glass windows up front and to the side of Visitors. Nobody comes to Visitors much anymore, they've written us off. What good are we anyway? Do we matter? If the hospital's shut down, which could happen, we'll be tossed out on the streets and left to fend for ourselves. They've been telling us that for a long time now as a way of keeping us in check. There won't be any rebellion in the ranks here.

"Hey, Brianna, good to viddy you," I open with a smile, forced, but still a smile.

"Hi, Jeremy," she says, giving me a hug, then pulling back.

"You look great." I'm eyeing her outfit, her scruffy cut-offs, hugging her hips like Saran Wrap, and her tight-fitting black T-shirt with the sequins around her boobs. Nipples protruding nicely.

Her hair is spiked and streaked orange, she's got a nose ring pierced through her left nostril, and about a half dozen rings on her right ear. Her lips are smeared with black splotches of lipstick and her eyes have big globs of paint or makeup of some kind under them. She's got that vamp look about her, like a goth, which was cool at one time in skolliwoll. I doubt she has any idea where Iraq is or who's there or why we're there, if she even cares. She's chewing gum, and cracks a bubble between her zoobies. The pop startles me. I'm hearing those rings in my ears again.

"What happened to your hand?"

"Gone, blown up."

"Why are you wearing that black patch over your eye? You a pirate, or something?"

"No, Brianna, I lost my eye, too."

"Oh, that's too bad."

"Yeah, I guess it is. What brings you here? How you'd find out I was—"

"It's a long story, Jeremy. Let's not talk about it, okay? I brought you some things, little goodies. Don't get your hopes up."

"My hopes are up just viddying you."

She's got a big shopping bag with her and she pulls out a few items. One is a carton of cigarettes, Camel Lights, another is a batch of comic books, a third item is a pair of undershorts in American flag colors, all red, white, and blue with stars. In big letters scrawled on front is MOBY DICK. She thinks I'm still a teenager, like her. A juvenile delinquent, worst of breed. She's trying to be real emo. I ought to break the news. "Hey, Brianna, I'm not seventeen anymore."

"What are you talking about, Jeremy? You're almost the same age as me. Remember, we went to skolliwoll together."

"That we did, we did. I'm old now, really old, like my dad. Maybe I'm even older than my dad, if you get what I'm saying."

She looks absolutely dumbfounded.

"You all right in the head?"

I resist saying anything else to her; she just won't understand. It'll go in one ear and out the other. "Thanks for the presents."

I want to tell her I don't smoke, don't read comic books anymore, don't even wear undershorts, just my green or white hospital wraparounds, but what's the point?

"You still like me, don't you?"

"Of course I do."

"When are you getting out of here, Jeremy?"

"Well, that's another story. I may never get out of here, way things are going. Takes a long time to heal."

"You wanna have sex?"

"Well . . ."

"Anyplace private we can go?"

In a flash I can't think of a single private place in the entire hospital compound, in the whole company. Every room's crowded, nurses roaming the floor, docs on call, deliverymen coming and going, cameras up in the corners or hanging from the ceilings of all the rooms, a thousand eyes viddying our every move. "If we had sex, we'd be on videotape and everybody would get to watch," I said with a sigh of resignation. "Perving can be a cheap thrill for some, I'm sorry to say."

"Doesn't bother me," she said, sounding rather chipper. "When you're hot you're hot."

"Brianna, I don't need the exposure. I'm trying to lay low. It's amazing you found me, but not unexpected. I'm glad you're here. I like the gifts you brought me, including the red, white and blue shorts; I'll wear them with pride. I love this country but I don't like what we've done over there, what I've done. I'm trying to figure out a way to live with it before it drives me crazy. You understand what I'm saying, Brianna?"

"Not really. I came all the way here to see you, Jeremy. I had to track you down, nobody knew what happened to you. And you don't seem to be in real good shape. How can you have sex with me when your left hand is missing and you've got a patch over your eye? I don't mean to sound like I don't care. I do. It's just that you're not what I thought you'd be. You're old, too old for me. I can see that, Jeremy. I'm sorry I came."

"Don't be sorry. You did what you had to do. That counts for a lot."

"Goodbye, Spoon," she said, turning away and heading out the door of Visitors. Probably everybody in the room had heard every word of our conversation, and that bothered me to no end. But there wasn't much I could do about it. Nor much I could do about my old high skolliwoll girlfriend, either. She was gone for good, I figured.

JOHN HART KEEPS TELLING one of the docs that Iraq is right next door to Kahleefornia, same border running north and south. I'm overhearing the conversation, not sure if he's just putting on the doc, trying to break up his headset, or if he's dead serious. But in any case he's getting the doc to smile, to loosen up a bit. I'm viddying this humongous smile coming across the doc's face, a half moon's worth, from one cheek to the other. I guess I'm making him feel good, I'm reading what John Hart is thinking, catching the seadrift of his thoughts.

"This is Kahleefornia," he says, pointing a finger at the doc. "And if you travel a few hundred miles to the east you come to the state of Iraq. Don't believe me, eh?"

"No, frankly, Captain Hart, I don't," says the doc, trying to keep a straight face.

"Seen any maps lately?" he needles the doc.

"No, I haven't," replies the doc, a bit irritated.

"Well, there you have it. Ask Ricki," John Hart says. "Ricki showed me a map of the world the other day and right there, as I was saying, next to Kahleefornia was the state of Iraq. Are we clear then?"

"Yes, sir." And the doc salutes John Hart. Meanwhile the rest of us are picking up on the conversation; it's being broadcast over the loudspeakers and we're all choked up with laughter. Come to think of it, maybe he's right. Maybe somebody's redrawn all the borders, or brought the state of Iraq over here and wedged it between Kahleefornia and Nevada. I'll have to viddy for myself.

I'M HAVING TROUBLE SLEEPING AGAIN. Only got a few hours every night for the last week, maybe a total of six or seven hours altogether. Should be enough to keep going but my nerves are frazzled. I hear everybody snoring on the ward and I catch bits and pieces of their dreams. Call me Spoon, the dreamcatcher. Pitch me your dream, toss it my way and I'll scribble down all of it in my notebook, where I keep fragments of this story for anybody who comes after us, who might want to know what's really happening during this time, in this place, of this world.

Because I'm wide awake, I viddy the stories of their lives flash right by me like in the movies, flickering in the dim light. I can tell you more than you want to know about the boys on the ward, especially the young ones who've come back from the war. Their dreams are always in color, with big splashes of red and blue and yellow projected on the walls of their rooms. I hear lots of explosions, particularly the ones occurring when roadside bombs go off. This is hard to take, and I've been begging My Doc to help me find a way to sleep. He's not too sympathetic, I can tell you that. Says it's all my fault and any drugs he might prescribe would only make things worse. I can't follow his logic.

They've got a list of things, scratched out on a board, for which they'll treat us. I'm not sure what category I fall into, probably wounded war veteran, or something like that. God, I hope I don't have what I fear I have: a couple of shells in my gulliver, stuck there, too deep to risk removing. I've noticed that wherever I go I set off alarm detectors: they come blasting back at me.

The way I figure it, I'll be out of here soon, sooner than anybody else. I'm on the mend. My wounds are healing. But that's not the way My Doc has me down on his chart. From his point of view, I'm not healed up at all, I'm still licking my wounds, which won't heal. There's no way to repair a broken soul, is there?

"Don't even think about it," My Doc tells me.

"So it's unthinkable," I say, repeating John Hart's words.

"I've heard that before and I'm sure I'll hear it again."

"Doc, tell me why you've got that big crap-eating grin on your face?"

He shakes his gulliver and keeps smiling. I know the answer to that one: all the docs and nurses in St. Richard's have been instructed to smile continuously when discussing anything with the inmates, especially anything baddiwad or controversial. One time I caught a glimpse of two docs being dressed down by their superiors for not smiling while telling one of the TBIs she needed to have part of her brain removed in surgery and more than likely would never viddy or hear right again. Baddiwad news is always delivered with the ice pick of a phony smile, a half moon face, and lots of bubbles in your voice.

❦

TIME IT TOOK TO GET HERE is something else; I was telling Ricki about this and she agreed. It's as if we each spent a lifetime to get where we're going, and now we're here and don't know what to do. She's got more of it figured out than

I do. For one thing, she believes in God, God's always there for her. "There *is* a God," she says, always in the context of righting some wrong, some injustice, some bending of the truth that's ruined our lives. God will fix it. That's her faith, her belief system, as I've heard it said. I'm telling her it's not as simple as that and she agrees with me.

Sometimes. Ricki's kind of weird, if you want to know about it. I mean, she dresses kind of funny, lots of long white gowns, hospital issue, and with her thick red hair, pure Irish on her father's side, all bundled up and curly, except for the metal plate sticking out of her skull. Nurse Mee is Ricki's only saving grace. If Ricki didn't have Nurse Mee to look after her, I doubt she'd be alive today. Ricki keeps talking about her poll numbers, as if she were a politician or something, saying "Okay, they're low, but so what?" She's on a mission of some kind, one that takes her to faraway places, geographies of space and time we know nothing about, she claims.

They'll come for me soon one day or another, but not if I lay low, keep to myself, and make sure none of the new arrivals can finger me for what I did on that night patrol in Ramadi with Skank.

❧

JETS STREAK ACROSS THE SKY in a thunderous roar. I hear the reverberations, as I write this in my notebook, deep in the echo chamber of my gulliver.

Ricki dances and sings and writes love poetry to her boyfriend Masood, the Afghan cabdriver she met at Bagram while on tour. Trust me, she does that. She won't say where the dude is living, though it looks like Fremont, across the Bay, in that Afghan enclave, but it seems like she's writing to him almost every day. I would be her boyfriend, too, if I could. Ricki's more like an older sister to me, so doing any kind of romance thing with her is weird. Besides, she's already got a boyfriend, although he's on the other side of the Bay. At least he's not in Iraq, contrary to what John Hart's been saying to the docs, namely that Iraq is right next door to Kahleefornia across the border beyond the Mojave.

In one of my dreams, Ricki's loose on the streets, moving fast, so fast I can't catch up with her. She's a demon in white clothing, and she can run even with one leg real and the other artificial, made of titanium and hard plastic. I'm out of breath just trying to keep up with her.

❧

RICKI COMES INTO THE WARD NOW and she looks to be about one hundred years old. I mean, she's got this horribly wrinkled face and all. She's old, really old. Her eyes are silvery, almost glowing like hot embers. She walks slowly, deliberately toward me on crutches, and she tells me with the movements of her body that she's ancient. I hate to think that I'll be one hundred years old some day, though I doubt I'll ever get there. Too many wounds from the war, too much lead in my veins.

Ricki looks young as can be. She's brightened herself up, dabbed lots of makeup on her face, dyed her hair blonde, and lightened her step. She's agile, thin as a matchstick (I guess she stopped eating completely two weeks ago, except for occasional snacks and lots of water). Ricki greets all the new guys, all the TBIs coming into the ward, with a polite hello and a big welcoming smile. She even shakes their hands. I viddy it happen with the new dudes. A little charm goes a long way, much longer than anybody knows.

Ricki likes to hide things, like a squirrel packing nuts in the ground. She promises to share everything she's hidden, though, so she tells me.

Is she a *madwoman*? Hardly, I would answer. Seems quite normal to me. One day she's like a big earth mother, another like a warrior princess. I eye her movements all the time. If she got out and drove across the border to Iraq, right into the heart of Baghdad, not the Green Zone where all us Americans are hiding behind concrete walls, she would bring peace to this troubled land. She would mediate the conflict, somehow. She would make peace with the Sunnis and Shi'a. I'm telling My Doc, just let her out of Kahleefornia for a day, and let her get in a car and drive across the border to Iraq, and you'll viddy what I mean. "Are you *kidding* me, son?" That's his standard response. I mean, why would I kid him? I'm dead serious. Ricki has a gift and a power and it's not being used properly.

❧

ONE OF THE GUYS ON THE FLOOR, a new metalhead, wants Kahleefornia to secede from the Union. He's going around with a petition, trying to get everybody to sign up. When he's got all the signatures together, he says he'll send it to the Governor. Ricki is opposed to this action.

Ricki is a beautiful actress, like one of those movie stars from the days when movies were in black and white, and sound wasn't so good, so their voices had a tinny quality to them but the women, lush babes with sensuous curves, were sexy as hell. Ricki is sexy, all right. I can viddy the guys on the ward giving her the eye, those elevator eyes cruising up and down her thin body. She's a babe, she's an actress, and she's got a lot of parts to play here. Her story is she got brutally gang-raped by some of our own while out on patrol in Baghdad; wasn't meant to happen but it did. Nobody in the ranks wanted to hear about it; the wounds festered until she got hit by those freaking improvised explosive devices, the ones wired together from 155mm artillery shells, IEDs about the size of a pizza box, deadly weapons of war, painted grey to blend in with the highway and planted in a pothole, then detonated remotely by cell phone when her Humvee rolled over it. The blast shook up her gulliver, cut off her leg, and hurt her in ways nobody'd want to know. I figure she got shipped back to the States so she'd shut up and be a looney TBI, not to be believed by anybody.

Like John Hart, she's got a big heart; she's generous with her time. She spent hours—I mean, *days*—listening to each of our stories, making them part of her own life experience, and even holding our hands. I could feel my wounds healing when she touched me and kissed me on the cheeks. And remember, I'm baddiwad, I'm the worst you'll ever meet, but I'm also angelic when I want to be.

Now she wants me to write a play for her, one she can star in and become famous again, she says. I didn't know she was famous before; a soldier, an officer in command of an army, yes, but not now. I thought once you were famous that meant you were famous forever. It stayed with you, stuck with you, because whatever you did to become famous was meaningful and would not be forgotten. But Ricki tells me I'm completely wrong about this. "Fame is fleeting," she says. And once you lose it, man, it's doubly-hard to get it back.

"The public is fickle," she says.

And I believe her, yes. Ricki is all sweetness and light this morning. It's as if she's basking in some kind of holy light, as if she's got an aura about her. I wonder how that came about, if I only knew. She's kind of radiant. Ricki is real artful about lying. She'll lie to me but it's okay because I know when she's lying and what she's really trying to accomplish with her lies.

❦

I OUGHT TO TELL YOU ABOUT DOGG. YOU SEE, Dogg's a man you got to know. Not only is he physically imposing; I mean, he's built like a tank from the ground up, ripped abs, arm, chest and shoulder muscles, every one of them buffed and polished. And he's motivated, working like a mad dog to get himself fixed right. When he got hit in Mosul he was lucky enough not to lose any body parts; all limbs intact, hanging together in one piece. But Dogg got hit hard in the skull: his metal plate is larger than mine or the rest of us metalheads'. It covers almost half his skull. He gets tired real fast, and dizzy, and hallucinates at times. The chemicals in his body are out of whack, way off kilter, however you want to characterize it. Dogg's gone on a big fitness program to correct the imbalance. He's built up his large black biceps, shoulders, chest, quads, and calf muscles to the point where he looks as if he's ready to take on the governor in a bodybuilding contest. I mean, he's strong as an ox. Two, three, even four times a day he's in the weight room, pumping iron, massive barbells, hundred-, two-hundred-pound weights with each hand, his body drenched in sweat, gleaming, black and beautiful as I've seen no other man in the company, and when he's there you can't interrupt him, even for a moment, without incurring his wrath. He talks about going back, returning to the frontlines in Fallujah or Anbar province. I forget if he was a corporal or a master sergeant in the Army, but I know he would set the example, lead men into battle, teach and train those under him, win any battle, engaging the enemy at will.

There's another side to Dogg, however, and you ought to know about it. He's sensitive, a caring man, and from what I can determine about his work habits and self-discipline, he's one fine writer, soon to become the best writer of his generation, black or white, yellow or brown. He lies on the floor in his room with sheets of yellow legal paper in front of him, pen in hand, scribbling away. "Dude, what do you *think* I'm doing? I'm writing a novel about what's comin' *next*," he tells me when I show up one day in his room and ask what he's doing.

"So what's coming next?"

"You'll have to *read* my novel. It's all *there* for you to see. Big *things* are goin' to happen."

"Like what?"

"What are you, *a reporter or something*? Spoon, don't be so *nosy*."

"No harm intended," I tell him as I move closer to viddy what he's up to. "You write with single sheets of paper, not with a typewriter or laptop like everybody else?"

"No way, man. For one thing, I don't have no typewriter or *computer* to work with, so I've got to do the *best* I can *with the cards I been dealt.* You dig?"

"Can I read it?"

"No. Critics come *later*. Right now, I've got to *finish*."

"Where's it take place?"

"You sure are *one persistent dude*. The place is never *named* in my story, the characters don't have names like *you* and *me*, or anybody else, *dig*? The streets and skolliwolls and hospitals in my story don't have names, either. I'm freaking sick of names and places. Crap like that. Can you, *for once*, understand?"

"What's it called?"

"*Un, think, able.*"

"Just like this place."

"It's unthinkable of a *different* order, but it's *still* unthinkable."

"I'm with you, man. Lay it on me when you're done."

"I will, *dude*. Now get the *hell* out of my room!"

❦

YOU'VE GOT TO SPEND A DAY or two here to get a feel for the place. There's lots going on, for one thing. My Doc, the smiling one assigned to me, stops by once or twice a week just to check in on me. Don't know what he's after; it's as if he wants me to spy on the other metalheads and report back to him. Okay, so I'm keeping an eye on Dogg, watching his every move. Dogg's a big man, like John Hart, about six foot three or four. He's in the room we call Weights, as I say, every day, lifting barbells, pumping hundreds of pounds of iron. He figures he'll get the metal plate detached from his gulliver in a couple of months, and then he'll be out of here. I mean, he's a tough soldier, with a sensitive side; comes from East Kahleefornia, grew up in Oakland with a lot of other young black men whose fathers got killed in the wars. And when he's not building up his body he's writing. The dude can write up a storm. There's that novel he's working on, he confides in me, and when he gets out he's sure he'll find a way to get it published.

"I'm sworn to secrecy," I promised him, even though My Doc keeps asking what Dogg is up to.

My Doc is more than a little curious; it's like an obsession with him.

"Where's he hiding the manuscript?"

"You been looking for it?"

"Spoon, unless you get a copy of it, I'm not sure I can prescribe any more painkillers for you."

"Is that a *threat*?"

"Call it what you will."

"I call it a threat."

He smiles as he sticks the dagger into my back and twists it around a couple of times. I feel the pain but I'm not bleeding, so I hold my ground.

"Okay, I'll do what I can," I lie through my zoobies.

"We knew you'd come around."

❧

THERE'S CAMP LIBERTY, NESTLED in the northern section of our complex surrounding the Baghdad Airport. *Marhaba*, hello. *Keef halek*? How are you? There are twenty, maybe thirty thousand of us living in this Emerald City within a city, a walled citadel, the mother of all fortresses. It's the Green Zone you hear about. We've got it all for us, all the conveniences of home: mess halls, shops, streets with familiar names, the works. There are street signs everywhere for easy navigation. No problem getting around; it's like Main Street, USA.

Outside the camp, in Ameriya, in northwest Baghdad, Iraqis have signs of their own. One, in English, spray-painted in black on a pink stucco wall, reads: "GET OUT WE HATE YOU."

❧

WE KILL AN UNTOLD NUMBER OF INSURGENTS in airstrikes and ground attacks in Yusefiya. It's Sunday and I'm there with my fellow jarheads. *Maca salama.* Go without fear, in Arabic.

Two of our airmen die when their helicopter is shot down during the battle. Two marines are also killed that Sunday in Anbar Province, where Sunnis still have control, west of Baghdad.

The battle is intense, a display of ferocity on both sides. We're stronger, with more firepower, but the resistance is smarter and equally determined. *Keef halek.* How are you? *Shukran. Al-hamdu li-lah. Wa ant?* Thanks. Fine, by God's mercy. And you?

On the ground in Yusefiya we attack an insurgent safe house under surveillance. I move inside and kill two Iraqis, known insurgents. Entering the house, we detain three others, all men, suspects, according to the latest intel. Inside, we've got to deal with the wounds of three injured civilians, all women. As we're evacuating the women by helicopter to a military hospital, our helicopter comes under fire from the ground.

We respond with rounds and rounds of fire, killing a gang of insurgents in flight from the scene. "We smoked 'em!" one of my buddies cries. "Blew 'em away!"

I spin on my heels and unload my weapon in a sweep, killing three men who are trying to come after us, close enough to do their jobs. One man detonates a suicide vest after he's shot dead. The vest explodes but doesn't hit us. His body is torn to pieces on the ground. It's not a pretty sight, my first kills of the war.

There's another explosion from a car, which was holding weapons and ammunition inside. Yusefiya is part of a string of towns south of Baghdad where insurgent activity is feverish, deadly. The surrounding area, including Arab Al Jabour, is controlled by Al Qaeda. *Hadatht.* What happened? *Mar-thu.* How did it happen?

At least the statue of Saddam in Firdos Square has fallen. At least we got Saddam in that rathole with a suitcase full of deng hiding in Tikrit. Maybe we ought to do a bit of *sahl* to him, if you know what I mean in Arabic.

❦

DOGG'S WORKED OUT AN INGENIOUS SYSTEM for hiding his work on the novel. He works at night, around three or four o'clock in the morning when the night watchman and a couple of night nurses are bored or half asleep and don't bother to come around to check the racks and viddy how we're doing. His girlfriend gave him a big packet of yellow legal pads because she works in a law firm somewhere in the city and a bunch of pens that write in invisible ink. He goes for a streak, scratching and scrawling on sheet after sheet of yellow paper, putting down his thoughts, always at night. I viddy him there with a penlight, a fine beam of dust particles streaming over his shoulder onto the paper. In the morning, he hides the sheets of paper under his bed next to a pile of old shoes. Nobody's figured him out yet, and I'm loath to tell the docs, even if it means going without my meds.

❦

TELLING YOU, IT'S HARD LIVING LIKE this, if you can call it living at all. I mean, if I were back in Iraq, at least some Iraqis, good people, *sadikis*, would look after me, in spite of my condition. Instead, they got me moving from one hospital to another, over there, then in Germany at a military base where they've got docs who can patch up the wounded like nobody else, then out here in my native land of Kahleefornia, where all the wounded warriors come to die. But I'm not dead yet, nor am I going to be, not unless it's by my own hand. You can be sure I'll look after Ricki and John Hart, in whatever way I can. That's how close I feel to them.

Did I tell you? Ricki's got the most beautiful eyes of any woman I've ever seen. Iraqis have beautiful dark eyes, bright with the light of the desert, dry and sometimes empty from shedding so many tears, dealing with so many losses.

When I was there I got to witness an entire family blown to pieces; I mean, I knew the father, the mother, their three boys, young daughter, cousin, a brother, two uncles, and a great grandmother who must've been one hundred years old, if she was a day. And when I came back to their house I found the rubble, the ruin, the body parts scattered in every direction, with nothing left of the family, a giant hole in the earth, smoldering from red embers, lives shattered into a million pieces, I could feel my guts coming out. You could reach across and pull my stomach up through my throat, without my saying a word, my pain impossible to match the pain of losing that poor Iraqi family. My buddies, the ones with me on that patrol, felt the same, or if they didn't it was because they had grown numb to the losses that fell their way each day. Ricki would understand; her eyes, as I say, are big and round and beautiful. She viddies it all.

Tell me. Am I making any sense? They've got us right where they want us, and soon, I'm telling you, they'll be coming for me. And Ricki, though she's pretty mean when it comes to authority; it still slides off her back, right down her spinal column like water off a duck, so I'm thinking maybe there's a chance, distant though it is, of heading them off at the pass.

❧

"YOU BEEN TO BALAD, SPOON?"

"No, never been there. Where is it?"

"About fifty, sixty miles to the north and west of Baghdad. You know, the freaking Sunni Triangle."

"Tell me about it."

"Well, what happens, what happens is we're riding back from Balad, and I'm with the gunner, on top of our Humvee, my eyes are peeled three-sixty, all directions. Straight ahead.

It's like I've got eyes behind my gulliver, but I must be blind, somehow, because I don't viddy it coming. I don't viddy it until it's too late, man. Bomb hits us, or hits me, because nobody inside gets hurt. I reel back, spin around, fall and then stand up again. Can't viddy a thing now. I'm thinking they've blown out my eyes. Then I open them again, and I don't viddy my hand. It's gone and when I look out on the road, the road behind us, behind me in Balad, I do a double-take because my hand is lying there in the mud, fingers pointed up, my good hand, the one I used to write those letters home. It's gone."

"Lost mine too," I tell the Lone Ranger, "if that's any consolation."

"It's not, man."

And the Lone Ranger walks away.

❧

IN MY DREAM, THE ANTS are crawling all over me, I'm covered in them, gulliver to foot, little nippy creatures, highly organized in their attack, up my nose, into my ears. I bolt awake out of bed. This is baddiwad, really bad, I'm saying to myself. It's a form of torture; I'm in enemy hands. I'm being left alive to be eaten by armies of ants. It doesn't get much worse than that, does it now? Oh yes, it does, another voice whispers in my ear. My gulliver spins.

Fresh-picked strawberries, juicy and ripe. For some reason, I dig the taste of them, but they're only in a dream. Food here is rotten and bland as hell. I can never get my hands on them. Who's got them? Where do they come from? In the Kahleefornia valleys to the east they've got the best farms in the world, and fields of strawberries for the picking. Let me out of here and I'll head over there for the harvest.

Dogg was here last night, I could feel his presence. I mean, you know when Dogg's around, he's got that gentle touch, like Jesus. Some say he is Jesus, and I guess they've got a point.

They say every man's got a family, but it's not really true. I'm an only kid, and my mom's gone. Dad's a sailor with his own boat and he's always floating on the water, sometimes out on the Pacific, riding the waves. One time he even took me out fishing; those were good times.

Light falls hard on my cell. I mean, it's not really a cell, or so they tell me. It's a room for myself, I got that much.

If it's late now.

If it's late now, there's no way to know.

On the street I hear they're setting up a protest march. Dad used to do that, back when he was going to skolliwoll. He had this thing about war: he hated war. So when I joined up after high skolliwoll, he hated me.

I'm not a big one for protesting, or anything rebellious like that. I'm keeping a low profile these days, trying not to rock any boats. Too easy to get thrown overboard into the Bay and eaten by the sharks. Lessons from Dad.

❦

ANOTHER METALHEAD ROLLED in yesterday, all locked up with straps in a motorized wheelchair; I spotted him during my daily rounds at Intake. The soldier's got no legs, at least none I can viddy. The guy's a goner. I'm speechless again, say nothing, stutter to myself and drop letters of the alphabet when I speak, and it all started when I wanted to talk about the events that went down in Ramadi with Skank. The words are buried in my stomach somewhere, dipped in acid, burning a hole in my gut. But luckily I'm learning from Dogg; he got me to start reading the dictionary, Webster's, rather than watching the idiot box in the big assembly room, as it drones on and on with everybody's damn opinion on everything under the sun. As if I care. I'm already up to the letter M, and it's a fat little dictionary, well-thumbed. Words are all we've got, all of us will ever have, when you think about it, so it makes sense to know them well. "Make 'em your own," Dogg tells me when he spots me holding my Webster's in one hand, flipping the pages. So I jot down new words I'm learning everyday, owning them, making them mine, mumbling them under my breath, and then hiding the words from my keeper, from My Doc, burying my notes and scribblings under my mattress at night, then moving them from one spot to another in my room. Words are my weapons now, my instruments of truth and justice, but to tell the truth, I still miss guns. Times are when I'd like to shoot again, hold my weapon against my shoulder and fire a couple of rounds.

What's Ricki doing here? I can't figure how she ended up here. This is the last stop on the road. From those roadside bombs to the Army hospitals to rehab to here, as I say. They must want her for something. Go figure.

❧

NURSE MEE HANDLES ALL THE PAPERWORK for the company; she writes the checks and does the accounting. I like her, she's cool. I mean, when she comes in everybody stands at attention like at boot camp and all the guys fall in line. If you've got control of the purse strings, you own the place. Deng is how the world runs, right? She made it known the other day that if we want to keep our privileges, if we want to keep taking the meds we need to kill the pain, we had better shape up. She reminds me of my drill sergeant in Camp Tombo before we shipped out for Iraq, yet she doesn't bark at you to get her points across. She just is. I mean, talk about inner strength and command of the situation. Nurse Mee's the one.

One time she tried to get John Wu to talk; she spoke to him in his language, Mandarin Chinese, but the Chinaman still wouldn't open up. Maybe he was licking his wounds, maybe he was like that Chinaman who stood in front of the tanks in Tiananmen Square, not moving to get out of their way, defiant, courageous. Chico's got video of the man's heroism, and it's a lesson to us all about standing up to the powers that be.

❦

I'M TRYING TO FIGURE OUT WHY Wu won't talk. It takes time but I'm putting the pieces together; Ricki knows what happened to him, knows others who know the details. You can't shake it out of Wu himself; the dude's silent, stone silent. Apparently, he got ambushed at night somewhere in the fields south of Baghdad. He was wearing a Kevlar vest and was sitting behind the driver of the Humvee when the explosion hit and tore up the vehicle, killing his two buddies in the front, and scattering pieces of shrapnel through his back and shoulder, and lodging in his left eye, which was later removed. The Iraqi interpreter in the Humvee was also killed, and that got to

Wu. He and the man were good droogs, bosom buddies, and Wu was learning to speak Arabic, studying the language and culture. The loss of the interpreter really got under his skin, but he said it was senseless, the man was innocent, only doing his job, trying to put food on the table for his wife and three daughters. Wu was stoic about his own wounds; the Kevlar had saved him but not the interpreter who worn none.

In the dark, Wu still recoils, because it brings back memories of that night, the flash of light and the brutal explosion that took the lives of three comrades, all good buddies in the war. Ricki says he keeps the chunks of metal that were removed from his eye in a bottle by his bed, as a reminder. He's got some other pieces of metal still stuck in his leg and back, but the docs say they're too dangerous to remove right now. He's got to live with them until they move or drift into less threatening parts of his body.

❦

RICKI'S NOT HAPPY WITH THE CRACKING and creeping of the floor above her gulliver where she sleeps. It's Private Dicky again, restless, having some kind of reaction to his meds that's forcing him to sleepwalk at night. Once Dicky is up, he's in the shower, the first of at least a dozen showers he takes every day, almost by the hour. Dicky won't come close to any of us for fear of germs or contamination, and if he does he'll jump in the shower. But Ricki needs her sleep and he's stopping her from getting any. She's complained but it's fallen on deaf ears among the boys in white. Nobody pays much attention when she starts on one of her rants. I feel all her pain and grief.

I raise my left arm but there's no hand. My gulliver is still trying to tell me I've got a hand, the one blown off by one of those freaking improvised explosive devices. The neurons, My Doc tells me, are running around, trying to fire synapses to get me to move my left hand, and those nimble fingers I used to have. I've got a dook of a hand now. And being left-handed, dominantly so, I'm out of luck. If one day they can build a really cool plastic hand, one that plugs into the stub of my left arm and hooks up to the nerve endings so I can feel some electricity flowing through me, I will be one happy camper. I'm waiting for that day to arrive. Maybe it will, maybe it won't. So I'm now hiding my left arm, wrapping it around the small of my back, and making my sorry adjustment in the only way I know how.

❦

THIS MORNING, AFTER BREAKFAST IN the cafeteria, I was called into a room by one of the nurses, I forget which one, probably Nurse Judy, the Irish girl with the swirl of reddish hair and those gigantic boobs that bounce up and down every time she walks by you in the long corridors of the ward. She told me to sit down and stay calm while I got outfitted with a new, synthetic eye patch. She removed the old black patch and, with a penlight beam, probed deep into the empty socket and told me I was healing well. "Pretty soon," she said, "you could get fitted for a glass eye. But in the meantime, wear the new patch, okay?" She gave me a lot of reasons, having to do with things I can't remember, mostly with infection. After peeling off the old patch and some bandages around my gulliver, a swirl of gauze and tape that fell to the floor, I reached up to the socket and poked my right index finger inside. It was gone, all right. Somehow, my missing left hand and my missing right eye connected for a moment and verified the loss with each other. Hey, I tried to be stoical, as they say, about the whole thing. Don't ask me where I learned the word *stoical*; I'm not even sure I know what it means.

Nurse Judy shook my right hand and gave me a little pat on the back. But she was in a hurry to get on with her round of appointments. I was another item to be checked off her clipboard. Nurse had to be on her way. Afterward, Ricki came over and said, "Hey, I like the new patch. You don't look like a pirate anymore, Spoon. You know, Johnny Depp? You look like the greatest writer of all time."

"And who's that, if I may ask?"

"James Joyce. He had really bad eyesight, poor man, and wore an eye patch across his forehead from what I caught in some of those cool portraits of him."

As if I had a clue as to who this Joyce cat was.

❦

IN THE AFTERNOON WHILE WE'RE ALL SITTING in the Large Assembly, about a dozen of us metalheads in various states of disrepair, Ricki gets agitated about something again.

She starts flapping her arms like a caged bird, a caged ptitsa. She wants to fly, to soar high in the sky above the clouds, she wants to land on the moon. Private First Class Daniel Dicky was bothering her again, I figured, driving her to the edge with his compulsive behavior, all those showers, handwashings, scrubbings, soap and leaves of tissue paper strewn about randomly on the floor in every room. Dicky's got under her skin with his antics, his latest being the washing of dishes by hand in the kitchen. They've got machines for that, but it doesn't matter. Sometimes, he runs around the company, skvatting everybody's dishes while they're still eating and then dragging them to the kitchen for washing in the big sink. After he's washed and dried everybody's cups and plates, knives and forks, pots and pans, he starts up all over again from the beginning. He's getting on her nerves. In Iraq, you never had the luxury of spotless dishes, the luxury of a dozen showers each day. Ricki is singing now, whistling. I mean, how can she fly away?

❦

JOHN WU WON'T SPEAK. HE'S INVOLVED in some kind of silent protest against the war, as I say. He writes these long notes to himself, and he corresponds with somebody on the outside, from the looks of things. But not a word falls from his lips. Half his face is disfigured, blown away, so I'm thinking it's affected his speech. His lips won't move, even if you shout in his face.

Ricki is the first one to speak in Circle. It's a bit like Montessori skolliwoll where, as kids, we used to sit around in a big circle and open ourselves up. What's on her rassoodock? She speaks for every one of us: "I want to thank the doctors for coming today. We agree we must all work together for the common good. We are still soldiers in arms, comrades of war. This is a good time to reassert our bonds of loyalty and brotherhood. Am I making sense?"

The doc looks bored.

"So I'll be finished with my therapy and then I can go home," says Specialist Vincent DiComo.

"Don't even think about it."

"You mean it's unthinkable."

"Yes."

❦

SO HE TELLS ME ABOUT HIS WIFE AND KIDS, John Hart does, and I listen closely, ears tuned into every word he says, which is a lot to digest, but I remember the details, not forgetting a sentence, a paragraph, a page.

They might shut down the hospital for lack of funds. We hear the rumors circulating among the docs and the staff; all the scuttlebutt, true or not, nobody knows for sure. Whispers at first, then louder and more open. I guess we'll be tossed out on the streets, like those vets from the last war and the war before that. I'm trying to think ahead and plan for the event. I know a good park in San Francisco. In less than the blink of an eye, I can bundle my stuff into a plastic bag, tie it together, and head out by foot to Golden Gate Park. I may only have the use of one hand and one eye, but at least, God willing, I've got my feet. Others might not be so lucky.

❦

RICKI LOST HER HUSBAND OVER THERE and it made her crazy. That's what I hear, at any rate. She won't talk about it but I've got my sources. Her man was a civil affairs officer with the Civil Affairs Battalion, in Ramadi. He got attacked when his convoy of Humvees approached Baghdad. The man was going for some kind of conference; he was this idealist type of guy, always planning for the future, willing to negotiate with different factions, settle any and all disagreements by working out some kind of compromise. Ricki, of course, is a warrior woman, more powerful than any woman I've met in my short and stupid life.

Evidently, he got hit badly, his legs shattered by the blast. The smell of it was foul, according to those who witnessed the explosion. This acrid stench in the air, you know? The blast had come up from the floor of the Humvee and taken out both his legs. The driver was dead, his face cracked through the windshield. Her husband apparently still had enough guts to skvat his weapon and begin firing. Parts of one leg were lying behind the vehicle on the road, covered in blood orange and bits of bone. They could not evacuate him in time, and he simply bled to death. She was in a rage about it, until she got hit herself.

❧

THE DOC WE CALL SHUFFLE IS NEVER AROUND. I'm not sure where he hides all the time but he does. Staff can't find him for meetings or appointments. He claims he's available by cell phone and I've seen him talking loudly on one such device, even if none of the buttons light up on the display or the batteries are dead. He pretends to talk on the cell is what it is. Of all the docs, he's the only one who's got a potbelly. If I didn't know better, I'd swear he was drinking beer every night. He loves that belly of his, rubs it with delight as if he were pregnant. Shuffle kind of shuffles along, wobbly on one foot, leaning against the walls of the white corridor to prop himself up and maintain balance. If you pushed him from behind, he'd fall flat on his face.

❦

DOC SHUFFLE IS sick again. He's got heart problems, apparently, and high blood pressure, owing to his habit of junk food eating. Not sure what's wrong exactly, but I'm worried. He's put on so much weight since coming back from Baghdad where he did some good things. I mean, he must be over three hundred pounds now, and he's not that tall. I can viddy him eating up a storm in the cafeteria, even when the food isn't much to write home about. I guess he's depressed about something but won't say what.

The morphs are at it again: that's what I call them, *morphs*. You can't tell one from the other. Nurse Judy somehow becomes Nurse Jackie becomes Nurse Jim becomes Nurse Jerry. I'm viddying one blend into the shape of the other. Makes it hard to know who's treating you, or whom you're talking to, doesn't it?

Nurse Mee understands this. She's very sympathetic toward us. Dr. and Mrs. Richards run the compound. If you want to know about them, I'll fill you in with all the gory details. Another round of TBIs are due tomorrow; that's what I'm hearing, as word travels fast. You know, metalheads like us. Our numbers keep increasing, jumping higher by the day. I guess the war's not going real well. Don't know how it could, really, given the politics of the place and rivalries between Shi'a and Sunni.

Major Pink won't forget. There's that night when he got hit by the RPG, when it exploded in front of him and all the blood orange and stench of the explosion filled the air. He cried bloody murder until his buddies in Infantry came to his rescue and wrapped a big tourniquet around his leg, but they couldn't save it. And after he was evacuated, at least saving his life because he could've bled to death, the leg was amputated, gone.

"I'm in the ward and all the guys next to me are blown up, missing both arms and legs," he says. "We're going crazy, feeling the pain and grief of it all, the stupidity of being in the wrong place at the wrong time on that midnight patrol around Tikrit in the freaking heat of August when the RPGs come firing at us in the pitch of darkness, out of nowhere, hammering our Humvee, rocking the crap out of it, splattering it with blood and guts. I lost two of my best buddies on that patrol. I feel bad I'm still alive, if you know what I mean, Spoon."

"Hey, man, I know exactly what you mean."

I try to console the dude in whatever way I can. He's a good man.

❦

THERE'S THIS THING I'VE been hearing about the fathers of soldiers not being allowed to look inside the caskets of dead sons. Major Pink told me this; he got word from one of the fathers whose son had been killed in Ramadi and he wouldn't get to viddy the body of his son because it was "unviewable," according to the officers who knocked on his door and told him his son was not coming back alive. The father got unhinged, burst into a rage, and almost beat up the officer, who kept shouting, "You ain't got no respect!"

His son had been blown to pieces by an IED but he still wanted to open the casket and touch whatever parts of his son's body he could. "Just wanted to say goodbye to my boy," said the father. Turns out the government was wrong: you can't deny parents the right to viddy their sons' or daughters' bodies in the casket. The father had to fight it out in court before he could.

Major Pink was steamed about this, as were John Hart and Ricki, both of whom are big on justice and honoring the rights of those who made the ultimate sacrifice. Major Pink hears about other complaints, too, like personal effects of soldiers being lost in transport, stolen, items of value, sentimental or otherwise, all gone into the ozone somewhere. Army's struggling to deal with it, Pink says, but they've got a long way to go to fix the system.

In Therapy, we got word one of our own died the night before. Nobody knows why; evidently, he'd been sucking fentanyl from a skin patch and he overdosed on it. They're beating up on us, everybody's sure of that, and sometimes the pain's so great, you go crazy, like this wounded soldier did, eating your painkiller on a skin patch.

There's a place called the G-spot. I never heard of it, but apparently Ricki has. It's on one of the roads in northwestern Baghdad, this big pothole you've got to avoid at all costs. There's a curve in the road where the enemy likes to target us and blow up our Humvees, as we're coming around the bend.

RAMADI'S STILL IN MY GULLIVER, I'm still living there. If you're cool with it, I'll tell you about Ramadi, more than you'll want to know, probably, but so what? Ramadi lies about one hundred clicks west of Baghdad, the southwestern point of the Sunni Triangle. Who knows the number of Iraqis in the city? Figure it's about a half million, more or less. A railroad takes you direct to Syria, so coming and going are a lot of foreign fighters, as well as local resistance to the occupation. You know all that, don't you? What you don't know is that we can't do anything to control the territory. Looming around every corner when I was there were Iraqis who hated our presence, hated us and called us all Jews, not Americans who'd liberated their country from the demon Saddam, but Jews. And that caused us some grief. You're there to bring democracy to an ancient land and you're lumped together with Israelis and their problems. I mean, give me a break, m'kay. If we're all Jews in their eyes, so be it. What's wrong with that? I'm there when Camp Blue Diamond is handed back to the Iraqi Army in the spring; it's one of the Saddam palaces and it's pretty much ripped to pieces from the bombing the year before. I'm on patrol at night, trying to ferret out the insurgency. Boots on the ground, knocking down doors, chasing after suspected Al Qaeda and foreign fighters streaming in through the Syrian corridor. Things got baddiwad during the siege of Fallujah when we lost a lot of Marines, noble and courageous warriors all of them, prey to ambushes and attacks in Khaldiyah.

We'd go into town and get hit for no reason while we were trying to protect the locals, provide security. This was eating us alive. An enemy using the mosques as ammo dumps and hammering us with RPGs and IEDs as soon as we showed our faces, I mean, that's baddiwad. Without enough intel to pinpoint the bad guys, without help from the locals, you don't stand a chance. Frustration levels soared through the roof. I'm not excusing my complicity with Skank in terms of what he did. He was brought in as a private contractor, a former soldier of fortune, a warrior from the last Gulf War, under the pretext of doing the dirty work we weren't supposed to do. We never thought he'd go insane, but he did. And we paid the price, all of us becoming in one night the worst of the worst—criminals of war.

❧

THE LONE RANGER IS THE ONLY SOLDIER on the ward with a silver metal plate attached to his gulliver. I mean, it *looks* like silver but could be some other metal, maybe a compound, that shines brilliantly when polished, reflecting light almost as sharp as a mirror. And he's got that black mask he wears, with cutouts for his eyes, hiding his true identity, or so he thinks. That's how he got the name Lone Ranger, I figure. That's also, from what I hear, how he operated in Iraq on his missions of no return, raids on insurgent safe houses in the most dangerous parts of the country—Ramadi and Fallujah—places where if you're caught by the enemy, you're sure to get brutally tortured and beheaded by your captors with your execution posted on the Internet and your mutilated body dragged through the streets in front of screaming crowds of Saddam loyalists, remnants of the fedayeen, and others who hate your guts. He and his buddy Tonto, as I hear, were masters of the dark, desert universe, knowledgeable in the ways and tactics of the enemy, outwitting them on every occasion when it came time to conduct nightly raids against young jihadists hiding in civilian houses, yank out those responsible for killing our troops, and deal with them—well, accordingly. Tonto was the scout, the Indian hunter brandishing his K-bar, who could sniff out the enemy with a single breath, while the Lone Ranger, in a manner of speaking, rode in on his white horse to finish the job.

Now Tonto and the Lone Ranger are TBIs like the rest of us, having served in Iraq on a couple tours of duty, and then returned to work as private contractors for a security operation over there before landing here at St. Richard's.

One day I'm with the Lone Ranger, without guns or weapons of any kind except a couple of picks and shovels, our trusty e-tool, the collapsible spade we used to dig ditches and set up camp in Iraq, when he and Tonto walk into the field next to St. Richard's. That's where John Hart and the others do their planting and growing and gardening. Tonto reconnoiters its perimeter, viddying what the flowers and shrubs and bushes are doing at this time of the year, if the field is hopelessly overgrown, if the big eucalyptus trees at the edge are shedding their bark earlier than usual, if the field can ultimately be secured. For the Lone Ranger, as he takes in the dimensions of the terrain, it's another field of battle, one that will engage the hospital staff and security guards against a platoon of us metalheads.

"It won't be pretty, Spoon," he tells me. "I can see it coming a mile away."

"What are you talking about, lone man?"

"Big fight ahead," he shakes his gulliver, then kicks up a patch of dirt on the ground. "They'll do anything to stop it. This is valuable turf. They'll pull out the heavy artillery and, if necessary, unleash the dogs of war. And they'll do it without hesitation, without honor, I can assure you, my good man."

"So, what's our recourse?"

"Bring in the A-team," he laughs a wicked laugh.

"And who's *that*, if I may be so foolish to ask, sir?"

"Why, whoever's brave enough to take them on."

❧

I AM IN A PERPETUAL STATE of becoming; I have to invent, then re-invent myself at every turn, and live by wits alone. There is nobody to fall back on. Not a soul.

The room is empty now and I'm waiting for Doc Shuffle to show up. He's always running late, never on time as he's supposed to be. It's a baddiwad habit, I tell him, but he doesn't pay attention. Will he change? I doubt it. Nurse Judy comes in before eleven o'clock, smiling, calm, nerves of steel. Her lips are kissable, sweet. I'm leaning back in my chair, sure of what she's going to tell me: "Sorry. The doctor's running a bit late. He'll be with you as soon as he's done with another patient."

What is it that he "does" with these patients? I'm tempted to ask but refrain.

All St. Richard's hospitals are the same, whether you're in Kansas or Kahleefornia. That's what Major Pink tells me, and he should know. He's been in practically every one of those hospitals since the war ended. Wait a minute. I caught myself in mid-sentence: *since the war ended*. Did it? That's what I hear from one side but still more soldiers are coming in, wounded, crippled, in desperate need of repair. Like me. I'm in need of gulliver repair. I'm not quite right in the gulliver. This war's one that'll never end, because it doesn't deserve to, because as long as it keeps going on you can't say we failed; it keeps going on because we want it to, we can't go on, we will go on. There's too much at stake to pull out now; it's easier to send the metalheads home and replenish their numbers with new recruits who, if the stats are right, will also become metalheads.

Doc Shuffle promised to help, he said he would do everything in his power to set things right, to fix me up. I believe him; there's no reason to doubt a word he says. The man is a god on earth (not true); he stands tall (a hope and a wish), walks with great confidence (when he doesn't wobble), carries a big stick (yes, a sharp needle).

I'm down on myself. I'm waiting for whatever because whatever's got to be better than what's now.

Who's the bird? Where is he or she?

A dream of flight is what I'm having, or had. Or will have, if all goes well. The other night I'm lying on my bed, half awake, eyes shut tight, lips sealed, body stiff.

I am soaring in the sky and viddy myself reflected in a shimmering silver cloud. I am a bird, a hawk with a broken wing. I have trouble balancing in the air because of the wing that won't flap. It only stays in one position. I try to swoop down to the house and viddy what's going on. A couple of teenage boys climb the back fence and go into the house, the same boys I saw at the convenience store, only they've got guns. Flashes of heat, red hot, emanate from their guns.

᭦᭥

THE NEXT MORNING I FIND RICKI in a despondent mood.

"She's looking pretty glum," says John Hart when he and I sit with her at breakfast. Not sure what to say, I say nothing. How can I cheer her up anyway? She's lost so much. I want to be the man in her life, at least the man who comforts her when she needs it most.

"Me too," says John Hart. "Same as I used to do for my wife Mary. I mean, I understand all about letting a woman cry, not rushing to her side when the tears are flowing down her cheeks and she's feeling sad about some event in her life or the lives of those less fortunate. That won't help Ricki, who stopped crying a long time ago, whose cheeks are gray and ashen, without the slightest hint of color."

"Understood."

I mean, at breakfast she sits at the table across from us and mechanically lifts spoonfuls of cereal into the orifice of her mouth, as if she's become a robot. Her mangled body, the loss of limb and the damage to her face and neck now seem to *repel* everybody who comes close. Something's changed in the way others viddy her. They want no part of her. But not me, not John Hart: it's what I most want to touch and hold, what I connect with and what gives me life and strength. Ricki has to know this; John Hart has to tell her, he has to. Yet that morning her demeanor is different, aside from the coldness in her body and expression.

I find out what it is later in the day. She's been planning it all along, as it turns out: meticulous planning down to the last detail. She's standing in the courtyard outside, near the garden of roses John Hart planted for her, dressed in pure white, a ghostly figure with lost limbs and a face turned to ice. There's a dryness in the air, a wicked blast of hot wind blowing from the East. Are these the dreaded Santa Ana winds like the ones they have in Southern Kahleefornia? The conditions are ripe for some kind of conflagration.

"I know from my days fighting fires as a National Guardsman," says John Hart.

During the morning I followed her by instinct from room to room, suspecting she was planning something, a wild action to wake up the hospital staff, to make a statement, and I was right. She's found lighter fluid somewhere, God only knows where in the hospital, and now pours it over her hair and face about twenty or thirty feet away from me. From her pocket she withdraws a cigarette and a book of matches. It's happening right in front of me, and I admit, I am slow to react. By the time she's lit up the cigarette, she's almost drenched in lighter fluid. I rush toward her, grab a blanket off a nearby bed, and wrap her in it to muffle the burst of flames she's set off.

My takedown lands her in my arms, as others in the distance run toward us. Ricki shouts and screams at me, her voice louder than ever before. "Get off me! Get off, you grahzny bratchny!"

The orderlies appear and take her away.

❦

WHERE Ricki GETS THE NEWS, I have no idea, but it comes to her on a daily basis, maybe from her Afghan buddy and boyfriend, Masood. He's tuned into everything, all the comings and goings in the community surrounding our asylum. It must be because he drives and drives and drives for hours everyday, shuttling folks lucky enough to be on the outside from place to place. I figure he makes at least three or four trips to the airport and back, and he's always yakking away on his cell phone. Ricki must've smuggled in a cell phone sometime, even though we're strictly forbidden to have one in our possession.

She must have at least a dozen in her locker, hidden there, or else scattered around the complex. Chico Rodriquez told me he tracked them all down with a scoping device, but didn't tell anybody because he didn't want to get Ricki in trouble. Chico is my savior. One day I know he'll do the same for me, because I'm planning on having a cell phone and talking to the outside again. So anyway, Ricki got briefed on a big event coming up at the local city council: a townhall meeting to discuss what to do about the vacant lot, that big empty field next to us where John Hart and a half dozen other metalheads have planted their gardens, now in full bloom, thanks to those seeds from Kamal. Apparently, the city wants to convert the lot into a condominium development and reap the benefits of that sale. The meeting is supposed to be a rubber stamping of the proposal by the city council members, according to Ricki. She wants us to protest, raise hell, appear in the council chambers with big banners and signs.

She's got it all figured out. "If we kick their butts, they'll come around," she tells the other metalheads. "Masood's coming at seven o'clock to take us there. We don't have much time to prepare, but I've got the paper and paint, all the materials ready for us to get to work. Are you with me? Say yes. Say you'll do it. Otherwise, John Hart's field of dreams is gone forever; no more plants or vines. No more gardening or basketball. Doesn't that field mean something to you? It's a breath of fresh air we all need, a place where we can rally our troops and do our singing. Now, everybody, let's get rolling."

Nobody moves a muscle. We're motionless in the Small Assembly, hearing her out but not doing a thing. What can we do? We're stuck here; there's no exit. You could say we're hunkered down but that wouldn't quite be true. Major Pink knows it's a noble cause to save St. Richard's Annex from further development; I can tell by the look on his face. John Wu wants to help out if he can with placards. Same goes for the Lone Ranger and Tonto. So there it stands. There you have it.

❦

NEXT DAY ALL'S FORGOTTEN. Now Ricki wants me to take her to the movies, but I can't and she doesn't understand that, so we're having a bit of a row, as the Brits say, or at least I heard the Brits say in Basra, where I met a British colonel in charge of their ground troops who never let his troops get in any rows. Ricki would know this if I could get her to believe me, but she doesn't. Not always, at least.

They've got the one-eyed glass monster blaring away in the Large Assembly room down the hall. You viddy how easy it is to get hooked on it. I mean, I started one morning after breakfast and couldn't turn it off until noon. Ask me what I watched and I'll draw a big blank for you.

Ricki's a sweetheart. I told her, "Ricki, I'm in love with you and don't know what to do." She just laughed at me and rolled her eyes, like some Madonna or Britney Spears pinup.

"The first twenty years of your life you spend collecting rocks and putting them into your backpack," she tells me. "The next twenty, with your back aching and sore, you spend taking them out, slowly and methodically, one rock at a time."

"Ricki, you know a lot more than I do," I say. "How'd you get to be so smart?"

"Easy, Spoon, I learned from experience, learned everything I could, especially in Afghanistan, which is the mother of all teachers."

❧

SECURITY VEHICLES PATROL the grounds, these Jeep Libertys, black with yellow lights on rooftops, gullivers sticking out of the side windows, dudes in aviator shades with bulging biceps and ratty faces, keeping track of us and our whereabouts, every movement made among us.

Security's in the parking lot now, a gang of some kind, on lunch break. A dense smog envelops the valley beyond the hospital; my eyes burn from the sting of the particles in the air. Hot smoke rises from the hills to the east. The day's infernal. I need to get away from everybody; of course, I can't wander past the fences on the perimeter of the compound. They're wired, electrified, with enough of a jolt to knock you out but hopefully with not enough voltage to kill you. Major Pink, being the daring soldier he is, gave them a try and got his hair set on fire, the ends burnt to a crisp.

When I turn, I viddy the gang of security workers playing

Hacky Sack—foosball—on the brown grass of the open field where, in the distance, I spot John Hart tending to his patch of garden, along with a few other green-thumbers among us metalheads. The workers speak some exotic language, Tongo, Boa, Keet, whatever, among themselves; hard to make out the words or even the tenor of the conversation. It's intense is all I know.

They stand in a large circle, kicking the small Hacky Sack cube from one droog to the other without letting it hit the ground. I wave hello to them but the crew ignores me. They have their own rites and rituals; most speak little English, anyway, so I am naturally excluded. This is their time away from grunt work, the security patrols, boring, detailed, covering the grounds of the factory. I don't really know them. But I've got a hunch they lead double lives: industrious workers by day, devoted gang members at night. After completing their shifts, I suspect, each droog goes home for a change of clothes, a little freshening up. You slick down your hair, put on your mirror shades and studded black leather jackets marked with gang colors and insignia. You meet the other droogs in a parking lot somewhere, climb into your custom vehicle and cruise the local neighborhoods in San Josey; if you want to be, you can be predators, tough guys taking care of business.

The business, in this case, may involve shaking down fellow droogs for deng, robbing and beating up on them if necessary, a little lesson in obedience they won't forget, not easily at least. Perhaps this is a fantasy on my part, a hallucination in the hot sun of Kahleefornia. Most are old people, I figure, folks who, mistrusting banks, keep large sums of cash at home, often hidden under their mattresses. If the whereabouts of the cash is not revealed right away, the gang members threaten to hurt or even kill their victims. The old people cave in and give up what little deng they have. Hello, Charles Darwin, welcome to my house. Let's viddy who comes out on top, survival of the fittest and all that. Next day, the gang returns to work in the factory, driving around in those Jeep Libertys, peering out the window, eyeing all of us, anybody suspicious, and then playing a round or two of Hacky Sack at lunchbreak as if nothing at all happened the night before.

❦

JOHN HART TELLS ME about Mary and his kids, sharing some of his grief: "They showed up every few days the first couple of months I was here, but then they stopped coming. Why, I can't figure. Do something wrong? Did I? Now I haven't seen Mary and the kids for the better part of a year. Go figure. Maybe I've been written off, discarded like a bag of old clothes. I'm still pretty coherent, all things considered. But they're gone, up in smoke. I told Queenie, our Head Doc, one day I'll get better and I'll be able to go home and she looked me in the eye, smiling, nodding her gulliver, but not saying a word, all the while appearing to agree with me, hear me out, and knowing it's not true. Medical ethics means giving hope even when there is none. Mary and the kids could at least show up once in a while and surprise me."

"Understood," I whispered trying to be in sync. "I'm with you, man."

"Mary and the kids will come see the garden I planted in the Annex, won't they?"

"Sure they will. They have to."

"Think so, Spoon?"

"Of course."

John Hart tells me, "The point of departure must be one's own personal history, that most elusive yet palpable of all subjects, at once so easily within one's grasp, at once forever receding in time's eye."

"You're a wise man, a knowing man, unlike me, who can't stand up straight as a man because of what I've done."

"Spoon?"

"What?"

"Remember the Loma Prieta quake?"

"No, what happened, man? Who got shook up?"

"I did," John Hart tells me. "Hey, I'm lucky to be *alive* and talking to you *right now.* The quake hits late in the afternoon, and I'm down in Santa Clara at a convention, lots of computer salespeople, when the entire building shakes and I run outside and find the parking lot undulating, like a giant wave at sea. It ripples through the lot and the cars roll. The building is all glass and I fear that large sheets of glass will crash to the ground, and I'll be sliced up like turkey meat in a butcher shop. The bridge collapses with a huge gaping hole in it that's taking forever to repair, and the freeway overpass where I've driven back from work everyday is now totally collapsed like a sandwich on the lower deck, killing a lot of people."

"Not a spectacle I'd care to revisit," I say.

"One time I was called to help out with the fires burning up in the redwood forests of my state, up north in Mendocino County," says John Hart, reflecting on his days as a National Guardsman before his tour of duty in Iraq. "Another time, when the quake struck and the power was out, the bridge damaged, freeways collapsed, my unit was called to action. We worked day and night to restore order. Before I could rest and go back to work I was shipped out on a Saturday for duty in Iraq. The air force base was mobbed and Mary and the kids gave big hugs and kisses to Dad. I'm standing there on the tarmac, in my National Guardsman uniform, duffel bags at the ready, proud to serve and do my duty. Tears are flowing, and then months later it all goes bad."

❧

THE WHALES, THIS TIME OF YEAR, do their annual migration from Alaska down the edge of the California coast all the way to the warm waters of Baja, where they spawn and give birth. I follow the whales, watching them as best I can with my antique Zeiss binoculars on the rooftop of St. Richard's, high above the crowd. I got up there secretly through the backstairs, four or five flights, spiralling into the stratosphere. Through the binocs I can viddy right out to the lip of the ocean, the cool waters of my beloved Pacific. I'm jonesing for those whales.

In my notebook, I write: "Buddhism teaches us that suffering, which we all go through, depends on a cycle of desire followed by ignorance, plain stupidity. We're stuck in that cycle and keep repeating it until death, and eventual rebirth. In the Samyutta-nikaya, it goes like this:

If this is that comes to be;
from the arising of this that arises;

if this is not that does not come to be;
from the stopping of this that is stopped."

In a book Dogg gave me, I read: "Hernando Cortez, who'd conquered the Aztecs of Mexico, named California after a mythical paradise ruled by Amazon warrior women. In the early sixteenth century, in search of gold, he found the garden of paradise in the coast of California. The natives were friendly, ran naked in the sun, and lived off the abundance of the land. The Baja Peninsula became the Sea of Cortez and first to the eyes of Cortez appeared as the island home of the black Queen Califa."

Is this true? Is Kahleefornia named after Queen Califa?

❦

I SHOULD TELL YOU about Chico. You need to know about him, really you do. He's a cool guy, very focused, a nice geek. Somewhere along the way he learned about networks, hooking them up, making connections, and getting different devices to talk to each other. I'm a bit envious, frankly, because he's got a real profession, knows what he's doing, and may viddy the light of day when he gets out of here. They've got him assigned to different jobs and they keep him real busy. One day he's hooking up the loudspeakers and audio system in the Large Assembly Room, another day he's troubleshooting the computers in the hospital network after they've crashed, owing to some virus attack, probably, or just plain stupidity on the part of the administrators who don't know diddly about using these machines.

Chico is around twenty-two or three, and like me, he got hit in Iraq. But he's not metalhead, or if he is, he's wearing a wig of some kind to cover up the plate attached to his skull. I'm not sure why he's here, except that he's got some ailment that makes him doze off spontaneously half the time. I mean, if the nurses didn't stop him from nodding off, he'd be lying on the floor sound asleep. So they like to keep him busy.

❦

BEFRIENDING CHICO RODRIGUEZ was not easy, I can tell you that. He tended to look down on me at first, a wounded and sorry-faced Marine, too young to know anything, yet cocky enough to think he knew it all. I can understand where he was coming from. That's the kind of veck I projected to him, with my daily antics in the Small Assembly and my general cynicism toward everything and everybody. He wanted no part of me until he met Kamal and Kamal's daughter. Things turned around fast after that. He and Kamal shared some stories about their experiences in Baghdad, particularly in the Green Zone where Chico had been assigned to wire up the buildings, despite the frequent power outages and spiky electricity in the city.

Chico was hit like me in Ramadi while on patrol in one of the outposts in Al Anbar province, but he lost no body parts. Only his gulliver was jarred, and shaken to the core. It took him three months before he could remember anything, and then it all came flooding back. Inside St. Richard's, he wires up the whole place, as I say, and he's always walking around with a backpack hanging from his right shoulder (he's got shrapnel still in the left, he tells me) that contains all the tools of his trade: spools of wire cabling, various meters for measuring power, computer disks in sleeves for starting and restarting the machines in the local area network, pliers, gloves, duct tape and the like. He's always repairing something in the complex, tweaking a connection, keeping the circuits clean and flowing with juice. The guy is amazing; quick hands, sharp focus, and this sixth sense when it comes to troubleshooting a problem. That's why the nurses and docs love him.

"NEXT DAY, AFTER HAVING lunch finally with Maria, I'm still in a state of shock," Chico tells me. Why, I don't know, but he tells me. "She's not what I expected at all, man. You understand? Her attractiveness, her presence—everything about her seems impossible. She's got this terrible, weathered look about her; I mean, those catlike eyes are so devious, even frightening. Her mouth and zoobies look ugly, as if she could rip into your flesh at any moment. 'I close deals,' she says. And perhaps that's why I'm still thinking about the jagged corners of her lips and mouth and those shark-like zoobies I saw when she first came into the restaurant.

"Hey, the way I figure it, lunch is not lunch, it's all about business. You're there to get what you want, at whatever price, it's business and it's carnivorous. 'Live with it,' she tells me in so many words. And I'm sucking on it like a cloud of black smoke, choking on it in fact. Something must be wrong with me, as if I didn't get it, man, didn't see what was coming right from the beginning. I'd perpetuated a fantasy, an illusion about who she really was. I'd seen her at first, on that dinner date, as a tall, attractive, beautiful Latina with a face scarred from life's struggles, from hard living early on, a broken marriage, yet a woman who had integrity, a grittiness but also a charm, a poise, an honesty. Maybe I projected all of that on her, man, wishing that she was some kind of ideal woman, not accepting the truth of the matter, which is that she's completely without any redeeming values. And there ends it.

"Strangely, afterwards I feel a kind of liberation, *a freedom*. For one thing, I'm not bound to be in Maria's movie, sucked into a world where my needs and desires get lost in the vortex of the other veck. No way, Jose.

"Where does it go from here? Where do I meet *women* now?"

"If I knew I'd tell you, Chico, really I would."

"C'mon, Spoon, you're a stud. Help me *out*."

"I'll do what I can, Chico."

❦

"SHE'S PLAIN BITCHY, that's all," Major Pink says, though his situation is not much better. His quest for women is also doomed to fail, as far as I can viddy. He's no hunk, not attractive, with a craggy, kind of ugly face, and some discoloration on his skin. He won't spend a dime on any woman, he's cheap. Maybe it's the Scot in him, who knows? Women want some gesture of expense, if not a bouquet of flowers, at least the willingness to spend on them. Pink won't do that. He always insists on going Dutch for dinner on the first date, he tells me, or even a movie afterward. Before he knows it, women want no part of a second date with him. They give excuses, typically of the variety, "Sorry, but I have other plans." The cool, snarky brushoff. He's heard that expression so many times that it's become a predictable chorus, a little ditty that makes him cringe at first, then laugh. Major Pink has given up on women. He's a gay man, probably, judging from all I've heard, but I won't ask, nor will I tell. Don't you, either.

IN THE LARGE ASSEMBLY after breakfast, we're supposed to sit down and write letters home. I've got nobody to write to, not really, as me and my dad aren't speaking much, but it's kind of weird sitting there at one of the tables and watching my fellow soldiers scribbling madly away on pieces of paper with big strokes of the pen while I'm twiddling my thumbs, trying to look disinterested, maybe even a bit bored with it all. Dad doesn't come to viddy me and I haven't heard from him since I joined the service. I figure he's still living on that sailboat, going out on the Bay and beyond in the Pacific with his buddies to ride the waves, catch a few fish and be free. I can't blame him, really; it's been too long and I understand how he feels. I'm a disgrace to him and his pals, now after Mom's death. He hates war and is unforgiving, and if he ever found out what happened to me on that patrol in Ramadi, we'd probably never speak again. So anyway, the guys are spitting out pages and pages to their loved ones, and at the end of an hour, some orderly in greens comes by with this big basket and collects all the letters.

You can bet they're screened before they have any chance of going out the door, if they go at all. Lately, I have the suspicion that they're being dumped into the garbage at night. I spotted a couple of letters buried in the compost John Hart's been building out in the field behind St. Richard's. John Hart collects bags of leftovers and other organic matter every morning, filling up a couple of plastic bags and dragging them out to the heap. I've got to tell him about the letters being thrown out like that; I'm sure he'll raise a stink, as will Ricki. She's the one who's got the most power among us; she was a colonel, after all, before she got hit and went all screwy. That ought to count for something among the higher-ups in the company.

❦

FOOD'S BEEN BADDIWAD, worse than ever, so it came as no surprise the other day when a big drat, a nasty fight, erupted in the cafeteria. Major Pink was the culprit who started it, and I have no idea what set him off; he threw a fit when he started to eat the porridge served again for the third day in a row. I mean, he scooped up a bowlful and tossed it at Ricki. She threw her slabs of white bread, which admittedly tastes like dried sponge, back at him. This unleashed a chain reaction among the twenty or thirty metalheads around four or five tables. I mean, the food was flying. It was like rockets bursting into the sky on the night of July Fourth, huge projectiles of eggs and burnt toast and butter pellets and banana peels, all airborne. The stuff rained down on my gulliver and the floor was swimming in milk and juice and leftovers. This thing was out of control, and the music began, loud as hell, full volume. The speakers in Cafeteria blasted Jimi Hendrix on electric guitar singing the "Star Spangled Banner," with lots of machine gun fire, screams in the night, voices from the unknown, cries and whispers, bombs exploding.

> O say, can you see, by the dawn's early light,
> What so proudly we hailed at the twilight's last gleaming,
> Whose broad stripes and bright stars, through the perilous fight,
> O'er the ramparts we watched, were so gallantly streaming?
> And the rockets' red glare, the bombs bursting in air,
> Gave proof through the night that our flag was still there;
> O say, does that star-spangled banner yet wave
> O'er the land of the free and the home of the brave?

My gulliver nearly cracked wide open; the metal vibrated like crazy, and everybody else felt the same thing. It didn't take long to quiet down the crowd. For hours afterward, all I could hear was Jimi Hendrix and nothing else.

"It's a technique they've been working on," Chico later told me. "You know, *crowd control*. They've figured out what works for every crowd, particularly one like ours, where you've got to herd cats to get anything done."

He reached into his pocket and pulled out the control device for the loudspeakers, which was oval-shaped and about the size of a car key alarm. "This is how they do it, man—with a flip of the switch and you're toast," Chico confided in me. "I've got my own copy as a backup in case theirs fails or needs repair. Cool, huh?"

Ricki was the only one the blast of music never bothered. I couldn't believe it. She walked around as if nothing happened, smiling from cheek to cheek while the music was driving everybody crazy as hell.

"Hey, what's your secret?" I asked when I ran into her in the Small Assembly.

"Look, Spoon." And out of her pocket came two tiny earplugs. "Specially designed. Custom earbuds. They deaden high decibel noise, like rocket fire, tank blasts, mortar rounds," she said. "I'll get you a pair, in case you ever need them."

"Thanks," I said. "You're the most resourceful soldier I've met."

"Learned a lot in Special Forces but it wasn't enough to stop a camel from kicking out my eye in Afghanistan."

"Tell me about it."

"Later, okay?"

❦

I'M THE ONLY ONE here who doesn't believe in UFOs. I've yet to be convinced.

Chico won't stop talking. You can't shut him up, no way. He goes on and on about his mother, as if she were some kind of saint, a Mother Teresa, and because of her he went to war, got into combat, fought against the enemy, bravely, valiantly, with great heroism, and his fate was what God wanted, what his mother wanted. I hear his voice in my gulliver but don't know how much to believe, or what.

❦

IN THERAPY, THERE'S A ROOMFUL of us, sitting on stationary bikes, spinning wheels, pedaling hard as we can. Sweat pours down our brows and backs and arms. Major Pink's only got one leg, the other's prosthetic, a metal and plastic job, so he's got it harder than the rest of us. John Hart's singing a happy tune while he pedals, stretching his arms, rolling his shoulders; he's in a good mood this morning. I wonder why, or how he manages to be so upbeat. There are miles to go on these bikes going nowhere.

"Pedal one, two, three . . ." I hear from the loudspeakers. "Again, now, one, two, three. Hup dee dup dee . . ."

One of the docs arrives to check us out. Who's due for surgery? All these wounds, loss of limbs in particular, require surgery, one repair after another. John Hart's had a couple, so has Pink. I don't know about Ricki, but I figure she's had at least three or four, judging by the prosthetic leg she's got and the broken hip and all that shrapnel buried in her gut. Docs fear infection the most, I'm told, fear all that bacteria spreading like wildfire through St. Richard's, a blaze out of control, eating us alive. And Ricki tells me, "Hey, Spoon. Ever wonder if the docs wash their hands?"

"No, always thought they did."

"Well, they don't."

"You're kidding. Thought docs were the cleanest dudes on earth."

"They're not. Look at their hands when you get a chance, Spoon. You'll be blown away by the number of creepy, crawling bugs on them."

"You know that? Seen it?"

"Yep. That's why I carry a bar of soap around with me at all times and demand whenever a doc comes close to be sure he or she washes their hands. Remember, they do all their work with their hands."

"How can I forget?" I smile and she smiles back.

❧

"IT'S A BAD HABIT," John Hart tells Nurse Mee, although I am not sure she's paying attention or in the least bit interested. "You know how difficult it is to break old habits? Once, my bathroom faucet broke, the one that turns on the hot water. I tried to fix it myself, but ended up twisting it badly with a wrench. I was embarrassed to call the landlord, figuring he'd come out and see how I'd messed up the repair. I said, 'Okay, I'll live with it. Let's see what happens.' I turned off the hot water underneath the sink. You know, everyday for a week I got up in the morning, went into the bathroom, and automatically turned on the hot water faucet, knowing damn well that no hot water would come out. Just a reflex. A habit. I even had a talk with myself about it. A little confrontation with my right brain, or left brain, whichever side was in charge of things rational."

❧

"WE'RE JUST THE SUM of all the neurons in our heads," the Head Doc, Dorothy McQueen, whom we call Queenie, tells us. "We think we've got free will but we really don't. Neurons do."

In Group, she tells us this. I figure she wants us to understand what's going on in our gullivers.

"Our brains are composed of cells, lots and lots of cells, something on the order of ten billion cells, give or take a couple million. That's what we're born with, ten billion, and we spend a lot of time hooking them up, making the connections, wiring them into a working, functional network that moves us forward, and enables us to adapt to the most difficult of circumstances. Each cell's got between a thousand and ten thousand synapses, which provide the connections, the wiring between those cells. That means we're looking at trillions of synapses.

"Well, the neurons can't shut up, they talk all day and night long, and they're highly specialized, grouped together to perform certain functions. It's a *monster dance*, with everybody holding hands and singing and chanting, and with luck, keeping it together. These neurons I'm talking about," she says, "have an intrinsic rhythm, they dance at a particular frequency, and they work together to define the external world, what's outside of us, every piece of information that we're constantly bombarded with, so we can understand what's going on.

"Deep down in the guts of the brain, you've got the thalamus." She says that if the thalamus is damaged, you have big problems because the thalamus is this gateway, and if there's a lesion of some kind, or a part that hooks up the visual cortex and that's damaged, you go blind.

"It's all part of consciousness, these connections between the thalamus and cortex, and there's a powerful feedback system between the two parts of the brain. They need to talk to each other, trade sensory inputs, compare and contrast experience. If that happens, you can actually raise consciousness.

"You've got to have rhythm, you've got to let go and dance. Brains need rhythm to operate properly. And there's this thing called *binding*. It's about pulling things together in the brain, firing in unison, with rhythm and purpose, so you can experience an event. The neurons know this, they like to work together and make things happen. That's the truth," she tells us. "And that's how you know you're alive."

She tells us about the brain and how it works, and all this business about cells in the brain having something known as *intrinsic rhythm*. I'm not sure what she means but it's all about having different frequencies, like vibrations, which I can understand, because I'm good at picking up vibes from people I meet. If the cells vibrate or oscillate real slowly, you fall asleep, and that's what's happening here. Everybody's asleep half the time; I say it's because of the meds, the downers, the painkillers, knocking us out and keeping us in a state of low energy, negative charges in the brain. "To wake up," she tells us, "you've got to *vibrate* at a higher frequency, and get those cells *in rhythm*, charged up, synapses firing away."

How to do that? I ask her. She doesn't have an answer, or if she does there's none forthcoming. She won't talk, won't say anything that's against company policy.

❦

IN GROUP WE SHARE memories of our experiences over there. It's one way to clear our gullivers, Doc Queenie tells us. There's Major Pink, Dogg, the Lone Ranger, his buddy Tonto, Ricki and John Hart, and occasionally John Wu. Each of us has got to lean forward, clear our throats and dig into our guts to spill the beans, what happened, where and how. It's the Therapeutic Way, Queenie says in her mellifluous voice (that's a new word I learned when I got to the *M*s in the dictionary, owing to Dogg's inspiration). So here goes:

Al-Asad is where I was stationed, I tell Group, and it's our Marine base, only for Marines, not the Army, which is out there in Tikrit. Thing is, you can't get from one base to the other without a lot of hassle; I mean, it's a major hassle, like, there are no connecting flights by helicopter. Crazy, eh? These reporters, guys I met like Peter Krill from the *Times* who followed us around for days and dug out the goods, are, like, trying to move between the two bases and cover the war but, hey, they can't get on any flights because there are none, or if there are, nobody's saying what the schedules are because the schedules are classified, as are the flight routes. "You've got to live with that," I tell this one news reporter whose name I can't remember, some lady from the *Times*, evidently, who works with Peter Krill. She's really unhappy about it, but there's nothing I can do. She starts pacing around our camp at Al-Asad, nervous because she's got to find the latrine. She's got to go. So she looks at me really funny and asks, "Where's the John?"

"John who?" I'm being caddy, smartass, too punk for my own good.

"Hey, can't you tell me where I can find the latrine *for women*?"

"You mean the Jill."

"Whatever."

The boys behind me all start laughing and it's embarrassing stuff. John and Jill are all the same, so you have to live with that.

"I'M IN CAMP AL QAIM," Major Pink tells us in Group, "when the temperature soars above 110 Fahrenheit, maybe 140 degrees in the sun, who knows for sure? A hot wind blows gusts of sand across the desert floor. And it's blown up my nose and all the way to the back of my brain, the deep recesses of my cranium; *sand for brains*, you dig? It's wearing me and my platoon down, *way down*. Day after day it's always the same. Hot from morning till night and even then it never cools. How can you have nighttime without cooling? Tell that to your science teacher. But I'm telling my boys, 'Hey, you can't let your guard down, ever. You've got to be vigilant, on your toes, understand?' I'm sitting on a chair outside Command Center, whistling Dixie, wondering when the hell I can get out of here and when my boys can go home. They ask me the same question: 'Major Pink, when can we declare victory and go home? My wife and kids miss me. They want me home.' And then it happens, I'm telling you, it happens when you least expect it, man. You've let down your guard for an instant, a split hair of a second. They start firing at us, snipers, out of nowhere, under cover, or lying on the flatbed of a truck. Luckily, they've got bad aims, can't shoot straight, although one of my boys is wounded real bad. He's got a bullet in his brain, along with the sand, of course."

❦

"MAN, IT'S THE WILD WEST out there in Al Anbar province," the Lone Ranger tells us. "I'm telling you, you don't want to go near the place. It's filled with little towns in the desert, like frontier villages built on the sand. Place is crawling with roving bands of insurgents, and I mean, these cats are mean, and smart as hell."

❦

"CAMELS ARE MOODY CREATURES," Ricki tells the rest of us in Group when it's her turn. "Nothing against them, mind you, even after what happened to me on that hot autumn day in the desert sun of Kandahar. You know about camels, Jeremy, don't you?"

"Only the ones I caught up with, long time ago, in the San Francisco Zoo." I try to be cute but she's not amused, not at all. Neither are the others in Group, as they stare me down and snarl at me with dirty looks. Everybody loves Ricki, and nobody wants you to be caddy with her; I can dig that.

"Two types of camels, okay? You with me?"

"Yes, I'm with you, Ricki, sir."

"Don't give me that sir crap, soldier."

"We still soldiers? I mean, what's the mission?" Nobody laughs at my feeble, lame attempt at a joke. All the missions are over, as far as we're concerned. We're finished, hanging on for repair work in the St. Richard's labs.

"As I was saying, there are two types of camels. You've seen them: those dromedary camels with one hump on their backs. I rode them in Afghanistan, like they do in Saudi Arabia. You can't ride the other kind, the Bactrian camels, with two humps. They're used mainly for carrying anything you can strap on their backs, because they can travel long distances without water.

"So a caravan of camels is coming toward our Humvee,

winding through the narrow roads outside Kandahar. They're kicking up sand, lots of swirls; dust all around us. And one of the camels makes a strange noise. Another grinds its teeth. Both appear friendly enough, at least from a distance, until they start spitting at us. I mean, these were like blobs of spit, almost rifle shots. We climb out of our Humvee to see what's going on. The one making strange noises is carrying a lot of cargo, transporting goods from the farms, maybe a couple of large sacks of grated poppies ready to be made into opium.

"I know something about camels, how they rarely perspire and why they don't pant. They're the toughest creatures on earth. They can tolerate really severe bouts of dehydration. And when they do get to drink, they can drain, I've seen it myself, a hundred liters in five or ten minutes. Any other animal would die after consuming so much water, but the camel is able to store the water in its bloodstream. Can you believe that, Jeremy? The water is then slowly released from their stomach and intestines.

"We start walking toward the camel caravan, me and my boys. Bad tempered, moody, and with large teeth. Yet capable of travelling great distances without food or water. I know all that, like you do.

"I'm standing next to it and it bares its teeth at me, turns sideways and kicks me right smack in the left eye. All of a sudden, I've got big trouble seeing, then I realize that my eye's flown out of its socket and hit the sand. A wind swirls and blows the eye away, rolling it in the sand. The pain's delayed, until I see the blood orange gushing from my socket. The camel runs away, making a loud noise in the distance.

"My retina's dangling there and I put my hand on it to push

it back inside the socket, but the eyeball's gone. Gone! Know what it's like when you lose an eyeball? You've got the retina, that thin tissue on the back part of the eye, is all. That's how I lost my eye, not in combat but at the whim of an angry, unforgiving camel."

"You do something to upset it?"

"Like what?"

"Just asking."

"Not that I know of."

❦

"BLEW UP IN MY FACE, taking out my left eye when an IED exploded in a tree next to my armored personnel carrier in Karbala," says the Lone Ranger, who worked as a private contractor, in Group. "Freaking thing detonated in my face."

"Baddiwad luck," chants the crew. "Baddiwad luck."

"The signature of the heat and the shrapnel took out my left eye. I could feel the heat searing my skin; that's why I'm like this, all skin-grafted, sewn together, burned to the bone. From the blast itself, I had a small skull fracture on the left side of my head, a subdural hematoma, the docs told me, plus a bruised brain. I'd never heard of anybody having a *bruised brain*, but that's what they told me. My right forearm was shattered at the elbow and wrist . . . and then, when I wake up from surgery, my left hand looks like an erector set of plates, pins, screws, rods and bailing wire, like the docs didn't know what to do and tried to make me into one of those half-man, half-robots from a *Star Trek* episode."

"Like the Borg," the crew cries in unison.

"Like the Borg *only more human*," says Major Pink.

"You'll get better." Queenie tries to console the Lone Ranger.

"Surgeons in Baghdad did all they could," the Lone Ranger continues with his confession. "Don't get me wrong—I'm not *blaming* them. To pick up where I left off . . ."

"That right, Keemosabee," says Tonto, the Native American among us, who worked with the Lone Ranger as a private contractor.

"So after a couple of operations in Iraq, I'm out of there and I land in Germany for more treatment; they're good to me and the docs are masters of repair work, replacing body parts, of which I could use a complete overhaul, and then I transfer to the States. I'm glad to be here, maybe I can go home to my dad's ranch in Sonoma and ride horses like I did before the war. Not going to happen, I'm told by the docs. My robotic arm needs maintenance, tweaking, fine-tuning. Stick around, give it time to heal. So here I am with you metalheads. Tell me if I'm making any sense, or if I've lost it completely."

There's a hush, a dead lull in Group. Nobody says anything, not a whisper. Finally, John Hart perks up and begins to applaud and soon the rest of the crew follows.

"Therapy sessions are good, I guess," says the Lone Ranger, a big, burly man with cowboy blood in his soul. "I need to ride again, be with horses, I need to recover use of my hands so I can hold the reins properly. If I can learn to see with one eye, like you, Spoon, and you, John Hart, I'll be okay on my dad's ranch rounding up cattle and such."

"And such," the crew chants until Doc Queenie calms everybody down, waving her arms in the air.

"Soldiers with TBIs," says Doc Queenie, in her most professional voice, calm yet direct, "need more time to overcome effects of brain injury than from other wounds. We can help you manage headaches and sleep disorders and work with you to deal with memory loss, like that. Most of you are taking stimulants such as methylphenidate or dextroamphetamine, uppers, strong but good, to handle any problems you may encounter with focusing and attention deficits or other kinds of tasks that require the processing of chunks of information. We realize this can be difficult; we're with you on this all the way. The staff and I are there to assist in whatever way possible. Don't be afraid to take these drugs. In some cases, we'll prescribe antidepressants or Valproate for migraines, and if you get real angry or pissed off about something, please be sure to let us know so we can increase the dosages. These memories of the war, which you men and women have so valiantly shared with each other, can be a bit of a bitch, a bob, to deal with. Yes, I said the word: a *bitch*."

"Nobody's ever the same," says Major Pink.

"I'm not," says the Lone Ranger.

"That right, Keemosabee."

"It's not funny, Tonto," says John Hart. "Some things just aren't *meant* to be told for laughs."

"You're too serious, man," says Tonto, leaning forward and shaking his head.

"We're here to make sure you make a full recovery," interrupts Queenie. "We'll do whatever we can to help. Be patient."

"We are, all of us, patients, that is," says John Hart. "We just know we'll *never* be the same."

BADDIWAD DREAMS LATER that night.

There's the base camp at Tikrit and I'm riding in that pink Humvee, the size of an elephant, when the vehicle gets hit. Hit hard from nowhere. The Humvee's driven over one of those roadside bombs triggered by remote-controlled cell phones, the weapon of choice among the enemy. Thing blows up from the bottom, right up from the floorboard, and John Hart's got shrapnel ripping through his arms and left leg, all up and down the side of his body. Some of it lands in his eye, which he later loses, and then another eye, which he also loses. He's walking around a blind man in Tikrit and speaking Arabic, but nobody understands a word he's saying.

The Lone Ranger, a private contractor, is with the 82nd Airborne on the rubble-filled highway coming into Baghdad when he gets hit. The pain in his leg is unfathomable, he's almost ready to black out. His eyes stay wide open. His left leg is chopped off at the knee and a titanium rod is placed in his right leg to help him walk and stabilize it. I'm trying to help him, as I've become a medic, but when I take one step forward my feet are frozen in the sand.

Doc Queenie is on night patrol when an RPG hits her directly in the eye, and riddles her body with shrapnel. She's a doc, she doesn't deserve to get hit, I'm shouting at Skank, who's laughing about the whole thing, spitting into my face. Skank, you're a monster, get out, leave before I engage in a bit of fragging, a bit of friendly fire, if you get my meaning. Half her skull is gone too. Her buddies in the vehicle are gone. She's counting her blessings, flipping a deck of cards that contain the names and photographs of the most wanted Iraqis.

In another dream, a soldier I don't know gets hit by an RPG while driving a truck on Ambush Alley, the most vulnerable part of the Baghdad highway. "I got hit," he tells me. I ask, "Who are you?" "I'm another you," he says. "I don't get it."

The window of the truck is blown apart, and glass flies in every direction, including his cheek and jaw. He yanks the glass out, blood orange pouring down his face and neck. One of his buddies has a large knapsack filled with bandages. He pulls one out and wraps it around the man's face to stanch the bleeding. The soldier who claims to be another me has a broken jaw and can never speak again.

I bolt awake, my body drenched in sweat. I'm shaking and trembling, cold as ice. I've had it with these damn dreams, had it with getting hit all the time. How long can I take it? Weren't we supposed to be greeted as liberators from the tyranny of Saddam? Greeted with showers of rose petals tossed lovingly at our feet? Another dream gone sour, another delusion of the war. Live with it, man, I tell myself.

Next day I see Doc Queenie as she walks into a conference room, carrying a yellow folder crammed with sheets of paper. She must have important things to say, things to communicate to the Brass. She's all right, thank God, her skull intact, her body not riddled with bullets and shrapnel wounds.

"Everybody suffers TBIs, about 62 percent of all soldiers coming back from the war," I overhear Doc Queenie tell the Brass in the meeting room. "All these brain injuries in combat are taking their toll on morale, sir."

"We don't care about morale," says one of the Four Stars. "We only care about winning."

"Amen," says another. "Our God is superior to theirs."

The Brass nod in agreement, sure of themselves, men without doubt. That's what I viddy through a crack in the door.

"And what is it, sir, if I may ask, that we're winning?" she asks, pointing a finger at the nose of the Four Stars, then tossing her sheaf of papers in the air and walking out of the room.

Next night, I'm lying in bed, wide awake, stone cold, eyes transfixed by the light of the moon when I viddy it all happening again.

There's a wild orange flash right there on the streets of Mosul. Tonto, the Lone Ranger's buddy, is out with some guys on patrol in their Humvee. The grenades hit the Humvee on the side, bounce off the door, and explode underneath the floorboard. The Humvee careens out of control, and Tonto can't move his legs, which are covered in blood orange. Other bombs go off, more explosions. Things are really, really baddiwad for Tonto. Luckily, one of his buddies gets to him and a chopper arrives to take him away. He lands in Germany, then is transported out here for repairs and recovery. He's missing one leg, and the other is pretty much gone too.

When Tonto gets home to his wife and young baby daughter, he thinks it's going to be okay. But it all goes wrong fast. The pain from his wounds is unbearable and his wife has no idea how to deal with him.

Tonto remembers almost bleeding to death from a mortar that ripped into his left arm and tore it apart. The right arm was hit too by shrapnel, and with both arms hurt he had no way to tie off the blood orange flowing from the wounds. Somehow, with the help of a buddy he got the bleeding to stop.

At home it's worse, so his wife tells the officers to put him in the hospital until he's better. They've been fighting about everything and almost come to blows a couple of times.

He needs a lot of physical therapy. "Iraq sucks," he says. "Twelve-hour shifts, living in hot concrete hangars, no toilet. Ready-to-eat meals most days. Then I almost died."

Next morning when I walk down to Mess, I spot John Hart, quietly eating breakfast all by himself at a corner table. I'm seeing him there and I'm seeing him in Baghdad, a double exposure. A grenade has fallen through his fingers. He's in a Humvee when it blows through his open window and lands on the seat next to his buddy who is driving. He skvats the grenade and is ready to throw it out the window, when it drops between his legs. He picks it up again and starts to toss it out the window but it blows up, blows to smithereens.

He's got a prothesis now with a two-pronged claw, which makes it hard to eat breakfast. John Hart is a kind warrior, a gentle soul. I respect him a lot and sit down with him to eat. We say nothing to each other, but he knows some part of me is living and reliving his life, being John Hart.

❧

JUST AS I FEARED, it happened. I'm doing my daily rounds at Intake, checking in on the new arrivals, when I spot him. He looks different, shaved gulliver, a bit of stubble, but he's the same, except for the robotic arm. It's Skank, all right; you can't mistake him, you can't deny it's him.

He's the one who committed those heinous crimes in Ramadi, the crimes I stood around and watched, pathetically, without doing a thing. I never came forward or turned him in to my commanding officer, as I should have done. No, I did nothing. I'm guilty by association, by being there and not raising my voice, going silent and dumb. What he did was an atrocity and he should be standing trial for war crimes, as I should be too.

Now he comes in, puffed up on drugs, no doubt, posturing, looking cocky as hell, proud of his robotic arm, this long, lanky mechanical device protruding from his shoulder. He's there and he viddies me. A wicked smile comes across his face, a big, crap-eating grin. I'm tempted to bail, run away, hide in my room, never come out, yet that's what he wants. We must cower in his presence, bend over and obey. BOLU: Bend Over and Lather Up. He's a power tripper, not a soldier, not a warrior like Ricki or Major Pink, not a warrior-diplomat like John Hart. He's a private contractor who went too far.

"Hey, Spoon! Look at me. Don't turn away. I'm talking to you."

"Well, Skank, fancy meeting you here." I'm trying not to blow my cool.

"Hey! My name's Travis," he smirks at me. "Nobody calls me Skank."

"That's the name you got over there."

"You call me that, Spoon, and I'll have to kill you, but don't worry. It'll be short and sweet. I'll keep the pain to a minimum."

"Like you did in Ramadi?"

"Shut your face, or I'll shut it for you!"

Skank's got a smooth, gleaming skull, a plate of aluminum metal attached like the rest of us to the part blown away or removed by surgery. Except for the arm, he's got all his other body parts in place and he's muscled up, pumped on drugs for sure, as he moves through the line at Intake. The docs are all over him; a good, working specimen.

"You and I are not finished," Skank tells me. "Stick around!"

I'm thinking he must've volunteered for some testing in the lab, brain work, probes, rewiring of old circuits, what they're doing now to make the perfect soldier.

He comes away from Intake flanked by two docs in white coats, tugging at his sleeves. He breaks away for a moment and pulls me aside. "Listen, Spoon. You know what I know, what I did, *so keep it to yourself.* You tell *anybody*—you're a dead man. Understand?"

"Yes. I understand, Skank."

"Don't call me Skank. Never call me Skank. Told you, I'm Travis T. Rex III."

"Yes, Mr. Rex. What can I do for you?"

"You're not thinking of ratting me out, are you, brother?"

"No, it's unthinkable, as we say around here."

"*Unthinkable.* I'll remember that."

"Swell."

"Hey, show me the ropes, m'kay. They're giving me some cool assignments while I heal and they do the necessary repair work, but I need to know more."

Part II

After that, I did my best to avoid Skank at all costs and when I did happen to run into the man, I fed him lots of misinformation about what was really going on in the hospital. To wit, I resisted telling him about the action out back in the big field next to the compound, the one called St. Richard's Annex. He had no business knowing what John Hart and the others were doing there.

One day I happened to be wandering about on the grounds, which stretched by my rough calculation almost the full length of a soccer field, maybe seventy-five or one hundred yards. I was stepping around the potholes and shrubs as carefully I could after a heavy rain but couldn't help getting my shoes caked with mud in the process. It was chilly outside. Behind me, I caught the watchful eyes of Security patrolling the perimeter. It made no sense because nobody was going to vault the wire mesh fence that circled the field and escape into the unknown. How could they when the thing was at least ten or twelve feet high, with spools of barbed wire on top and probably with enough electricity flowing through the mesh to fry you to a crisp?

In one corner I spotted John Hart diligently working on his compost heap. I mean, the guy was obsessed; every day he'd hike out to that corner to feed the heap, always under the watchful eye of Security, guards in black uniforms sitting patiently in their Jeeps with binoculars in hand, scanning the horizon, ever watchful, ever vigilant. He'd carry a big green plastic bag over his shoulder with leftovers from the kitchen, all the scraps of discarded food, uneaten veggies, balls of cabbage, leaves of lettuce and whatever else he was able to scrounge from the garbage bins in the kitchen—until he'd find the spot. I followed him a couple of times, and on one occasion, even helped him carry a few extra plastic bags. He'd unload the bags, stomp the contents into a big hole he'd dug up, then rake it over with a modified broom until it was properly groomed. I figured the dirt in the field was pretty rich already in swarming bacteria and lots of dead bugs and dog crap accumulated over the years, so the added stuff was like icing on the cake, as it were.

John Hart loved building this compost heap, I could tell by the look in his eye; he was beaming. And the look was contagious. I started beaming too when I saw him like that: sweat rolling down his brow, his lungs puffed up, heart pounding, fingernails covered with dirt. The big day came for him when he dug into the soil and found it black with loam; that meant the compost was ready to be spread for fertilizer, ready to give birth to plants or flowers. He wanted a flowerbed and he talked about it to me, said he'd been in Holland one spring when the tulips blossomed and the land was covered with them, a sea of gold and red and white.

Two days after Kamal came to visit and I talked to him about John Hart and his compost heap, he said he wanted to meet John Hart and had a surprise for him. There was another surprise too: Kamal's daughter, Leila, who accompanied him. I wanted to catch a glimpse of her because I'd heard a lot about her when Kamal and I were in Iraq: he was the proudest dad on the planet because his daughter was coming to Kahleefornia to study at the university nearby and follow in his footsteps as a scholar and teacher. In Visitors, I introduced Kamal to John Hart and right then and there I sensed the two men understood each other. Kamal, with his shock of white hair, thick white beard, and penetrating dark eyes, exchanged knowing glances with John Hart, man to man; I felt small by comparison. I was just a kid, a baddiwad kid at that. These were large men with commanding voices, leaders of the pack, alpha males who wanted to do great things. I owed my life to Kamal after that explosion in Baghdad.

Kamal's daughter, wearing a white headscarf, white blouse and tight-fitting jeans, sat at his side in the lounge area of Visitors and said very little. I could feel myself drawn to her; she was probably close to my age, if not younger, and her shyness and gentle smile touched me where I live. I could not get her out of my gulliver for weeks afterward, but that's another story.

"Captain Hart," Kamal said, "my gut tells me you're a good man and in need of some help with your garden."

"That's true, I could use some help."

"Well, my daughter Leila and I have brought some seeds from our garden in Beirut and a very special rootstock from the city of Shiraz."

"So Jeremy told you about my compost heap and my plan to plant a flower bed?"

"Indeed he did," said Kamal, reaching into a large basket. "We brought you many varieties of seeds, enough for flowers, an herb garden, and some simple vegetables. Of course these will need some watering at first and the proper staking to the ground. Is that possible out in that field behind the parking lot?"

"I think so," said John Hart. "Look, there's a patch of city land and a school yard right next to it and last year they dug up the field, laid down a whole bunch of pipes, and set up a watering system. Don't tell, but I think I can re-route some of that watering to the garden. Nobody's supposed to know."

"As long as it's not illegal," said Kamal lifting a skeptical eyebrow.

"What's a little water among friends?" said John Hart.

Both men laughed and smiled at each other.

"How long were you in Iraq?"

"Ten months, National Guard, before I got hit and my mozg got shaken up like all the other soldiers in this compound."

"What do you intend to do with the fruit and vegetables you harvest, if I may ask, Captain Hart?" said Leila, leaning forward on the table.

"Hey, have you tasted the food here? First time and you'll know why some fresh herbs and fresh vegetables, grown organically, will make a difference. I'm getting sick, sicker each day on this diet of pablum they serve in Mess. I ate better in Iraq, no offense intended. All of us could stand to get healthy by eating right."

"Well, these are from my father's garden in Beirut," she said, handing him a series of packages with seeds, explaining in detail the source and origin of each item of fruit.

"Sounds pretty exotic," he said, not knowing really what to say, except to thank Kamal for his generosity.

"There is one more thing I ask of you, Captain Hart," said Kamal. "This rootstock. If you would be so kind as to plant it in your garden. It needs a stake. It's an ancient vine from the vines of Shiraz. You'll grow grapes from it and a friend of mine at a local winery will purchase those grapes when they're ready to be picked. It's a bit of an experiment. I was in Shiraz and found them there, owing to another friend who was growing them discreetly, against the wishes of the local government. You know, of course, wine was first made in the land that is now Persia, thousands and thousands of years ago. The Shiraz grape travelled to France and then Australia and even here in California. Can you do this?"

"No problem. Does it take much water?"

"Actually, not. I'm told many of these vines grow wild in the hillsides above the city of Shiraz, where it's dry, wedged between the desert and the mountains, and survive quite happily on small amounts of rainfall. Use your judgment. The rootstocks, my friend told me, are at least five hundred years old."

"Well, Kamal, you've really done a lot for me and for my fellow soldiers here at the base. Think we're in business and ready for a good crop; soldiers make great farmers too. I don't know how to thank you."

"You don't have to. God thanks us both," he said, "if not in this life, then in the next."

❦

SO KAMAL BRINGS BACK the twigs, the rootstocks, long, sinewy ones, from the ancient city of Shiraz, wrapped in a big green plastic bag. I'm not sure where Shiraz is on the map, but I figure it's pretty important because Kamal knows all about it.

"This is precious cargo, Spoon," he tells me. "But it'll serve you well. After you plant and harvest, you'll find the grapes have healing properties. The twigs are more than five or six hundred years old, only a few having survived the centuries. This will make the most potent and powerful wine in the world. A glass or two, I'm told, will work wonders and heal. Trust me on this. You know the irony is that they come from a country that forbids the drinking of any alcohol, yet that's where wine was originally made nine thousand years ago. Go figure."

I'm not sure I understand everything Kamal is talking about. He's got a way with words, he's a poet and scholar in addition to being the best translator of Arabic we ever had in Baghdad. I'm willing to give the twigs a try.

"Remember, you can't tell anybody about this."

"Why?"

"Keep it a secret," he says with a wink. "I'll be back in a few weeks to check up on you guys and see how things are going. Hang in there, buddy."

I'M TURNING OVER IN my rassoodock what Kamal said about the field out back, alongside the parking lot, behind the hospital, which hasn't been used for years, lots of weeds and shrubs and dirt, yet still ripe for John Hart's compost heap. Out there Kamal is looking over the stretch of land and talking to John Hart about it. I can't quite make out what he's saying, something about "terroir," this thing the French always talk about when they talk growing vines and making wine. "It's not only about the land," Kamal says. "It's about a combination of elements, the richness of the soil, yes, but also climatic conditions, the slope of the field, the interplay of temperature, hot in the day, cool at night, the way water drains from the vines. But of course, much depends on the quality of the rootstock, the woody trunk of the vine, how well it handles the water and other nutrients in the soil, of which there are many, thanks to your efforts, Captain Hart."

❧

KAMAL SEEMS TO KNOW a lot about growing grapes and making wine. "It's in my blood, and the blood of my ancestors," he tells me. "When I went to school in England I studied other things, language, literature. I lived in Iraq for many years under Saddam and it was a desperate time; I am sorry for your loss, Jeremy, I understand this is no war for any soldier to fight honorably. Going house to house, door to door, pounding and slamming your way through the civilian population, looking for so-called insurgents, we're told, is a recipe for disaster, and not worthy of a military man. Now I am old, and my daughter lives in Beirut, travels to the States to see me and attend the university here. She tells me I must do more for my American friends, the ones who sacrificed for my country. I must honor them with good deeds. Growing wine is one such deed."

❧

MIDNIGHT AND I'M OUTSIDE in the field of broken dreams, as Ricki calls it. I've got the three plants, dirt and roots and all that in my green plastic bag. This is a stealth operation. I'll vouchsafe the security. I'm getting ahead of my story. Bear with me.

This field behind the hospital, St. Richard's Annex, is semi-abandoned. I mean, it's overgrown with weeds and lots of shrubs, as I've been saying. Nobody's bothered to look after it. It's like a giant compost heap, one of those we had once in our Sunnyvale backyard when I was growing up in the Valley.

The grapevines are going to take a lot of watering, despite what I've heard, and I've got no way to deal with that. Until Kamal appears a day later and tells me, "Oh, by the way, Jeremy, forgot to tell you. Don't bother watering these vines. When I got them from the Persian dealer in Shiraz, he told me nobody watered them at all. Well, maybe just a little. They're pretty hardy and resilient, and all that, so don't panic."

Man, was I relieved. Thoughts hit me of having these dying vines on my hands. Another disaster, another loss.

Somehow, I'm thinking, these grapevines are going to set me free. How, I don't know exactly. Shadows fall. There's a thin beam of light in the garden. I can viddy it from my window. They've got all the windows locked, with metal bars from top to bottom. I can't open anything. I'm a prisoner in here, for sure.

❦

WHEN KAMAL COMES to visit, my spirits are lifted.

He was my interpreter in Baghdad, as I say, a man in his fifties or sixties with a shock of white hair and equally shocking burly white beard. He's like the father I never had, but I'll save that story for another time if you're with me. Nobody comes to visit; it's one of the reasons everybody is so down, feeling blue. Kamal shakes everybody's hand, the whole sick crew, all of us in Group, Major Pink, Dogg, Ricki O'Brien, John Wu, Chico, and of course the best man among us, John Hart. He throws his arms around us in a series of big bear hugs one after the other. He's got all this billowing and booming well of emotion for us—in contrast to the docs and nurses who run the company, where everything is technical, clinical, a function of lab tests and reports. Kamal looks us over and asks how we're doing and if there's anything he can do for us. I say, "Hey, can I talk to you in private?" He agrees.

We take a brief walk outside, under the watchful eyes of Nurse Judy; she's got her binoculars focused on us, peering across the parking lot and into the field of compost John Hart created. Maybe she can read lips. What I tell Kamal is that I'm hearing some buzz of secret lab experiments on soldiers, and I'm watching my back because this war criminal Skank is part of it and out to get me, so I'm concerned we're being used and maybe soon we'll be out on the streets, begging for food, living underneath some freeway or out in the public parks. He screams in anger: "But you're heroes of the war! You gave your life for your country! Okay, you're wounded. Somebody's got to help you."

Nobody's going to, I tell him. This is business, all business. Government funding wants results and we're a bunch of lab rats and we won't be able to survive and maintain and keep things going here for too much longer. Kamal's gulliver is spinning. I can viddy he's processing all this information, taking it in, trying to figure out some kind of solution. That's part of being a translator, an interpreter: you take one language and turn it into another, you find the equivalents of one in the other. I like Kamal; he did a lot for me in Baghdad before I got blown up and lost my hand and my eye and some part of my rassoodock.

We walk back to the hospital slowly, his arm around my shoulder. He whispers in my ear: "I'll do what I can. You can count on me." I know I can, Kamal's word is gold. He's a man of his word. But realistically what can he do for us? I mean, we're hosed. The writing is on the wall. Maybe some of us will get transferred to another hospital, maybe not. The lion's share will have to get ready for a life on the streets. It won't be easy, but we'll find a way.

Two days later Kamal returns. He's got a backpack strapped over his shoulders. I don't know how he got it past security up front, but somehow he did. Kamal is crafty, a magician when it comes to getting what he wants. I've been with him in Baghdad, plying his trade.

"I've been travelling through the ancient lands," he tells me, "and I've got something that ought to help you."

I'm wondering if anything will grow in that field, the soil's so baddiwad, but Kamal thinks otherwise.

He explains: Grapevines don't require rich, fertile soil to thrive. Soils too rich, too full of nitrogen and nutrients, produce abundant grape crops, but these will be grapes suitable for eating, not for making wine. The fruit will be too simple and sweet and lacking in complex minerals, sugars, acids and flavors. The world's finest wines are invariably produced from poor quality soils where few other crops would be worth planting. The great wines of Bordeaux are produced from soil composed largely of gravel and pebbles, on a base of clay or chalk. The great Burgundies come from acidic, granite soil on a base of limestone.

The reason for this anomaly, where you've got poor soil

producing great wines, is that the thinness of the soil naturally restricts the quantity of the crop, so that fewer grapes are produced, but of higher quality. Poor, free-draining topsoil encourages the vine to send its roots deeper in search of water and nutrients. As the roots reach further down, complex minerals will be absorbed that add complexity to the grape and, eventually, to the wine. Vineyards tend to be situated along river valleys, on gentle slopes where they have maximum exposure to the sun, where the soil is free draining, and where, historically, the rivers could be used for transport.

Kamal's got it all figured out; he's smart as hell, yet I never thought he'd be going into the wine business like this. I mean, he's taking advantage of that good field out back, unattended, fenced in, with baddiwad soil and all, plus our labor in tending to the vines. So what?

In time John Hart will be happy growing a vineyard along with his herb and vegetable garden because he's determined to make us eat better. "We should grow what we eat and eat what we grow," he says to the crew. Meanwhile, when the vines are ready to harvest, the grapes will look ripe, all set to pluck when somebody gives the word. Kamal will collect all the grapes and take them to the Sage Mill Winery where a droog of his, he claims, has the machinery in place to crush the grapes and store the contents in these huge oak barrels in the basement of the winery. They've got to be stored at the right temperature and monitored until they're ready to be poured. Kamal says wine tasting is a big event at the Sage Mill Winery; and this Shiraz will receive high marks. He's very confident. The future will unfold as he says, so he says.

KAMAL WAS GOING TO fall by yesterday but he could barely get out of bed, poor man; he'd been lying flat on his back for about three days, owing to a fierce and throbbing pain in his lower spine, he told John Hart. It's obviously due to a lack of exercise, I figure from his account, and from those extended periods of sitting that involve his daily work at the computer, writing and translating documents from the government of Iraq. He sleeps on the floor of his apartment. That helps a little, he says. He has not eaten much, he adds, because he's lost his appetite and has trouble sitting upright for any length of time without enduring back spasms and a pain that runs up and down his spine relentlessly.

BEYOND THE FIELD NEXT to the parking lot is a small local elementary skolliwoll. I wandered out there one day and hung on the fence, observing the kids at play during one of their recesses. These were the cutest kids in the world, a mix of every race and ethnic origin known. They made a lot of noise, shouting and screaming and shrieking, which bothered me at first, my gulliver being particularly sensitive to even a few decibels above normal. After a minute or two I was able to block out the sounds, and just watch the pattern of movement, the running around, the small legs and feet hitting the ground. There was so much energy and life I felt dead by comparison.

A day later I saw the kids, a troop of them coming into Visitors. I had no idea what they were doing here, on my turf, with my droogs lounging around, gullivers bobbing, muttering under their breaths, drooling and spitting, some of the worst writhing in pain, wheelchair bound, limbs missing, metal rods and weird wired contraptions replacing them. What was going on here? Were we some kind of a freak show to be laughed at and mocked by these kids? Who let them in? A couple of nurses whom I didn't recognize led the pack, pointing at various fixtures in the facility, while the programmed TV set, this monster plasma display, locked into a single source, pumped out the latest fair and balanced news from the Pentagon channel. My buddies tried to pay attention to the stream of little kids flowing through the corridors, out of Visitors and into Mess, and back away from Weights to Counselling, and then Reception. I followed their paths, more out of curiosity than anything else, and because I got a charge from viddying the future youth of the country, little people now, darlings who had not yet become monsters like the rest of us.

Things got weird when, out of the crowd, emerged a man dressed as Bozo the Clown. He was large, larger than John Hart, and his outfit seemed made of some kind of inflatable plastic, so his arms and legs and torso were puffed up, like the Michelin Man in those television commercials. His face was smeared with white paint, his lips circled with black outlines and his nose a bulbous red ball of fire. He had on a crazy wig, so his fake hair spiked outward into big curls of white. I figured he was one of the teachers from the skolliwoll, trying to make the kids feel right at home, but then I got a baddiwad vibe from the dude. He actually frightened one of the little girls by dropping his pants and wiggling his bottom. I stepped forward and wanted to say something, like, "Hey, asshole, back off.

You're screwing around with my kids."

But I decided not to. Instead, I hung around the fringes of the group, slinking down the corridor at the tail end of the phalanx. Bozo the Clown led the pack, pointing at my buddies and then laughing up a storm. The laughter was contagious and the kids roared. This was insulting, mockerous. Who was this clown anyway? How did he get in here?

After a minute of laughter, the clown disappeared, splitting off from the group, as the nurses led the kids to Exit. I was tempted to follow the clown and check him out, but resisted the temptation. Something was going on here, and it would take a while to figure it out. Time was always on my side. I had the patience, like my buddy Vincent the sniper, who could sit in the bush for hours and hours a thousand yards away from his target, waiting to get the right shot.

My shot would come, too.

❦

FOR SOME REASON I'M beginning to think we're all lab rats here at St. Richard's. They keep changing the meds on me, one day green pills, another day orange, and the effects vary. I'm breaking out in fever, the chills, a rotten stomach, coughing and wheezing. When I tell Nurse Judy she smiles at me: "Oh, you'll live. You're taking your meds, aren't you, dear?"

"Of course I am, but it's knocking the holy crap out of me. Can't you get the doc to change my prescription? C'mon, what's the problem? Why are my meds different every day?"

She had no answer, not a peep. And she went on her merry way, checking in on all the metalheads, one by one, with her standard are-you-taking-your-meds-dear interrogation. I know something's up when they blast the air-conditioning full bore at night while we're sleeping. I'm drenched in sweat and then I'm hit with rockets of air chilled almost to freezing.

Half the metalheads wake up out of the dead of sleep and try to throw blankets around themselves while their bodies are literally shaking to the bone. The blankets are thin as paper, standard Army-issue but not wool, just plain cotton, no fluff, and when I look around I viddy a whole bunch of blankets missing. Standing on the threshold of our room, which houses about twenty-five of us on Army cots, I make out the silhouettes of Nurse Judy and one of the docs I don't recognize. This is an experiment, all right. The metalheads shout, "Turn off the freaking air conditioner!" But the air still streams through the vents and causes the sweat on my body to turn to ice.

This goes on for a couple of nights, then subsides at least temporarily. When I do a quick count of blankets I notice only half of our crew have them; the rest have disappeared.

A day later, still chilled to the bone, sneezing and wheezing, I can't believe whom I'm viddying when my name is called to come to Visitors. I'd been thinking about her, dreaming a couple of times, and now there she is: Leila. She's wearing a blue headscarf and a long dress, almost down to her ankles, but I can still catch the curves of her breasts and hips. She's got a big brown shopping bag with a Bloomingdale's logo on it. I've never been to that store; heard about it but never been there. It's out of my range. She greets me formally with a little handshake and a sweet smile: "Hello, Jeremy. Nice to see you again."

"Oh, call me Spoon. Everybody else does."

"I prefer Jeremy, if you don't mind."

"Jeremy's fine. What brings you here, Leila?"

"Many things. Can we talk in private?"

"Not easily. They say the place is bugged, we're under surveillance, and if you look around carefully you'll see where they've got the video cameras placed. My buddy Chico gave me a map of them."

"What are you saying?"

"Listen, if it's really important I think I can find a dead spot, a gap in the line of fire."

"Forgive me, Jeremy, but I still don't understand what you're saying."

"Leila, come with me."

We walk out of Visitors and down the hall past Reception and into the Large Assembly. The docs and nurses are giving her the once-over as we stroll by. She walks with a certain grace, her movements lithe and smooth. And she's got presence. Man, does she have presence. I can feel her strength like I felt the strength, the aura, of certain great Marines in boot camp. You knew they were true warriors by the way they carried themselves. After we stop I notice there's something angelic about Leila, an aura about her; it pulsates with blue light and a band of gold around her body.

Inside the Large Assembly we sit down at a far corner away from the other metalheads, yet close to the blaring beast of television. Our conversation will be drowned out by the roar of the beast, the jacked up volumes when those TV commercials come on. Chico's map ought to be okay; after all, he installed the surveillance system, or at least was one of the ones who made it operational. I've committed the map to memory, so this is the spot where Leila and I can be private, out of earshot, out of view, according to my calculations and previous reconnoitering of the terrain in St. Richard's. She sits down at the table and opens her bag, pulling out a large wool blanket.

"We heard you were being frozen to death the other night," she says with a look of deep concern on her face.

"That's what I'm thinking too. We're lab rats, I guess, ready to be eaten alive or experimented on. So it goes."

"No, so it does *not* go."

"Hey, that rhymes. Cool."

"Listen, Jeremy, along with the blanket I've brought you some vitamins and some power bars for energy, in case you need them for your health. When Babba and I were here last he said he thought your health was bad, *deteriorating* was the word he used, and he couldn't understand why. It made no sense. So I asked if there was anything we could do and he said, 'Leila, there are things we can do, but we must be careful.' He would not elaborate, so my heart told me to bring warm blankets for you and vitamins and other sources of protein. Babba knows how important you are to Captain Hart, John Wu, Chico, Ricki, Pink and the rest. He knows what you've done but doesn't blame you for your acts of violence in Ramadi; he says you were drawn into a plot unsuspectingly, without your knowledge. In fact, you might've been set up and kept on a string, so you wouldn't talk."

"Your father, Kamal, is a wise man, all right. I mean, he saved my life in that car bomb. He told you, didn't he?"

"Yes, but not the details."

"I don't believe what I'm hearing from you. Somebody cares? You care? This place, St. Richard's, is the end of the road for us metalheads, the ones without family or droogs, anybody to look after them on the outside. I'm finished."

"That's *not* the way we see it. Not at all."

She reaches over and touches my hand and pulls it up to her cheek. Her lips move to my fingers and she kisses them. My other hand, the missing limb, now gone phantom, feels jealous. Twinges of what can only be described as joy, something I have not felt in months, probably years, begin to find their way up to my gulliver. Even the metal plate on my skull vibrates. A shiver runs down my spine, from the base of my neck to the seat of my pants. I can feel a zillion nerve endings getting excited, maybe even heated up. Leila's got some kind of power, an angelic gift.

"So, Jeremy."

"Call me Spoon."

"I prefer Jeremy, as I say. Jeremy, others are depending on you, and you won't be any good to them unless you take care of yourself now. I'll bring you other things when I return next week, okay?"

"You're coming back? *Nobody* comes back here after their first visit, which is usually perfunctory, a matter of hello-goodbye, hope you don't die too soon. They're grossed out by our condition, our state of rassoodock, our missing body parts. Pink says it's all Darwinian, whatever that means. Survival of the fittest, and we ain't very fit anymore."

"See you next week, Jeremy."

When Leila returned the following week, I was outside in the field with John Hart, watching the vines grow and the herbs and vegetables begin to sprout up from the ground, showing their new faces.

"THEY SEARCHED MY BACKPACK at the Reception entrance," Leila tells me. "I had to take out every item, in this case a lot of poetry books, and spread them on a table for examination. I felt violated, Jeremy, because after that I was strip-searched in a room next to the Reception hall. A woman in a nurse's outfit—I'm not sure if she really was a nurse or just a security guard pretending to be one—made me take off all my clothes and stand naked before her while she reached into my body cavities and poked around with a cold rubber glove. I thought, why are they doing this in a hospital for veterans of the war? What's going on? It was humiliating, I can tell you that. Then she asked me questions about my headscarf and why I was wearing one, was I a Muslim, what was I doing here as a visiting student at the university, why was I seeing you, how did we meet, was I trying to convert you to Islam, and when I told her my father was an Arabic translator in Iraq working for the Americans, she laughed at me and said, 'I don't believe you, honey. You're lying, aren't you?' I was shocked by the treatment. Here I am studying business and finance in America, in an American university, a straight-A student, modest, unpretentious, trying to do good, trying to live up to my father's high standards, his international reputation as a scholar, teacher, translator in Arabic, Hindi, Persian, and other languages, and I'm treated like a terrorist. When they stopped me from seeing you, I told my father and he was outraged. He said something was wrong with St. Richard's, as you call it, something bad was going on there that the authorities didn't want us to know about, and he was going to investigate. Justice would be served."

"Don't believe it," I said, stunned.

"Believe it, Jeremy. I'm telling you the truth. St. Richard's is not what you think it is. Did you get my books? The ones I left with the people in Reception?"

"No. The funny part is that my ex-girlfriend from high skolliwoll was here the other day and she left me a bunch of new action comic books, without any trouble. I guess I know what they want me to read."

"I'll find another way to get you those books, plus the new vitamins, power bars, and some other things to build up your strength. This woman Ricki told me about her Afghan driver friend, Masood, and gave me his number. Meanwhile you can be sure my father will do his part to find out what's really going on in your medical center."

"Leila, you're a great woman," I said, almost embarrassed as the words rolled off my tongue. "All I've known are teenage girls, forever teenage girls, and they don't give a crap about me. They look at my missing left hand and that piece of plastic and rubber and metal on my gulliver, and start to puke. They can't take it, and want no part of me. I was good enough to go to war for them while they shopped the malls and bought new clothes and made themselves real pretty so they could screw a lot of boys. Now that I'm back and licking my wounds, in a state of disrepair, I might as well be thrown out on the junkpile of humanity, a discard and reject from my high skolliwoll crowd."

"I'm sorry, I feel your loss and grief," she said. "Really I do. We've got to work together on this. Promise?"

"Okay."

"Let me know when you get the books. Inside one of them is a cell phone I've smuggled in for you. It's got all the numbers you need for speed-dialing. Are you with me?"

"I'm with you, Leila."

"Call me at night, any time really, if you need me, but better at night while the others are sleeping. We can talk quietly through this. I'll let you know what my father finds out."

"It's a plan. Okay."

TWO DAYS LATER I got a package from Ricki delivered by her Afghan droog who was going to take us surreptitiously to the City Council meeting. Ricki, I realized, was not under surveillance, as I was. She had free rein at St. Richard's, mostly because of her warrior spirit which she carried with her like a sword and shield on her back. If she didn't like something, she spoke up and let the powers that be know it. After she had rallied the troops to attend the City Council meeting—at least in spirit but not physically—and raised hell about the city's plans to build condominiums on the open field next to the children's skolliwoll, her stock had risen considerably. She had the admiration of all us metalheads, and docs and nurses in power, including Nurse Mee, feared she could cause a revolt in the complex at will, and the whole shebang might come crumbling down.

Nobody wanted to cross her. So when she came into my room with a big brown Bloomingdale's bag and handed it to me, not a word was said. It had got through Security without a peep, though I'm sure the video cameras had got a look at it. The bag had a couple of books of poetry by Hafez in translation. Leila had told me that in Iran every Persian family kept a book of Hafez's poetry on their living room table, reading and memorizing large passages of the text, and always asking questions of the book, then looking inside to see what Hafez's answers, in poetic form, would be.

I resisted opening the books in Ricki's presence for fear the cell phone Leila had promised would suddenly drop out, and an explanation would have to be made, which I couldn't make. So I reached in and skvatted the other items. There was a small bag with a string you could pull, and it contained a dark blue shell parka for warmth at night. I unfolded the parka and pulled it over my gulliver; it was made of some kind of insulating material and felt crisp to the touch. Just what I needed to fend off the air conditioning attacks at night.

Unpacking the rest of the items, I found a bottle of vitamins, several power bars, which I was sure were loaded with protein, minerals, and other things to build up strength, as well as another bottle containing plain white aspirin tablets (something we were never given), and what looked to be a lock of her hair. She had attached a brief note to it with a paperclip. It simply said: *Jeremy, be brave and be in touch. Leila.*

Ricki skvatted the note out of my hand and looked it over. "Well, well, Spoon, looks like you've got some babe on the outside who likes you. Good for you, kid."

For the next two days I read and re-read the poetry of Hafez.

I had hidden the cell phone underneath my bed at first, then transferred it to another spot in the ventilation system down the hall in one of the storage rooms. When I thought about it I realized I had no connection to the outside. Our little protest effort, which Ricki had orchestrated so skillfully in collaboration with her Afghan driver droog, was probably the last time I would have a chance to see anybody on the outside. Security had tightened up in recent weeks; new cameras were installed, according to Chico, and our short excursions to the parking lot and the open field where John Hart and John Wu tended their gardens were heavily monitored.

I realized why the next day when the clown appeared in the Large Assembly. He was the same Bozo the Clown who had practically mooned the little kids from the neighboring elementary skolliwoll and who had given off such baddiwad vibes I wanted to run down the corridor and hurl myself through the glass in the front lobby of Reception just to get away from him. Bozo was back. He found Private First Class Dickey at one of the tables and took him by the arm and led him off. That was the last anybody ever saw of Dickey. And when I asked about his whereabouts, about where he was and what happened, nobody would answer me with a straight face. All I got were smiles cheek to cheek, followed by suppressed laughter, as if it were some kind of joke. Nurse Judy said, "Oh, Spoon, you ask too many questions. Private Dickey's gone off with the clown, simple as that. You can live with that, can't you?"

How could I respond? What to say?

Not that Private Dickey was a droog of mine, or anything like that. He had a nasty temper, as I recall, and he'd served three tours of duty in Iraq before getting hit, before his gulliver went all wonky and he started yelling at everybody and threatening to take action if they didn't answer him back. How can you come down on a soldier like that?

Too many *thats* in the last paragraph, as I can viddy in my notebook. My gulliver's not working right, so I'm going to nibble on one of the power bars Leila smuggled in.

❦

A WEEK LATER LEILA came for another visit, this time accompanied by her father Kamal. I mean, I caught a glimpse of them standing in Reception, talking to the security guards. Kamal's an imposing figure, a man of authority and presence, his shock of white hair and white beard giving him an aura of power. I sensed from a distance how much he loved his daughter Leila and how offended he was at her treatment during a recent visit to me. He got the security guards somehow to laugh at one of his jokes, or something like that because he and Leila were given a free pass to Visitors, without any body check or search. She was carrying a shopping bag from Macy's with a big wool blanket sticking out. Kamal himself had a big thermos of what I thought was tea or coffee hanging over his shoulder, along with a backpack I suspected was filled with books and writing materials. Under one arm was a small black typewriter, an old manual job with the name Underwood in silver letters. He had heard from John Hart, no doubt, that Dogg was writing a book on sheets of yellow legal paper, and whatever else he could get his hands on, so I figured the typewriter was for him.

What could I say to Leila? She had smuggled in a blanket, bottles of vitamins, books of poetry, and a cell phone in case of an emergency, all of it on my behalf. Nobody had done that for me, not in my short and unhappy lifetime, and a feeling of deep appreciation, a stirring of emotion, came over me such as I'd never experienced before. People really did these things, unselfishly, without expectation of anything in return. I mean, what could I possibly have to offer Leila? She was the daughter of a famous Arabic scholar, translator, teacher, and world traveller. The man was a gift to our soldiers; he had saved my life from a fate far worse than I had experienced. I owed him that, yet he had never asked for anything in return. These thoughts filled my gulliver as they walked toward me, waving and signaling to meet them in Visitors.

Leila wore jeans, tight fitting ones, and Nike running shoes, and a thin white blouse that was more than a bit revealing. Her white headscarf was pulled back a notch or two from her forehead, and her jet-black hair jutted outward above her light blue eyes. I greeted her father with a handshake and a word of thanks for his efforts on my part; I suspected he might be behind his daughter's risky behavior, her smuggling of contraband into St. Richard's. Kamal had a devilish side too.

I leaned forward to kiss Leila on the cheek but she turned away. It was not appropriate, certainly in the presence of her father. This was a family bound by custom and tradition, a family with deep roots in the past, even though they had made their way, at least temporarily, to the land of milk and honey, where the past fades into yesterday's sunset. Leila, instead, shook my hand and held the phantom limb of my left. The neurons from the phantom fired in my gulliver, dancing in the limelight and singing joyously. Those neurons, as one of the docs had told us—Doc Queenie, I think—needed to be awakened every now and then, and reassigned to another part of my limbic system.

"Jeremy, good to see you," said Leila.

"My daughter tells me you've gone through some difficult times at night, with blasts of air-conditioning and no blankets, and she tells me the staff aren't tending to your needs, you're eating badly and your health's getting worse."

"That pretty much sums it up, Kamal," I said. "Thought we'd have a chance for recovery here in Kahleefornia, but it doesn't look that way."

"How's John Hart's garden doing?"

"Well, you'll have to viddy for yourself. We can walk it if you like. He's even got me doing a patch. I planted tomatoes and cauliflower and some lavender the other day. I mean, I'm a city kid, all bricks and concrete, and here he's got me being a gardener. John Hart's amazing. I know it wouldn't have happened if you hadn't got the ball rolling and given him all those seeds."

"Where is John Hart, by the way?"

"Haven't seen him in a couple of days. Maybe he's in surgery to remove those chunks of shrapnel he's got embedded in his gut. Hope he's all right."

"So do I," said Kamal, with a skeptical eye. "Things may not be on the up and up in this hospital, this repair facility, from what I'm hearing."

"Jeremy, we brought you a thermos of," said Leila, her voice trailing off into a whisper, "wine. It's from Shiraz and it's the same rootstock my father gave to John Hart to plant and harvest. The wine is ancient, and was used by Persian warriors for healing purposes. Try it if you like, but don't tell anybody. Just between you and me."

She handed me the thermos and smiled, "Well, if it's anywhere near as good as the vitamins and power bars you passed along to me, I'm one happy camper, I can tell you."

"And the man who calls himself Dogg?" asked Kamal. "How's he doing?"

"Okay, I guess. He's been writing this great American novel, he's bragging to everybody in the compound, doing it at night, I hear him scratching away on these yellow legal pads, as I told Leila."

"What's it about?" asked Kamal.

"The next thing. A coming disaster as a result of a hole in the ozone layer, or something like that. It does a lot of damage but not in ways you think, he told me. That's all I know."

"Would he need a typewriter like the one with me?" said Kamal. "I wrote my first scholarly book on it years ago and it may have karmic value if I can pass it on to a young writer like this man Dogg. Does Dogg have any outside friends or contacts?"

"Not many. There's a beautiful black woman, I mean she's a knockout, don't mind my saying, who comes and visits every few weeks, but they usually argue, drat about something, then kiss and make up. She leaves but she never brings him anything because I always see him going back to his room empty-handed after her visits. It kind of makes me sad. Here's this big powerful man with a plate of metal over half his skull and like the rest of us feeling the pain of shrapnel and other metal object in our bodies, and nobody seems to care one way or another."

"We care," said Kamal. "Can you give him my old Underwood typewriter and wish him luck on his novel-writing efforts?"

"Sure, glad to."

"Does he have a title for the book yet?"

"Yes. It's called *Unthinkable*."

❦

THE FOLLOWING WEEK WHEN Leila came for a visit, I was blown away by her appearance. I mean, there she was dressed to the nines in cutoff jeans, her bellybutton exposed, wearing a haltertop that accentuated all the right curves and nipples, with globs of makeup on her face. She was almost unrecognizable, and dare I say it, she looked like a hooker. At Reception, they told me, "Spoon, there's a babe here who wants to catch your act. Says her name is Brittany. You know her?"

"Sure, sure," I lied. "Used to know a lot of babes, even one named Brittany. She must be from Vegas."

"Well, come out and get her," said the voice on the loudspeaker.

The other metalheads, on hearing the news, were up in arms. "Hey, Spoon, who's the babe?"

"Didn't know you were a stud, man," snarled Major Pink.

"Awesome, dude." The Lone Ranger patted me on the back. "C'mon, be sure to introduce us."

"That right, Keemosabee," chimed in Tonto.

When I got to Reception I turned and spotted Leila. She looked at me, winked, then whispered: "Don't say anything."

I shook her hand and took her to Visitors.

"Please forgive me, Jeremy, but this was the only way I could get in without raising any questions," she said apologetically. "I made myself up to look like a woman hired to turn tricks, you know?"

"That's the easiest way, I figure, to get inside St. Richard's. Welcome all hookers."

"I'm glad you think it's funny."

"What's up, Leila?"

"Well, I thought we could have some fun," she smiled seductively at me.

"Haven't had any fun in months, maybe years, and I'm only a twenty-something kid with a missing hand, a glass ball for a left eye, and a gulliver full of metal. Soldiers like me don't have fun. We can't get it up, for one thing."

"I brought along something to help you out," she said.

"What's that?"

"My father's Viagra," she said. "Here, take one of these baby blue pills and let's find someplace where we can be private, okay?"

"Leila, this all comes pretty suddenly. I don't know if I'm prepared."

"Oh, you can do it."

I popped one of the blue pills and an hour later we were in the room adjoining Weights with the door locked behind us. I had not been able to get it up since getting hit in Baghdad, figuring I was doomed to impotence for the rest of my days. But Leila knew otherwise. We kissed and made out and got to touch each other's naked bodies more tenderly than I had ever touched Brianna, my ex-girlfriend from high skolliwoll. Leila was a woman, not a teenager, and for the time we were together in that room making love on the cold floor while soldiers lifted weights next door, pumping pounds of iron, I began to feel like a man again.

LEILA TELLS ME: "Before the war my father took me on a pilgrimage to Shiraz, the city of poets. Do you know Hafez and Sa'di? Both poets come from the city; Hafez was born there. You know a copy of his poetry sits on the living room table of every Persian family, and is consulted when the family must make an important decision. The members of the family ask, 'What would Hafez say?' and read lines of his poetry for answers.

"Babba and I visited the mausoleum of Hafez, which was filled with Persians reciting lines of poetry, always by heart. They love his poetry. The beautiful light fills the city courtyards and the roses are in full bloom.

"We found the Bagh-é Eram, the Garden of Paradise. There was a large garden and a palace inside. Mosaics on the walls told stories about the life of Shah Abbas the Great. It was really moving stuff and that's why I wanted you to read the book of Hafez's poetry I gave you."

"Haven't read the book yet, but I will. Can I ask Hafez how the hell do I get out of here?"

"Okay, we'll have to read his poetry to find out. Are you with me?"

"Sure. You're the best thing that's happened to me in a long while, Leila."

IN GROUP, RICKI SHARES A DREAM: "I am on a pilgrimage with Masood, my Afghan interpreter, guide, lover, ancient tribesman and Northern Alliance warrior. Yes, my lover. Are you surprised? You already knew that, didn't you? A pilgrimage is called a *ziyarat* in Dari. Do you speak Dari? Masood taught me and I am forever grateful.

"We must travel to the northern part of the country through the Tashkurgan corridor in Samangan province. The journey is perilous, yet with Masood as my companion I have no fear. Semper Fi.

"Because the Salang Pass tunnel is closed, under heavy construction, we are told, we must shift directions and travel through the Shibar Pass. The road is wicked, tortuous, and serpentine in the extreme, made only of dirt and rock, riding on the edges of cliffs. On both sides, we're embraced by the high Hindu Kush mountains. Huge trucks move back and forth, in counter directions, spewing black fumes, engines roaring and grinding, making the road almost impassible in our Humvee.

"Several days and nights later, we arrive in Balkh province and its capital Mazar-e Sharif. In Dari, *Mazar-e Sharif* means 'Tomb of the Noble One.' You need to understand how important this is to Afghan Muslims. They believe that Ali, the fourth caliph of Islam and the first infallible imam of Shi'ites, lies buried in Mazar-e Sharif. This is an Afghan belief, powerful and deep, even though other Muslims believe Ali is buried in Najaf, in Iraq, not Afghanistan.

"Our pilgrimage is probably like that made by hundreds of thousands of Afghans over the centuries to the shrine in Mazar-e Sharif. 'When you get there you must read the opening chapter of the Qur'an over the grave of Ali,' Masood tells me, 'and ask the shrine's inhabitant to plead to God on your behalf.'

"I am not a Muslim," I tell Masood.

" 'Don't worry. I will pray on your behalf, Ricki,' says Masood, in his voice of greatest assurance, 'and ask forgiveness.'

"Mazar-e Sharif still bears the scars of war left by the Soviets and the Taliban. Fear runs through the streets, especially among the women who are veiled in blue and white burqas, even after the ousting of the Taliban. Being unseen, hidden in the afternoon light, Masood says we must understand their desire to protect themselves from the prying eyes of soldiers loyal to their warlord masters.

"We find the Imam Ali mosque at the center of town. The tomb resides in the middle of a beautifully crafted tile mosque, in a marble courtyard. The turquoise dome is tranquil, offering the promise of solace and prayer, communion with God. Masood recites the words of the *fatiha*, the opening of the Qur'an, taking in and exhaling the words with each breath, and tears begin to form, until he weeps uncontrollably. 'I still cannot believe I have come this far on our pilgrimage,' he tells me, 'you and me, soldiers of the mountains, united against the oppression of the Taliban. And now I am pressing my forehead against the tomb of Ali. Is this not incredible or what? I find a oneness with God I have not seen or felt before. Soon I join other pilgrims in asking forgiveness.' "

❧

THE GOVERNOR IS COMING. Can you believe it? He and his troops will be here any moment, I hear the nurses chattering among themselves. Everybody's got to be on their best behavior. He's coming with an army of staff and news reporters and TV crews with cameras and lights. They're going to watch his every move, record it for posterity, clip after clip. He's famous for being famous and you can't take that away, at least not easily, I tell myself. What does he want? What *would* he want?

In the distance I viddy him come into Reception, flanked by members of his staff, all decked out and neatly dressed in dark business suits and ties. Their faces appear to have been scrubbed and polished like fine silverware and they wear permanent smiles. Not a single one is sad or frowning. In their eyes the world's nothing short of perfect. This is the day to mount an aggressive PR campaign and show the Governor as a sympathetic amigo with the wounded and lost, the poor souls who got blown up in war, over there, not here in Kahleefornia, although if you ask John Hart he'll still tell you Iraq is right across the border from Kahleefornia, a stone's throw away, a short drive by car beyond Yosemite and the Sierras.

I try to get a peek at the Governor as he moves in and out of Reception, shaking hands with the docs and nurses, and occasionally signing autographs. Wait. Who's that with him? The others?

"Oh, I know who they are," Ricki bumps into me from behind.

"Well, who are they, then?"

"You really don't know, do you, Spoon?"

"Said I didn't."

"Look. Look closely. Those are the heads of the five families, the men in black suits wearing sunglasses. They pull the strings, run the state, and probably, on a good day, even the country."

"Power brokers, eh?"

"Well, more than that. Selectors. They choose the politicians they want to run for office, fund the campaigns, smear the opponents, and curry the necessary favors to get what they want. They own the country, always have, always will," Ricki tells me with a deep sigh and some pained grief in her voice.

"So what are they doing here?"

"Good question, Spoon."

"Let's go find out."

Ricki and me move toward Reception, ambling down the long corridor from the Small Assembly to the crowd around the Governor. All of a sudden Security jumps in front of us, blocking our path. Two bruisers with guns stand sentinel and push us away. Nurse Judy appears out of the gloom and says, "Hey, Ricki. You can't go any further. You're not part of the plan."

"What?"

"I suggest you and Spoon turn around immediately and go back to your rooms. You've seen enough of the Governor and his party already."

"But we just got here," I tell Nurse Judy.

"C'mon, Spoon, let's get something to eat. Aren't you hungry?"

"Of course I am," I tell Ricki with a wink and a nod, like my dad.

"This is truly an honor for me to be here. All Kahleefornians should be proud of this facility and how we're treating our boys coming home," says the Governor, shaking the hand of Doc Richards, the founder, as the cameras record the event. "This should serve as a model for other hospitals dealing with the injuries of our young men and women coming home."

"Ain't war a bitch?" says Major Pink in a loud voice that

everybody can hear.

The Governor picks up on it and doesn't skip a beat. "Yes, war is bad, bad for everybody. You men and women have made the ultimate sacrifice to serve your country. I am proud to stand here next to you."

"What about some more funding for the hospital? Can you get that?" cries a voice in the crowd.

"Doctor Richards and I are working closely with those in Washington who control the purse strings. I can't give you an answer right now but my staff will be on top of this. Now if there are no more questions, I want to visit your rooms and meet each and every one of you."

Everybody knows it's a PR event, brilliantly orchestrated to pump up the Governor's poll numbers. He's getting photographed now with John Hart, Major Pink, Chico, the Lone Ranger, Tonto, and the rest of the crew. John Wu's nowhere to be found; he's disappeared down a rat hole somewhere. Small matter. I've never seen so many star-struck folks falling all over themselves to be photographed with the Governor. They're in love, is all I'm thinking. The man's a lovable metalman, maybe like John Hart, when it comes right down to it. He struts through the corridors of the compound, shaking more hands, patting us on the back, asking how we're doing. Of course, all he hears are the same replies: "Governor, we're doing fine. Healing well. Soon we'll be going home." Of course, none of it is true. Not a word.

I'm curious about the heads of the five families, the men accompanying the Governor on the tour. They linger in the background, then disappear into the elevator at the far end of the compound, which takes them not up, but rather down into the lower level facility, the one that's only available to those who have a high security clearance. The heads are on their own, breaking away from the Governor and his tour. They've got bodyguards flanked on both sides, and those guards are packing heat, lots of it.

What's down there? I'm thinking to myself. I've never been and curiosity is sure to get the better of me, cat that I am. Where's the elevator going to take them? I want to ask Ricki, who knows it all, but maybe I'm afraid to get the answer.

❦

ON THE FOURTH OF JULY, I'm telling you, the wildest thing happened in Mess. You won't believe it but it did. It got me to thinking about how easily we can get freaked out.

You know about IEDs and all, don't you? They're the defining weapon of the war, the game changer, so to speak. You'd find a lot of them in abandoned cars or on the roads and highways leading in and out of Baghdad stuck in potholes or buried in cinderblocks, always detonated by trip wires or cell phone calls. Nobody was safe, not even those in armored tanks. You're driving all over the place outside the Green Zone, in convoys, at checkpoints, doing house-to-house raids, and at any moment your Humvee could be hit by one of those IEDs and blown apart, and you with it. We're all metalheads because of them, because nobody prepared us with proper armor to protect us from those blasts. Flak vests and Kevlar helmets were not enough. Insidiously, the blasts occurred underneath our vehicles, like some volcanic eruption, and tore off our legs and arms, or if we were lucky enough to be out of range, our limbs would be saved, only our gullivers jarred.

And they cost about five dollars to make. And they were about the size of a pizza box. The cost of war for the enemy. Go figure.

It's around six o'clock and all of us are lined up and ready to enter Mess for dinner. I'm at the back of the line, wondering, ironically, if I'd ever get to viddy any fireworks again on the Fourth of July. That's what me and my Dad used to do, sitting on the dock of the Bay, catching the burst of rockets and Roman candles over the water.

Major Pink is at the front of the line and he spots ahead of him a couple of dozen cardboard pizza boxes on the tables where we eat. Each box has a small, plastic American flag sticking to it, standing upright. The flagpoles are not made of wood but tubes of metal. That's the first clue.

"We've got a situation," says Major Pink calmly, so as not to upset the troops waiting in line. Just the opposite happens. Maybe he's putting us on, seeing if we're sharp enough to recognize any and all signs of the enemy. A ray of light from the overhead glints off one of the metal flagpoles and hits Chico in the eye, triggering some kind of flashback.

"Holy Jesus! IEDs!" he cries, almost freaking out. "Head for cover."

"We're under attack!" shouts somebody from the back of the line next to me.

"How'd they get in here, man?" says the Lone Ranger, in his best cowboy voice, looking more puzzled than worried.

"That right, Keemosabee," says Tonto, doing his Indian bit.

"Am I losing my mind or what?" says Dogg, also having a flashback to the war. "This *can't* be happening. Tell me it's *not* happening."

I'm viddying the scene in Mess and notice the staff behind the counter have all disappeared. Nobody's serving us. Okay, it's the Fourth of July: they must be off from work, I figure, gone home to be with their families and celebrate.

The Lone Ranger and Tonto walk slowly inside. Tonto scouts the perimeter, as he usually does.

"There's an unattended cell phone on a chair over by that table," says the Lone Ranger, pointing his finger.

"Somebody's going to detonate these bombs and blow up the entire frigging Mess Hall and all of us along with it," says Major Pink. "I'm not *happy* about it, soldier. Not at all."

"Hey, who the hell left the cell phone there?" shouts Chico.

When I glance up, I spot a banner draped across the counter on the wall that reads: RAMADIO'S PIZZA WISHES OUR BRAVE SOLDIERS A HAPPY FOURTH OF JULY.

The boxes are stamped with the name RAMADIO'S in big red letters.

"Don't you *get it*, man? Wake up! They're from Ramadi, the enemy," says Major Pink, trying to hold back a big grin.

"Hart was right, after all," says Chico. "They've crossed the border from Iraq into Kahleefornia. They've taken over the hospital, infiltrated the ranks and are ready to blow us all up. The invasion of the enemy has begun."

"They're starting from here to make sure justice is served and those who attacked them will now be avenged and won't be able to defend the civilian population," says another soldier in line.

"You get near that pizza box, I'm warning you, and it's *kaboom*, bang, bang, bang, you're finished!" says Major Pink.

Hart chimes in. "Told you I was right, but you never believed me!"

"Wait a minute," says Ricki, appearing on the scene, unruffled. "Don't you idiots *smell* anything?"

"What are you talking about?" says Major Pink. "Lost my sense of smell a long time ago, matter of fact in Fallujah."

"Me too," says Dogg. "Lost it there on patrol."

"I smell *pepperoni*," cries Ricki. "I smell garlic and herbs and mozzarella cheese. Yum-yum. It's wonderfully aromatic. *Let's eat!*"

And she muscles her way to the front of the line ahead of Major Pink. As she moves toward the tables ready to grab the boxes, Chico shouts, "Ricki's going to blow up the whole place. Let's get the *hell* out of here!"

One by one she opens each pizza box and lifts the slices to her nose, inhaling the powerful scent of its ingredients. The smell is so pungent from this RAMADIO's donor that all of us, from the looks on our faces, are beginning to imagine the reawakening of our lost sense of smell as if we were standing next to the oven in a pizza restaurant. "C'mon, it's okay," she says, taking a bite. "Tastes terrific!"

A moment later, Doc Shuffle appears, looking somewhat bewildered, and asks sheepishly, "Anybody seen my cell phone?"

Chico pounces on the cell phone and shouts, "Stay back, doc! Traitor! You were going to blow us all up!"

Dogg, reacting wisely, wrestles Chico to the ground and yanks the cell phone away from him, then gives it back to Doc Shuffle.

"C'mon, guys," says Ricki, waving a tiny plastic American

flag in each hand, "get over your paranoia and celebrate the Fourth. Life is better with pizza!"

❧

IT'S HAPPENED AGAIN. I'm telling you there's no mercy, no hope for us metalheads. We're freaking *doomed*. The moment we make any progress, any so-called positive steps forward, the company staff take issue, and if they don't like what we're doing, they take action.

We're out in the field when all of a sudden it starts to rain. I mean, it's a cloudburst or something, a wicked wind kicks up and batters all of us out there planting new seeds. At first, I'm tempted to race inside, as are Pink, John Hart, and Tonto; rain won't help us and besides, who wants to get drenched and all? Then the pellets of rain come down harder and start pinging the metal plate on my gulliver. It's like I'm in an echo chamber, the rain amplified in my skull, bouncing around and ricocheting inside. I like the sensation; feels good. It's music, I'm thinking, it's loud and soothing and heavy. My forehead's dripping wet, my clothes soaked. It's the best feeling I've had in ages. And the rest of the crew feel it too. Smiles all around. It's the rain that never fell in Iraq, the rain in the desert we all dreamt of, the rain that never came.

Pretty soon the docs and nurses charge outside, yelling at us to come in. Nobody moves. John Hart opens his arms to the sky, thanking God and whoever else is responsible for this downpour. Pink dances around in a circle, yelling "Whoopee!" Tonto's got his mouth open wide and he's drinking the rain. The nurses try real hard to shuttle us back inside. There's concern the rain will damage our gullivers, get inside our metal plates, or mess up the prototype mechanical arms and legs we've got. Rust never sleeps, I'm thinking. If my titanium hand gets wet, will it rust?

Before we know it, they've got Security on our case. The Humvees pull out of the parking lot and drive across the field, running over the gardens that John Hart and the rest of us have planted. A couple of guards jump out of the vehicle and move toward us for the roundup. John Hart is furious: "You're crushing my plants! Go away! Get the hell out of here!"

Nothing's going to stop them. So we're hauled inside, dried off with big white towels, and given a lecture.

❦

IN THE PARKING LOT adjacent to St. Richard's, where all the nurses and docs and hospital administrators have their marked spaces for their vehicles, John Hart was able to find a free corner to set up his makeshift basketball court. Ricki had ordered the backboard, hoop and net, using one of her many credit cards, and had it delivered to the company by truck. John Hart took some time assembling the portable device, which rolls on wheels with a metal post that stands the regulation ten feet high and a glass backboard attached to it, and making sure the hoop was the right height from ground to rim. I watched him out there in the parking lot, standing on a ladder, getting the hoop and net in place, so all of us could have some fun outside for a change. He filled the base with a couple of gallons of water for stability and moved it at an angle away from all the cars zooming into the lot. Ricki ordered three basketballs and a pump to inflate them. Our first game paired up Major Pink with Ricki and John Hart, against Dogg, John Wu and me. The Lone Ranger and Tonto cheered from the sideline while Chico videotaped the action. None of us could move very well, I can tell you that. We hobbled onto the court, broken warriors, with banged gullivers and bodies. But I'm telling you, it sure felt good to shoot a couple of baskets and watch the ball swish through the hoop, all net, all good. Nobody kept score.

FORGOT TO TALK ABOUT SKANK. He's been real quiet of late. None of us have seen much of him, so I figure he's been laying low, or getting special treatment from the docs in the Repair Shop, the lab down below in the bowels of the joint.

Skank's not in Group and I don't viddy Doc Queenie pulling him into one of her therapy sessions. One time I spotted Ricki and Skank getting into an argument of some kind, shouting obscenities at each other, a face-to-face snarling confrontation, but I don't know why. All I know is, I've got to watch my back.

Spoke too soon. Skank just showed up in the Large Assembly with one of the clowns the hospital has hired to entertain the kids from the skolliwoll on the other side of the Annex. He's walking around with the man in the clown outfit, as if they're buddy-buddies. Go figure.

This place gets weirder by the day. One time, a while back I spotted Skank with his big mechanical claw of an arm testing the doors, the windows, the security on the perimeter. Just to viddy what was vulnerable, what was not, I'm thinking. He's got something up his sleeve.

Part III

JOHN HART WAS WITH the US Army Stryker Brigade, manning a submachine gun on the back of a truck rolling through northern Iraq as part of a convoy transporting Iraqi volunteers to Mosul for military training. When the convoy rolled into the town of Talafar, he noticed the streets were unusually quiet: no children ran toward the vehicles, like they usually do, demanding sweets. John Hart got on the radio and warned others in the convoy: "Something might happen. Look out, I've got a hunch. They might have some plan for us." Moments later, as the convoy slowed at a traffic circle, an improvised explosive device (IED) went off right next to his truck, knocking him unconscious for a moment.

John Hart's version of what happened next is patched together from his own memories and what others told him later. "I remember waking up and wondering who the hell I was, where the hell I was, and why can't I see or hear? A soldier screamed for me to get out of the truck and I told him no, because it hurt too much. So he literally threw me out of the truck and guided me to a Stryker," a lightweight armored vehicle.

The blast wave and fragments from the explosion had blown out John Hart's left eardrum, fractured his skull, injured his left eye, and caused a severe contusion in the left front temporal area of his brain. His fellow soldiers rushed him to the nearby military base, where he partially regained his vision and tried to walk before again losing consciousness. He was medically evacuated, first to a combat support hospital in Balad and then to one in Baghdad. There, neurosurgeons performed a craniectomy. He remained unconscious and remembers nothing about his stops in these hospitals.

A craniectomy was performed to permit brain swelling after Traumatic Brain Injury. Some surgeons leave the dura mater intact; others open the dura to give the brain more room to swell. The excised piece of skull is implanted under the skin and subcutaneous tissue of the abdomen, outside the muscle wall, so that it can be replaced after the brain has recovered.

"The next time I came to, I'm at St. Richard's—like, fourteen days later," John Hart remembered.

He spent about six days in Intensive Care, sometimes mistaking nurses for CIA agents or believing he was back in Baghdad. Then he was transferred to a room in Neuroscience at St. Richard's. At some point, he became alert enough to realize he was having difficulty speaking.

"Just trying to say something," he told us in Group, "but no such luck." The nurse asked him questions and waited patiently for him to answer but left to check on other patients. About a half hour later she returned, and John Hart managed to articulate his message: "My head hurts."

When he was first evaluated, seven days aft

er his injury, his speech was limited and nonsensical, and he could not understand or follow commands. During the following week, his profound receptive and expressive aphasia rapidly resolved as the brain swelling abated, so he told us. Once his language deficits had improved, his therapists were able to test his cognitive skills and found that the traumatic brain injury had led to defects in reasoning, memory, and problem solving. He attended daily cognitive-therapy sessions and went to group sessions three times a week.

John Hart got better much more rapidly than many patients with TBIs, some of whom had severely impaired function and showed little progress. The doc told him his residual cognitive defects were "mild." His headaches abated. Although crowds make him uncomfortable, he won't always socialize with the rest of us, staying in his room for long stretches here on the hospital campus.

The key event from his childhood, John Hart tells us in Group: "When I was six years old, or was it seven, I forget, I had been playing in a neighbor's yard with their kids, when the parents came out and others in the neighborhood. They had seen a nest in a tree, and the birds, robins, flying back and forth to the nest. They goaded me to climb the tree and take the eggs out of the nest, which I did, in full view of a cheering crowd. What was I doing? I had no idea. I thought I was pleasing the crowd, and then when I came down from the tree with the eggs, they all turned away and abandoned me. I had taken away the robin's eggs and the mother robin would now never return to its nest."

"WE NEED TRIBBLES! Get me some tribbles!" John Hart shouts one day in the Large Assembly, as we're viddying that episode of *Star Trek* on the telly, the one in which these cute, fuzzy little creatures, balls of white fur, begin to multiply like rabbits on the Starship *Enterprise*.

"Why do we need them, Captain?" asks one of the metalheads, raising a skeptical eyebrow.

"Stay loose, soldier," he replies. "You'll know once we get them. I have a plan."

"Aw, get them yourself," answers another droog.

"Ricki, can you help me?"

"Sure, Captain Hart, whatever you say," says Ricki.

A day later her Afghan boyfriend Masood arrives with this huge container, the size of a wine barrel, filled to the brim with old tennis balls. John Hart has meanwhile collected big wads of cotton from one of the medicine supply cabinets, along with several tubes of Elmer's white glue. He and Ricki get to work. On a big long table they spread out the tennis balls, then one by one attach tufts of cotton to them with swabs of glue. With a heavy marker pen John Hart draws smiley faces on the balls and brushes up the cotton with shapes that look like hair gone wild. When he and Ricki are finished, they hand out a dozen tribbles to each member of the *Enterprise* crew, as he now calls us. "Look, in case you haven't noticed, I'm doing my best to play the part of Captain Kirk," he cries. "It's time to have some fun on board this spaceship!"

"Agreed," says Ricki. "All hands on deck!"

"I get it. We can barter with them," says Chico. "Use them for money in poker games. I see you two tribbles and raise you another two. Cool, man."

"How about just for companionship," says Major Pink. "I could use a few for that. You know, tribbles could make great pets!"

"I could use a pet," says the Lone Ranger. "I do get lonely from time to time."

The lads begin bouncing the tribbles on the floor, rolling them around, tossing them into the air, throwing them at each other. I've never seen so many converted tennis balls, now tribbles, bouncing off the walls of the compound. It's become a craze. Pretty soon, after another delivery by Masood, the number of tribbles in circulation around the hospital multiplies. They're all over the place, like in that *Star Trek* episode, lovable and adorable critters yet impossible to handle, impossible to control. The docs and nurses are going crazy, stumbling and tripping all over them. I'm thinking, Hey, John Hart was just trying to do good again, and look what happened. It's not fair, but whoever said life was. All's fair in love and war, right?

🌿

THE TRIBBLES DON'T LAST long before Skank gets into them.

One night he goes on a mighty rampage and destroys every one of them. Nobody can stop him; it's as if he's out there on patrol, eyes glazed from heavy drugs, lips swollen and drooling with an unquenchable thirst for destruction. He dumps the tribbles sitting by everybody's bedsides into a big green garbage bag and races outside to dispose of them in the trash bins by the parking lot. Security is on his tail and Ricki comes after him and clobbers him over the gulliver with a broom from the kitchen.

He keeps shouting, "Nurse Mee gave the order! Just following orders!"

"Liar! Liar!" Ricki shouts back.

"Doing what was I told to do! That's all."

Security has to break up the drat and lock down the ward. John Hart is stunned. He's been trying to do good, as I say, and all he gets for his efforts is destruction. In Group, we talk about it with Doc Queenie, and she does her best to soothe the open wounds we all have from losing what John Hart has worked so hard to create. The tribbles are gone now and we've landed back on planet Earth.

❦

MAJOR PINK WAS IN intensive care for about a week, flipped out, all wiggy and bent out of shape, running scared because he thought the nurses were CIA agents out to get him. He said, "You can't break me. No way. I'm hard as rock, tough as nails, and soon as I get a chance, I'm out the window and over the fence."

He could not talk real well, slurring his words every time he tried to describe the throbbing pain in his gulliver. He blacked out a couple of times, and woke up blind, vision blurred in a dark haze with pulsating beams of light coming at him. That's when he knew for sure he was being tortured, even though they'd taken him to Reid in DC.

Pink's now in Recovery and making progress. You can viddy that already; he speaks more clearly and the brain injury is healing, although he's still got that metal plate on the right side of his skull. "Tell me they're going to replace it soon with some kind of artificial plastic," he tells me. "Speech therapy helped a lot. I knew what things were but I'd forgotten their names, or how you name them. I'm learning."

"That's good."

"Soon as my brain swelling went down a bit, I could remember more, more coming to me. Us TBIs forget a lot but also we can't reason too well, if you know what I mean. You try to figure things out when there's this constant ringing in your head and every time you try to think about anything, you can't connect the dots. Therapist did her job and got me thinking again, but when I asked, 'Hey, think I'll be out of here soon? I'm making progress,' she looked at me with a big smile and said, 'Oh, dear, that's not something you ought to be thinking about right now. We have a long way to go.' I looked at her and said, 'Go where? Tell me that, Nurse.' She went silent, cold as ice, and walked out of the room. I didn't see her again for two days."

Pink got some homework assignments and a book of crossword puzzles to work on, and there he is, sitting in his car, pencil twirling in his lips, nipping and chewing on the eraser end, wheels in his gulliver spinning as he tries to figure out the day's crossword puzzle. I feel for him, I really do.

❦

KEVLAR BODY ARMOR and helmets are one reason for the high proportion of TBIs among soldiers wounded in the current conflicts, Doc Queenie tells us. By effectively shielding the wearer from bullets and shrapnel, the protective gear has improved overall survival rates, and Kevlar helmets have reduced the frequency of penetrating head injuries, she says. However, the helmets can't completely protect the face, gulliver, and neck, nor do they prevent the kind of closed brain injuries often produced by blasts. As insurgents continue to attack US troops in Iraq, most brain injuries are caused by IEDs, and closed brain injuries outnumber penetrating ones among patients.

A blast creates a sudden increase in air pressure by heating and accelerating air molecules and, immediately after, a sudden decrease in pressure that produces intense wind, she says. These rapid pressure shifts can injure the brain directly, producing concussion or contusion. Air emboli can also form in blood vessels and travel to the brain, causing cerebral infarcts. In addition, blast waves and wind can propel fragments, bodies, or even vehicles with considerable force, causing gulliver injuries by any of these mechanisms.

Now I know what's going on inside my gulliver. If only the docs could somehow find a way to fix it.

❦

US METALHEADS HAVE all got some form of traumatic brain injury.

That's for sure, as Doc Queenie explained. We've been hit violently by some external object, jarred out of our rassoodocks, or worse, had our skulls pierced by an object that jabs into brain tissue. They tell us our symptoms can be mild, moderate, or severe, depending on the extent of the damage to the brain. Other symptoms include headache, confusion, lightheadedness, dizziness, blurred vision or tired eyes, ringing in the ears, baddiwad taste in the mouth, fatigue or lethargy, a change in sleep patterns, behavioral or mood changes, and trouble with memory, concentration, attention, or thinking. A veck with a moderate or severe TBI may show these same symptoms, but may also have a headache that gets worse or doesn't go away, repeated vomiting or nausea, convulsions or seizures, an inability to awaken from sleep, dilation of one or both pupils of the eyes, slurred speech, weakness or numbness in the extremities, loss of coordination, and increased confusion, restlessness or agitation.

If it's baddiwad, you've got to have surgery as soon as possible after the injury because a blood clot can mean increased intracranial pressure (ICP). Some clots must be removed; others must not be removed because of the danger of disturbing them. Subdural hematomas and intracerebral hemorrhages may also increase ICP, sometimes requiring immediate surgery.

Swelling in the brain (edema) is monitored and treated. Brain edema can have dire consequences, causing increased pressure inside the gulliver (intracranial pressure or ICP). Because the skull is hard, ICP can compress or squeeze the soft brain tissue against it, preventing blood from circulating adequately in the brain tissue and causing damage to brain cells. Most edema subsides within a few days or weeks, but a few minutes or hours of excessive ICP can cause permanent damage.

To manage this condition, a device called an ICP monitor can be inserted through the skull to provide physicians with a constant pressure reading. If the ICP rises too high, medications are administered to draw fluid out of the brain and into blood vessels, decrease the brain's metabolic requirements, and increase blood flow to the injured tissues. The patient also can be placed on a ventilator to ensure an adequate supply of oxygen (hyperventilation), which is necessary to promote healing. When brain swelling is particularly severe, elevated pressure can only be relieved temporarily by surgically removing a portion of the skull. This allows swollen tissues to bulge out, reducing the risk for pressure-induced damage.

A buildup of fluid inside the brain is also a concern in acute treatment. If the fluid-containing spaces in the brain (ventricles) experience blockage, a neurosurgeon must insert a tube called a *shunt* to drain the fluid build up (hydrocephalus). This allows the ventricles to shrink and restores normal function to brain cells. Elevated ICP due to swelling, hydrocephalus, or blood clots significantly impacts recovery from TBI.

Seizures may occur seconds, weeks, or years after TBI. A seizure can be a minor twitching of one finger or limb, or a complete loss of consciousness accompanied by involuntary movements of the entire body.

❧

THING YOU'VE GOT to watch out for, I'm told, is seizures. All TBIs, all metalheads, are pumped with some kind of anti-seizure medication.

Your whole system gets out of whack; you've got more sodium in your body than you need, more sugar, more calcium, and if they're not treated, you get seizures, like epileptic fits.

Infections can be baddiwad too, I'm telling you. Who wants to die of pneumonia? Well, it can happen, happen real fast, if you don't watch out and get treatment for baddiwad coughs, lung problems, wheezing, and general fatigue.

There's loss of physical and mental function caused by neurological impairment, meaning decreased ability to interact with others in socially acceptable ways, you can't walk, carry or manipulate objects, process or retain information, viddy clearly, use your fingers or legs in a coordinated fashion.

❦

JOHN HART'S WIFE IS COMING, I know she is, I can already pick up the vibe. There's something in the air. And John Hart feels it too, after not viddying her and his kids for a long, long time.

So Mary shows up one day, unexpectedly, without the kids. She's all dolled up, dripping with makeup and a fancy new hairdo, from what I can viddy, spying on her as she struts through the entry corridor of the hospital and down the hall to Reception. For a moment, John Hart doesn't recognize her. I viddy her, knowing it's her, but he can't or won't, or doesn't want to. If he's changed, she's changed even more, he's thinking to himself. I read his thoughts.

There's an awkward moment between them as they adjust and readjust their respective character armor. She wiggles, squirms, then speaks: "John Hart, I'm here to say goodbye." She hands John Hart the papers, a big batch of legal papers clipped together with those hideous clips lawyers all think they've got to have to prove their power and authority. "I've filed for divorce."

"Why?"

"You know why."

"No, Mary, I don't. What have I done? Huh?"

"It's not what you've done but who you are."

"Well, who am I?"

"Don't know. You've changed."

"Mary, I lost my hand and my eye and probably some part of my head but I'm still the man you married."

"That's another question."

"Where are the kids? Got to see them, my kids."

"You can't."

"What do you mean I can't? They're my kids."

"Not anymore."

She stands up, slapping the divorce papers on the table next to John Hart's chair. He's too groggy, too stunned by the cold exchange of words to run after her, his gulliver's spinning and flashing like a Ferris wheel gone berserk.

❦

WITH MARY GONE AND done with John Hart, he's got no connection to the outside world, except Kamal. Hard to believe, his interpreter and mine, a generous, intelligent Arab man living in Kahleefornia, is his only connection. He's thinking about me. And it's come to that.

Meanwhile, Ricki's got a lot to say, always does, so I've got to hunker down and listen. I struggle to concentrate, to hear what's on her rassoodock and how she viddies things.

She says to John Hart, and her voice is loud enough to

overhear, "There comes a time when you've got to accept the state of affairs, John Hart, and say, 'Okay, this is how it is now. What can I do next?'

"You don't have to be a victim of the situation. I know you're grieving and there's a kind of emotional paralysis from it that you can't avoid. Take action! Look at your own needs and when the timing is right for you, when you're out of here, out of St. Richard's, you'll get on the road and move back to the house with her and your kids. I know how much you love them; they love you too. Be strong! Be smart! Your own self-worth has to come first before your family. I know that's hard to accept, but you won't be any good to them until you've reconnected with yourself. You'll be linked for a long time just because of your two sons. If your relationship is right, you'll have a long time to mend it, a whole lifetime, in fact. You have two kids and therefore a reason to make it work. You need to show independent muscle now, and that's like entering a whole new world on your own.

"There's always a strong tendency to give up and just wallow in the grief. That's easy. Out of this grief will come that muscle. It's good to grieve, even if it takes your appetite away, you feel all that pain, and it gets you physically wrecked. Give yourself a little hope when you're not grieving. Give yourself a little success every now and then. The old way won't work; you can't mend it with band-aids. It's the death of the status quo, not the marriage. You have to be sure that you don't get into a situation where you're going along with her just to please her, signing the papers blindly, thinking that'll get you back together again. What's important now is to fight for your best interests."

"But Ricki, I already signed the papers," says John Hart. "I'm finished."

"Only if you think you are."

"I think I am."

"So it's unthinkable to think you aren't finished."

"Yes."

"Why?"

"Don't ask why. Don't know. I've lost my wife and my kids and it's over. What can I do?"

"Give yourself more hope to enjoy life, to have fun, to be your own veck. Grieving has its own life, its own period, and there's not a lot you can do to speed it up. It's got to run its own course, like the flu. What you have to find is some way to restore your own personal integrity, like picking up the gems on the floor that are truly pieces of your life and what's important to you. It's like reclaiming yourself, but not to anybody else's specifications. It's making yourself a whole and desirable human being again. And when you've grown up always pleasing others, always accommodating, doing what you think will make others like you, then it's doubly hard. You have no role model, no example of how it ought to be done, so you're completely out there on your own.

"It's like re-creating yourself all over again, without having anybody to tell you these are hoops you must jump through."

"How? That's what I want to know."

"You'll figure it out."

Scientist Predicts 'Mini Ice Age'

ST. PETERSBURG, Russia, Feb. 7 (UPI) — A Russian astronomer has predicted that the Earth will experience a "mini Ice Age" in the middle of this century, caused by low solar activity.

Khabibullo Abdusamatov of the Pulkovo Astronomic Observatory in St. Petersburg said Monday that temperatures will begin falling six or seven years from now, when global warming caused by increased solar activity in the 20th century reaches its peak, RIA Novosti reported.

The coldest period will occur fifteen to twenty years after a major solar output decline between 2035 and 2045, Abdusamatov said.

Dramatic changes in the earth's surface temperatures are an ordinary phenomenon, not an anomaly, he said, and result from variations in the sun's energy output and ultraviolet radiation.

The Northern Hemisphere's most recent cool-down period occurred between 1645 and 1705. The resulting period, known as the Little Ice Age, left canals in the Netherlands frozen solid and forced people in Greenland to abandon their houses to glaciers, the scientist said.

❦

CHICO, WHO KNOWS SCIENCE, thinks that this dude Abdusamatov is right on the money, like, his bit about climate being controlled by magnetic forces on the sun. "I studied it, Spoon," he says, "when I was in skolliwoll, even wrote a paper about it, so it's coming, all these little ice ages when the sunspot count drops to zero. We're screwed, man. I told C.J., I mean Dogg, as he wants us to call him, and he's predicting other big disasters ahead for us because we're messing around with climate and all that warming business. Dogg's got a novel he's writing, and when he showed it to me, I said, 'Hey, it's true, it's coming.' "

The future. Jagged edges of San Francisco, a grid of steep streets, a maze of winding lanes. I'm levitating. I'm viddying the flow of blood orange into the city. Cool, I'm thinking. Aliens rule, so be careful about where you fly. Be real careful. Stay under the fog.

❦

RICKI TELLS ME THIS STORY: Outside Kabul, about sixty kilometers away in Bagram, if you want to know, is where I met Masood, a soldier with the Northern Alliance who was working as a jack of all trades: teacher, interpreter, truck driver, construction worker. He had a family of four daughters to feed and a wife who wanted more children. Out of the blue, and you have to understand, Spoon, there is no blue like the blue of the Afghan sky, he began teaching us at Bagram a few basic phrases in Dari, figuring we might need them if he were in the field with the locals.

"Salaam."

"Chetor hasten?"

"Now you say, Khoob astam."

"Naam-e-ma Masood ast."

"Naam-e-shoma cheest?"

"You say, Colonel Ricki."

"Khosh shodam az mahrefee tan."

Masood reached into the woolen bag he had strapped over his shoulder and pulled out a hat. "This is for you, Miss Ricki," he said. "You are one of us."

It was a very special hat, indeed, the same one worn by Ahmed Shah Masood, the great Afghan leader of the Northern Alliance who had been murdered by bin Laden's henchmen two days before the 9/11 attack on America. Masood's men wore the very same hats when they were up against the armies of the Taliban. "This hat is called a pakol and comes from Chitral," he said. "If you look on the map, you'll see it right there, a tiny village, up in the northwest region of Pakistan."

The hat felt nice when I put it on, all woolen and round as a large saucer. All the Afghan warriors wore these hats, so I thought the men and women in my platoon ought to wear them too, starting with me.

"Masood's home," said my Afghan jack of all trades, "was in the Panshir Valley close to Chitral, so he got the hats from there where they became very popular among our fellow Afghans, many of whom had fled the country through the city of Chitral when life with the Taliban became impossible. I want you to have this hat, Miss Ricki. I love you. You are a hero to us and you would serve Masood proudly, if he were alive today, as an American-Afghan warrior."

❧

KAMAL'S DAUGHTER LEILA smuggles in a book of stories during her next visit, as part of my new diet of reading material.

The stories are famous in the Middle East and beloved by children, she says, these little fables and parables from Mullah Nasruddin.

"How old are you, mullah?" someone asks. "Three years older than my brother," he replies. "How do you know that?" "By reasoning. Last year, I heard my brother tell someone that I was two years older than him. A year has passed. That means that I am older by one year. I shall soon be old enough to be his grandfather."

Mullah Nasruddin goes into a shop to buy a pair of trousers. Then he changes his rassoodock and chooses a cloak instead, at the same price. Picking up the cloak he leaves the shop. "Hey, you have not paid," cries the merchant. "I left you the trousers, which were of the same value as the cloak," replies Mullah Nasruddin. "But you did not pay for the trousers either." "Of course not," says the mullah. "Why should I pay for something that I did not want to buy?"

One day Mullah Nasruddin enters his favorite teahouse and says, "The moon is more useful than the sun." An old man asks, "Why, mullah?" Nasruddin replies, "We need the light more during the night than during the day."

❦

WE'VE BEEN HARVESTING the Shiraz grapes, plucking them off the vines. There's a real art to knowing exactly when to do this, so the sugar and acid content of the grapes are in balance. They've got lots of cool instruments to measure this, but we're left with our own instincts. Who decides? Ricki took a walk out to the vineyard, to the field one morning, a casual stroll, and picked a few off the vines. I watch her do this. She's barefoot, wearing hardly any clothes at all. It's been hot and cold, days and nights, so the grapes have been getting stoked by the summer heat, then cooling off when the sun goes down. Ricki's been studying the seasonal changes. She knows what's in the air. I think it's because of her keen sense of smell; she picks up the scent of things from great distances. She smells when I'm perspiring with droplets of fear. She looks in my eyes and tells me to be calm, everything's cool. It'll be all right. I get these anxiety attacks all the time; they come right out of the blue. So she's there in the vineyard at the crack of dawn, I viddy her from a distance, and she nibbles on the grapes, tasting, then spitting out the grapeskins after she's had a chance to examine each one.

She comes running back to the compound, waving her arms in the air, laughing and crying at the same time. I'm there to catch her as she steps inside before anybody can viddy her. My arms curl around her thin, bony figure, and I kiss her on the cheeks. What's up? I ask. She's absolutely jubilant, jumping up and down. One moment she's dancing like a ballerina, doing a pirouette on the tips of her toes, another moment she's sobbing like a newborn. I'm sad and happy, happy and sad, she tells me. Don't you understand?

Of course I do.

"Now's the time, Spoon, to harvest the grapes."

"You know that for sure?"

"Yes."

"How? How'd you come to that conclusion."

"Just do it."

In the next hour I'm inside skvatting John Wu and Chico

Rodriguez and Major Pink out of their beds, along with the Lone Ranger and Tonto, handing them each these big green plastic garbage bags. I tell them to get moving, we've got to start picking. I've prepared for this day: clippers for each veck, which I've smuggled in from one of Kamal's buddies.

Frankly, I wasn't much of a wine drinker in high skolliwoll. Most of my droogs liked to sneak shots of Johnny Walker from their old man's liquor cabinet or chug a six-pack of Budweiser when the parents were out of the house. Drinking booze was always, to my rassoodock, associated with an act of rebellion: something you did against your parents. I never figured it had any medicinal value, but that all changed when I took a sip of the wine Leila had smuggled in. Man, it was strong; deep, dark red, this Shiraz. Almost immediately, I felt relaxed, calmer than before. Everybody thought I'd taken up drinking hot coffee from the thermos Leila had given me. It was a cool disguise, and nobody suspected anything until one of the metalheads— think it was Major Pink—took a gulp when I wasn't looking. "Hey, Spoon. This is no shot of coffee, man. This is red wine."

"Well, I'm not sure," I lied. "Given to me by a droog who said it's old red wine, grown in a region of the world where they had a lot of battles and the soldiers drank it to heal the wounds of war."

"I like it," he said, taking another gulp.

The two of us sat there in the Small Assembly at a back table, sipping wine in the afternoon sun. I think we finished the entire thermos, if I remember correctly, and we talked and talked about things we never talk about, like poetry and food and girls who used to go out with us. That night I refused to take my meds, hiding them in the back of my mouth, then spitting them out into the toilet in the Men's. When I fell asleep I had great dreams of doing good things, like John Hart was doing for the crew. I was speaking into a microphone to a huge crowd of folks who were cheering me on. It was all about telling the truth; they cheered me on because I was "telling the truth, not making it up."

❦

AFTER WE'VE SPENT THE ENTIRE MORNING picking and bagging grapes, with sore backs and all, Kamal pulls up in the parking lot in his van. I wave to him but he doesn't viddy me. In a few minutes he comes out to the vineyard and we hand him the bags packed to the top with Shiraz grapes. We stuff them into his van, my crew at work in an assembly line.

Kamal drives away now and we wave goodbye to him in the distance. He honks his horn, a couple of loud, deafening blasts that shake the ground in front of the compound. I stick my right thumb in one ear but have no hand to block the sound in the other. Like all the other TBIs here, I can't take the sound of anything above a few decibels. Sound rattles my brain and sometimes triggers baddiwad memories.

But this is good stuff, indeed. The crew celebrates the bumper crop of grapes. The vines are plucked clean now, not a single grape left in sight. The docs come out of the compound, observing the spectacle, half curious, half puzzled. By the looks on everybody's faces, I can viddy we're doing something they don't quite approve of.

The vines are stripped bare and there's a wave of sadness around that. I mean, we worked like dogs to bring this crop to harvest and now it's all gone. Kamal had assured me once the grapes are weighed and processed we'll be compensated for our work, a check will be in the mail. He's taken the bounty to his droog's place at the Sage Mill Winery, not far from the compound. There they've got the equipment to crush the grapes and process everything and make wine. They've got row after row of big wooden barrels down in the basement to store and ferment the harvest. He's still puzzled about how we knew exactly when to pick the grapes, right down to the precise day and hour. I told him Ricki did it. She knew and we followed along at her command, mobilizing the troops for action and getting the job done. I keep telling him we failed in Iraq but he doesn't want to hear that. Not your fault, he rebuffs me.

Maybe we got something right here, I tell myself. Allahu akbar, indeed.

🍂

SKANK DOESN'T LIKE ANY of what's going on in the field. So one day I'm out with John Wu working on the vines. John Wu's got a big broom he's converted into a rake when Skank shows up. I tell Wu to avoid the creep, stay out of his way, particularly if he's in a bad mood, but Wu is oblivious to what I'm saying. He's not even aware of Skank's presence until he viddies a long samurai sword unsheathed from a case on the man's shoulder. How Skank got to hold on to his sword, the one he used in Ramadi, I have no idea. Soon the sword is flying in the air right at Wu. This is getting nasty; I want to intervene but Skank pushes me away into a bush of vines.

"Y'all didn't invite me to the party, did you now?" snarls

Skank. "Thought I wasn't good enough, maybe, eh?"

John Wu says nothing and holds up his wooden broom to block the sword thrown at him. I'm ready to call Security when I notice Security is watching yet not doing a thing. The Jeep Libertys are parked at the far end of the field, headlights beaming, windows rolled down. They're enjoying the spectacle: a six foot, ten inch tall man of Asian descent confronting a warrior gone berserk. Skank, meanwhile, goads Wu on, circling around him, a crouching tiger, throwing dirt in his face, and quickly skvatting his samurai sword.

This is blood sport for Skank, a chance to measure his mettle. He won't be satisfied unless he chops up Wu into small pieces. He must have a pact with Security, a deal of some kind. Wu dodges swipes of Skank's sword, holding up his wooden broom to the man's steel blade. I'm thinking he's another Chief Bromden, whose statue visitors pass by in the lobby. If Wu doesn't do something fast, he'll be a statue too. It's a losing battle, all right.

In a flash I remember that Chico has the device that controls the loudspeakers in the hospital and blasts waves of Jimi Hendrix music at earsplitting volume. Where is he? I race back inside, panting and screaming for Chico. He appears out of nowhere. "Hey, man, what's up?"

I babble incoherently about what's going down in the field outside between Skank and Wu. "Security won't get involved. Turn the switch on *right now* for the loudspeakers and direct the sound at Skank! He's our target. *Paint him.*"

"Sure, man. No problemo."

I pop the earplugs Ricki gave me. Chico and I run outside, he flicks the switch, and the sound explodes in a giant sonic boom across the field. Skank is stunned, grabbing his gulliver, sticking both fingers in his ears. Wu sprints away down the field, taking long strides, like a champion runner until he gets to the side door of the hospital and disappears inside.

For days afterward there is no sign of Skank. Everybody breathes a collective sigh of relief. Sitting on his bed I catch John Wu as he throws three coins and reads what the coins mean in his dog-eared copy of the *I Ching*:

33. Tun / Retreat

———
——— · above   Ch'ien The Creative, Heaven
———
———
— — below   Ken Keeping Still, Mountain
— —

The Judgement
Retreat. Success.
In what is small, perseverance furthers.

The Image
Mountain under heaven: the image of Retreat.
Thus the superior man keeps the inferior man
at a distance,
Not angrily but with reserve.

The Lines
Nine in the third place means:
A halted retreat

Is nerve-wracking and dangerous.
To retain people as men- and maidservants
Brings good fortune.
Nine in the fourth place means:
Voluntary retreat brings good fortune to the
superior man
And downfall to the inferior man.

❦

"IT'S ALL IN YOUR GULLIVER," says Major Pink in Group. That's how we got to using the word gulliver to mean what it means.

For Major Pink, it happened on returning home from Iraq, from his second tour of duty, still licking his wounds, struggling to heal and to understand the meaning of his experiences in war when, after a motorcycle crash, his life was saved by a colony of little people known as the Kocholoo. I'd heard him tell the story before, at least a couple of times, mostly to new arrivals at St. Richard's. Nobody believed him when he first told of his strange encounter with the Kocholoo; everybody just laughed and laughed. Who could take any of it seriously? The man's hallucinating, they said; the man's high on something. But then things changed, changed fast. I wasn't around to viddy it for myself, but others did. They swore that a band of Kocholoo showed up one day at Group and got to work on Major Pink's wounds.

❦

THE ROAD WAS TWISTY and fraught with danger, lined on both sides with dense rows of redwood trees, tall, imposing giants of age and beauty. Before I knew what happened, my motorcycle spun out of control. I don't know if I hit a hole in the road or what, but I missed a turn and was flying, airborne, into the unknown before I could figure out what hit me. When I awoke I was flat on my back in a redwood grove. The trees towered above me, hundreds of feet in the sky. I could not move a single limb, as my body was firmly tied down with long strands of nylon cord, crisscrossing my legs and arms and stomach like fishnet for big ocean tuna.

Three Kocholoo with long needles in hand stood on my chest, stitching me up. About twenty or thirty men, along with half a dozen women, stood around me, looking me over, as if I were a huge chunk of fresh meat. Each one was no taller than a foot or fourteen inches. The three on my chest wore doctors' smocks, the others wore different clothes: stovepipe jeans, muscle shirts in all colors of the rainbow, and tiny white tennis sneakers. Although awake, I was drowsy, my head clouded up and my eyes unable to focus clearly. I winced at seeing this long, silver sewing needle move from one side of my chest to the other. Another Kocholoo held a hot cloth to my forehead, still another unlaced my shoes. I thought I was hallucinating. At any moment these Kocholoo people would suddenly burst into full-size humans.

But they did not. They went about their work methodically, with great care and precision. A few nurses poked and prodded me in my rib cage. It tickled. They pored over every nook and cranny of my body. My kneecaps, bruised and bleeding, were tested by two Kocholoo doctors. The nurses had pulled down my zipper and checked out my genitals. I sneezed and almost knocked down one of them. I was starting to panic. Was I a giant guinea pig for a round of medical experiments by some crazy cult? The leader of the group emerged, sensing my displeasure. He was slightly larger than the others, perhaps a foot and a half tall. He gave commands to the others, but I could not make out the words. Slowly, I began to make out what he was saying.

"Is your gulliver all right?"

"My what?"

"Your gulliver?" And he pointed to my forehead, my balding pate, the wisps of hair protruding from my ears.

The work on my body continued busily, then halted for a moment while he spoke. I shook my gulliver, as he called it, from side to side and felt a sudden twinge of pain in my neck. This was it, I thought. My neck's broken, I've gone mad, seeing all these Kocholoo. I'm going to die right here and all the great things I was going to accomplish in life will never, ever happen, like in my father's case, a major killed in the Vietnam war. "Keep cool," he said, as if reading my thoughts. "Everything's going to be all right."

Then he explained that I had no internal injuries they could find, after stomping on my body for a while. Just minor cuts and bruises. But still, I was lucky to be alive. His crew wanted to help me. They were not sure if I could even walk, so they wanted to take things slowly. The leader, who introduced himself as Mike Choo, had studied medicine, but now devoted all his time to keeping the group together.

He explained that, because of their size, the group had dropped out of American society; they were outcasts, freaks.

They discovered that their children grew up very fast; in only a few years they were already adults, so their numbers had multiplied. They now formed their own colony in the redwood forests north of San Francisco in Mendocino County. Their reason for taking care of me was that, if they nursed me back to life, I would owe them a debt of gratitude; they could then count on me for supplies and support. "Look at your motorcycle," said the leader. He held a mirror up for me. I glanced at it and saw my trusty bike completely disassembled: the handlebars were pulled off, the gas tank, the seat cushion, the wheels, motor, all gone. One motorcycle engine was enough power to supply the heating needs of the Kocholoo colony.

I squirmed. The Kocholoo sensed my discomfort and tried to ease my tension. One got a couple of aspirin, another filled a whiskey shot glass with water. They climbed on my chest, opened my mouth, laid the aspirin on my tongue, then poured water from the shot glass. I gulped and swallowed the pills. I fell asleep, and when I awoke a few hours later, I felt much better; there was a good vibe in the air. A little fire in the distance, and I sat up and looked around. What I saw astonished me: a small village of houses, geodesic domes, tree houses, all tucked into a grove of redwood trees.

The Kocholoo workers moved parts of my motorcycle back and forth; fires burned. Different dress: Indian, Latino, with ponchos, striped colors, space men, doctors. These were like frontiersmen of another age. "Our numbers are growing," said Mike. "And everybody gets along."

"Are you sure it's not all in your gulliver? I mean, the part about everybody getting along."

He broke into laughter, but then turned serious.

"We live without war," he said with studied calm. "Of course, we have our conflicts, disputes and internal dissent. Nothing is ever perfect, now is it? But," he took a deep breath, "we do not wage war on one another."

This piqued my curiosity. How was this possible? War had taught me that we were hard-wired to fight, to defend ourselves, to protect our loved ones. Life wasn't just about everybody getting along, was it?

"We live without war," he repeated. "It can be done; must be done and we've found a way to do it."

"By magic, eh?"

"It's all in your gulliver, isn't it?"

I was hungry, and my stomach growled. Two of the Kocholoo came with a bowl of soup, and a couple of spoons. They fed me. The cook and his assistant appeared. I slurped the soup, and it warmed me up a bit. I felt better, though there was no way to know what would happen with these Kocholoo. Mike paid special attention to me; he directed all the actions. My chest was now stitched up, the cuts on my hands and face cleaned, swabbed with big balls of cotton and alcohol. My headache was almost gone. I could sit up but could not get up, as my feet and arms were anchored, like a ship in port. What did they want from me? In the distance, I could see the pieces of my motorcycle scattered about, along with a torn up copy of the philosophy book I was reading, strapped onto the seat with the bungee cord. Mike tried to allay my fears. He brought the members of the colony to my side and introduced them one by one.

There was Bobby, the village teacher, along with three of his pupils; the council of elders who ran the society, three gray-haired men and one woman who smoked cigarettes that were half the length of standard Marlboros. The society had to wrestle with the stark reality of being outsiders. They also had to make everything from scratch, gathering materials, carving and shaping things to fit the sizes. A hot item was a Swiss Army knife, which their small fingers could handle dexterously. Everybody learned to handle the knife, and its various tools, with ease. Wood was carved, holes drilled. There was little chance of the colony ever being absorbed into mainstream society. Most of the Kocholoo, said Mike, were resigned to this. They were free to leave the colony, but knew without help from each other, their chances of survival were dim. Even a small dog or cat could be a threat.

"How long are you going to keep me here against my will?"

"You're free to go anytime you want," he said. "The only thing we ask is that you come back a few times with the items on this list. That's not asking too much now, is it?"

He handed me a piece of paper, with a laundry list of food and supplies. "No problem," I told him. "You guys saved my life."

"Well, it'll take a few days to get your motorcycle working. It's still pretty bent out of shape."

"Hey, I appreciate all your efforts," I said, reaching out to thank him. "How can I repay you?"

"You don't have to," he said. "Besides, everything repays itself over time. It's a law of nature."

The Kocholoo untied the nylon cable around my arms and legs. For the first time, I stood up. I am a little under six feet tall, and when I looked down, I towered over the Kocholoo like a giant in the circus. They immediately dispersed in all directions. I suddenly became very conscious of my steps, every movement of my legs. I did not want to hurt them.

Standing up, I was a little shaky, my body wobbled, my gulliver began to spin.

A crew of workers in white jumpsuits surrounded my bike. One worked on the engine, another on the wheels, another on the clutch, using little toolkits, hammers, and wrenches. Mike explained that the community had a team of mechanics who worked on the sewer system, the communications, the vehicles, the bicycles like in Holland. Mike said that the Kocholoo had studied the Dutch and the Chinese, people who ride bikes, and determined that these were the best means of transportation, the most efficient, and the ones that kept the inhabitants in the best physical shape. Mechanics were like gods in the community; they were treated with reverence.

On my last day, my bike fixed and my body repaired, the entire community of Kocholoo gave me a fond farewell, standing up and chanting:

We are Kocholoo
You are too
We are Kocholoo
So are you

❧

"THE KOCHOLOO ARE GIANTS, taller than all of us," said Major Pink in Group. "Last time I heard from them they'd all grown over six feet and were getting even taller. When you don't have a lot of wars to fight, you've got more time to grow.

Like Mike Choo said, 'It's all in your gulliver.'"

🍂

SKANK'S OUT THERE IN the field, stomping around in the gardens; I can see him from a distance. He's killing the tomatoes, the herbs and vegetables planted by the crew. How to stop him? If I call Security, they'll show up fifteen minutes later, too late to do anything. Skank's got my number, all right.

So I'm stuck like I was in Ramadi, when I stood by and did nothing while Skank went on a rampage. I'm motionless, frozen in my tracks, a Marine who can't stop a private contractor from committing a war crime. How'd I ever get to be like this? What's happened to me? I mean, this poor, innocent Iraqi girl is coming home from skolliwoll and Skank targets her, this tall, thin girl with blue eyes, rosy cheeks and those sweet lips. Skank's made sure her father was arrested two days before and dragged off to prison on some phony trumped up charge of participating in a militia and firing on us, and being part of the militia that killed Bill, so he knows it's only the girl and her mother in the house. I'm getting sick to my stomach. I hate these freaking private contractors and how they've tainted our men in uniform with their acts of violence.

The streets of Ramadi are, for some reason, quiet that afternoon; folks are scared, hiding away in their homes. Skank's got something screwed up in his gulliver about this Iraqi girl, she can't be more than fourteen or fifteen. He wants her, he wants to take her down, and he's dragged me and another Marine, whose name I won't mention for fear of implication, into his twisted plot for rape and murder. Skank's high on some evil substance, uppers, meth, crack, who knows?

He's made us into co-conspirators, saying he's got orders from his superiors to take out this girl and her family, to eliminate all traces of them. I'm ready to radio my commanding officer when he comes toward us, as the Iraqi girl is going into her house, and tells me: "Spoon, this is personal, private business, understand? You got to turn away from it if you can't take it. This girl and her mother are members of Al-Qaeda, they're terrorists, and I have my orders. You have a problem with that?"

"Not if you're sure of their identities, if you've got proof," I tell him.

"Don't need to show *you* any proof? Who the fuck are you?"

"I'm a Marine, like you used to be, and I follow the rules of engagement, the code of honor, the principles I was taught when I became a Marine."

"Orders is what I've got. Now either you're for me or you're against me," Skank growls in my face, then lifts the barrel of his M-16, aiming at my crotch.

Me and my buddy back off. And, without saying a word, we step away, a dozen feet outside the Iraqi girl's house while Skank goes in. And then we hear the screams, the cries for help, the rape and murder of the girl and her mother. He's emptied his M-16, a full round. He's smoked 'em. Dark shadows fall on the house when Skank comes out, his face turned flaming red, his lips breathing fire. He's panting and wired to the sky. A few moments later he tosses a grenade into the doorway and it explodes with a pop and a bang and puffs of foul smoke in the air. Before you know it, he's set the house on fire and skvats me and the other Marine, to disappear under the cover of twilight.

At the base he says, "Spoon, you tell anybody what I did and you won't live to see another day in Ramadi. You know what I mean about friendly fire? Fragging? Got it?"

As I turn to walk away, he pulls my arm: "I'm talking to you, kid. You hear what I said?"

"I heard."

"You get it?"

"I got it."

Part IV

IN GROUP, I'M TELLING QUEENIE about Mom. How Doc Queenie got me to open up like this, I'm not sure. This stuff's real personal and no amount of prodding can shake it loose from me, yet that's what she's done. Okay, live with it. Maybe she's going to pry open the wounds of war, my guilt about what went down in Ramadi, though I had no part in it, except as an observer, a witness, and one day, I swear, I'll bear witness and fry Skank and the others who were there.

You see, I remember Mom walking along the Avenue, remember it real well and what happened. She's taking a morning stroll when she sees him again, huddled in a doorway, shivering in the morning cold. He's homeless. His face blackened, his feet bare, he sleeps in doorways. Eats from garbage bins. And he's always there, in the neighborhood, near the shops, not far from campus. The Green Man. She calls him the Green Man because of the dark green Army fatigues he wears. She can't figure out what to make of him. Is he a prophet of doom? A holy man? He preaches no message. He simply gropes along, a primitive, desperate man. Does he seek salvation? Are the streets his only home? she wonders. He's a man of no season, no winter or spring, for he wears the same ragged green clothes, despite the heat, despite the chill in the air.

She brings him food and he looks her in the eye knowingly. He's sitting right in front of the drugstore now; inside, at the soda fountain, the mayor is holding court, talking with a couple of city council members dressed in blue suits and white Oxford cloth button-down shirts and rep ties. It's a strange juxtaposition of worlds, she thinks. She loves politics, loves to debate the issues of the age, but her interest is in the fate of the Green Man.

There's a sparkle in the Green Man's eyes, a kind of spiritual light, as if he's seen something no one else has seen. Perhaps a glimmer of the divine.

What's your name? she asks. He grunts. She asks again. John. And he lets out a laugh before muffling it with the cup of his right hand, which is bruised and scarred.

Each day, I remember, as she strolls College, wearing her pink raincoat and carrying a grocery bag with food for the homeless, she sees the Green Man trudging along, his body twisted and bent out of shape, his gulliver bowed. He sometimes pushes a shopping cart, filled to overflow with a collection of his meager belongings wrapped in sheets of dirty plastic. She waves to him but he does not wave back.

Across the street she stops at that candy shop, to buy a birthday present for me, then the corner 7-Eleven to redeem a coupon she's clipped for a bottle of Diet Coke. Despite the crazy quilt of shops and restaurants, the parade of people on the Avenue, her eyes are always pulled in the direction of the Green Man. He must be about my son's age, she's no doubt thinking, maybe older. The Green Man is one of the walking wounded, she tells herself. A victim of war and poverty. And neglect. Surely he won't starve to death on the streets, she wants to believe. Surely he won't be homeless forever. Someone will take him in. I wish I could but I'm too old. Winter's mild, he'll survive, she thinks.

Being dispossessed, she mutters under her breath, is having—having no season.

Then one day the Green Man disappears, drops out of sight. She has food for him, but he's not there in the neighborhood. What's happened? Where's he gone? I'm the Green Man now, she tells me as I sit with her in the dining room of her upstairs apartment. I'm old and vulnerable. Forgotten too. A sadness comes over her. She trembles, and starts to cry like a baby.

"Don't be melodramatic, Mom. You're not forgotten," I tell her but she doesn't believe a word I say.

NEXT TIME DOC QUEENIE gets me to tell more.

She waits for me at her window. I know because she always waits for me there, peeking through the blinds expectantly. I ring the bell and she comes downstairs to open the door for me. She shakes my hand, smiles and I step inside. It feels a little strange, as an eighteen-and-a-half-year-old getting ready to report for duty with the Marines, to shake your mother's hand, but that's what I do. Really, I want her to kiss me, if only a peck on the cheek. I hold back a smile; she's got water boiling in the kitchen.

We sit in the dining room at her large circular table. She pours hot water into my cup and passes Instant Decaf my way. I hear the roar of traffic, cars zooming by outside. Traffic's so terrible, she complains. So many cars in the city. Day and night they pass by. I can't sleep. Try closing the windows at night. I have but it doesn't help. Nothing helps. She's not a complainer, though she sounds like one from time to time. I resist the temptation to offer a solution, having heard this litany before. I keep silent.

A lull occurs in our conversation, broken only by the sound of cymbals on the street below, accompanied by chanting voices. My friends. She laughs. *Hare Krishna, hare Krishna* … The chanting recedes in the distance. So many crazy people. That's the city, all right. The walking wounded. I see them all the time from my window. I feel sorry for them, they're lost on the streets, no place to go, she says.

She scratches the top of her gulliver, wincing at the pain. She's opened up a couple, three sores, which are almost like wounds. I know she does this when she's nervous about something, as she is today because I've come to take her to the doctor and because she's had some pelvic bleeding that she hasn't told anybody about; I'm both angry and worried about that. Dad's on his sailboat and he sees her every few weeks, even though they separated and divorced a long time ago. Because she hates to go to the doctor, fearing that he'll find some condition beyond cure, worse than what she came in for, she stays at home, waiting for it to go magically away. It's just the way she is. I can't do anything about it, much as I'd like. I've got to accept her, stubbornness and all.

We should try to get going soon. No, we haven't finished our coffee. What's the hurry? She's slightly irritated with me, as if I'm forcing her into an action that she doesn't want to take.

I pull back, regain my composure, trying to stay as calm as possible. A cool wind blows through the living room window. Kids play in the skolliwoll yard across the street. It looks like rain. I feel as though I'm coming down with a cold, fighting off a bug of some kind. It gets like this in December. I want to hurry up and take her to the doctor's because there might be traffic on the bridge and we'll be late. She's deliberately taking her time, stretching out every moment.

Don't worry, Jeremy. We have time. I don't want to rush anything. It's a test of wills: who can remain calmer under pressure, who can stare in the eye of the storm without blinking.

Okay, Mom. If we're a little late, then we're … well, a little late. I don't want to—tears suddenly well up, as if they've come from someplace deep inside, and she begins to cry—see the doctor. I'm frightened. Let's split. Okay. It's a little joke between us, the way I say, Let's split. It gets her laughing, if only for a moment or two. She's a pretty hip mom when she wants to be.

We're on the bridge and she's sitting beside me in her pink raincoat, leaning back. Rain pounds against the windshield. I hold tightly the wheel of the VW bug. I keep thinking that in a rainstorm you've only got four handfuls of rubber between you and the road. A powerful gust of wind picks up and bends the car counter to the direction I'm turning. Boy, is it slippery! Be careful driving! At the doctor's office we sit in the waiting room, along with a pregnant woman who looks as if she's about due any moment.

The nurse pops out and says, Sorry, but Doc Stone is running a bit late. I pick up another magazine from a stack on the table, leafing briskly through its glossy pages. Mom seems pretty calm, all things considered. She won't even take off her pink raincoat. She strikes up a conversation with the pregnant woman, trading comments and gossip about Doc Stone. Is he married? That's a hot topic. How old is the doctor, really?

When did you last see him? Mom's always one for striking up conversations with strangers, like she did with the Green Man and other homeless folk, and making friends rapidly. Two more women, both in their twenties, join us in the cramped quarters of the waiting room. Doc Stone, the OBGYN, finally comes out, this large man with a big gulliver of thick curly hair. He's got on your standard hospital-issue white smock, which doesn't quite fit him properly: it looks baggy and too stiff from all the starch. I say hello, and he greets my mom, extending his hand.

A current of warmth, such as I haven't seen before, flows between them. Good to see you. He kisses her hand. Thank you, Doc Stone. How have you been? Oh, just fine. Kissing Mom's hand is hot stuff, she loves it. He always makes a big hit with her that way. In a few moments she's gone. The two women, who are both pregnant, chain-smoke nervously. I cough and cough, feeling as if I'm about to suffocate. The ceiling's turning a nauseating yellow. I look up at the streaks.

Pictures of Mom's pelvic exam on that cold white table in the doctor's other room dance before me like an early morning dream. I begin to sweat, for it's been a while. I hope she's okay. Is there a phone where I can make a call? Outside, down the hall to your right, Mr. Witherspoon. The nurse speaks methodically but in a friendly tone of voice. My body drips heavily with sweat. I duck out to catch my breath. When I get back to Doc Stone's office Mom's just coming out, looking pretty good, even smiling a little. I'm jittery, trying to hold back the trembles. Hope it went okay. Fine. What's the problem? What did he say?

An hour later we're sitting across from each other at McDonald's; her pink raincoat is slightly damp from the winter rains. I'm eating a cheeseburger, with fries and a Coke. She's waiting for a bowl of chili, fidgeting with some items in her purse. So we'll know more when the results of the test come back? Yes. I'm glad. There's nothing to worry about, he said. I'm glad. That's a relief. She eats her chili slowly, savoring each mouthful, this small, large, round woman with white flowing hair, crystal blue eyes and soft cheeks. I want to give her a big hug, a pat on the back, something. Just for courage.

❧

I AM STANDING IN THE LIVING room, across the hall from where we sleep. The long corridor leads upstairs. The landlord, his wife and their son, who is a year younger than I am, live on the second floor. The family is Italian, and unlike us, they like to romp and stomp and shout at each other. By contrast, we are quiet, shy and withholding. Mom hates all the noise when she comes home tired from work, hates the slamming of doors, and one day, I overhear her complaining to the Italian mother about all the drats going on upstairs. She is trying to be reasonable, and in her cool, calm voice, she asks if the Italian woman would mind not slamming the doors so loudly the house shakes. The Italian woman takes offense, and barks back, "I want you out of here in three months! Do you hear me? Get it?" Mom is offended, and I begin to realize we must move again, pull up stakes, pack our belongings in suitcases, and find somewhere else to live.

❧

LYING ON THE LARGE ASSEMBLY room floor, eyes focused on the ceiling, I begin to remember the days when I took her to the hospital. It's all coming back to me now.

We drive across town and up the road to the hospital and treatment center. It's cool and I feel the chill of that January morning in my bones, with the hills above the hospital still enveloped in dense winter fog. The air cuts into my lungs. In the car we hardly speak a word or two to each other; Dad's on his sailboat, sick with a cold. If anybody in the family's called offering to help Mom with her cancer treatments, I haven't heard about it. So it's on my shoulders. Mom senses this and looks at me out of the corner of her eye. She seems disappointed in the whole lot of the Witherspoon family, as if to say, "Where are they when you need them?" I can feel the pain of her disappointment, her mix of emotions coming to the hospital, not knowing what to expect, worried about her condition.

When we park in the underground lot and step out of the car, she pulls her arm through mine. We walk together slowly, taking small steps, one at a time. I realize at once, despite the present circumstances, what a remarkable woman she is: strong, determined, and I wish I could find another way of doing this because I know it's going to be painful, it's going to test that inborn strength and pull her down. Luckily, her mood, which was sour when I arrived, has changed a bit; there's been in just the last hour a visible transformation. She had wanted to go by herself, rejecting Dad's offer to drive, telling him not to bother or take his germs from his cold to the hospital and spread them around. I'm the default solution, but there's a caveat: I can take her, doing a son's good deed, but I must agree not to watch while she gets her first dose of radiation to zap the cancer cells in her breasts.

The hospital is a big, modern steel-and-glass job, rising a couple, three stories on pillars of concrete, layer by layer, upward against the pale winter sky. I'm cold, but not as cold as Mom; she's trembling, so I quickly wrap my arms around her and try to warm her up. I'm not sure if she's losing her nerve, or what. I want to tell her that she's got to keep up her courage. We get to the front desk and ask for information.

"Where's the radiation treatment lab?"

"Lab or center?"

"I don't know which one it is," I tell the receptionist, feeling slightly peeved. "For cancer patients, that's the one."

There, I've said the dreaded word: cancer. I wince with pain, Mom's pain, and I'm choking up, holding back a flood of emotions.

The receptionist drops her gulliver, then looks up, her eyeballs white and popping. "Downstairs, one flight, and to the right. Follow the signs."

I know I've said the wrong thing. Mom quivers at the mention of cancer; she hasn't come to the stark realization yet that she's got cancer, I'm thinking to myself. But then, neither have I.

She stops dead in her tracks, like an ox. "That's it. I'm going to die right here. No further for me. Let's go back."

"We can't"

"What do you mean, we can't? I want to go home, Jeremy."

"Mom, you have an appointment."

"So?"

"We've got to honor it. You need treatment."

"To hell with treatment," she shouts at me.

"Not so loud, Mom."

"I'll say what I want to say."

"Okay. You want to die right now. Listen, nobody dies at the Information desk of a hospital."

"Maybe that's where I was meant to die," she says. "You ever thought about that?"

"Sorry I said the C word."

I realize if Dad were here, he wouldn't apologize. Okay, I've said something very stupid; I have second thoughts about it. Okay, I want to retract it but it stands. She breaks into tears for a moment, then regains her composure.

Downstairs at the Radiation Center, we stop together at the front desk and lean over the counter. The nurse is almost too friendly and accommodating as she checks out Mom's name in the computer, nimbly clicking away at the keys, then hands Mom an array of forms to fill out. We sit down in one of the green vinyl chairs and wait to be seen by the doctor while I fill out the information requested. Mom's too jittery to hold a pen, so I skvat it and fill in the fields of the consent form and the questionnaire attached to it. Beside us, sitting in one of these green vinyl chairs, is an old geezer with a bald gulliver that reflects specs of fluorescent light on the magazine table; the man looks as if he's ready to kick the bucket before sundown. His face is tattered, his eyes almost frozen, unblinking. He can hardly move his arms or gulliver. Mom turns away from him, repelled by the sight, fearful that that's what she'll look like after she's been radiated. She moves to another chair, as I continue to fill in the blasted form. Mom drops her gulliver into her lap, holding back tears.

"He should be here soon," I tell her.

"Hope he never comes."

"Why?"

"Then we can go home."

But it is not to be. Before we know it, Doc Goldman pops in from the other room. Under his arm is a big clipboard with Mom's medical record attached to it.

"I'm so pleased to meet you, Mrs. Witherspoon." He smiles, extending a hand.

"Hello."

"Your doctor told me all about you. You're in good hands." He scans Mom's report from the clipboard. "Let's get you going today. Okay?"

She introduces me to Doc Goldman.

"Hello."

"Hope you'll take it easy on Mom," I say, shaking his hand. "She's the only mom the Witherspoon family's got."

Doc Goldman, dressed in a white smock that looks all stiff and neatly pressed, fidgets with Mom's report. I notice there's a blue nametag prominent on his chest and that he's middle-aged, with streaking gray hair and black tortoise shell glasses. Not as large as Mom's primary care physician, nor quite as charming, but still imposing and the best, so I'm told. And that's what I want for Mom. There's a string of patients waiting, in rows of chairs, before us. We wait and take our turn before walking slowly, hesitantly into the radiation room around the corner. Doc Goldman accompanies us to the radiation machine, which, from a distance, looks like a giant cement mixer, only white and smoothly polished and gleaming a bit in the hospital light.

"This is my baby." He laughs a muffled laugh as he speaks the word baby.

I put my arm around Mom and squeeze her tightly; she's shaking like a leaf. I feel protective and wish the rest of the Witherspoon family were here to provide some comfort. "What can I do?"

"Just wait. It won't take long," says Doc Goldman.

He points to the machine, which is an awesome piece of work, a huge contraption half the size of the room, and explains that once you're strapped into it, with the target areas on your body marked out plainly for treatment, a beam of X-rays, all invisible of course, zaps you for a minute or two.

"Two minutes, in your mother's case."

"Why?"

"That's what we've determined your mother needs."

I ask if the treatment is painful. He says no. I ask about side effects because I'd heard they're horrendous.

"You can expect nausea, dizziness, some chills afterward. Be sure to call us if the condition persists."

"You can bet we will," I say.

"She has to go once a week, for a month. That's how long the treatment is scheduled to last."

"Wow. That's a long time."

"Listen, Jeremy, I don't think I'm ready for this. Why don't you just let me die in the operating room after surgery? It'll be better for the whole family like that."

"Stop being melodramatic, Mom. This is going to help you. It's going to zap the bad cancer cells to kingdom come. You'll live, they'll die. Simple as that."

"What if the machine misses the bad cells? Ever think of

that?"

"I can assure you, Mrs. Witherspoon," interjects Doc Goldman, "this is a targeted assault on the cancerous cells."

"But it'll kill the good with the bad, and with the ugly."

"Mom, this is no time for a debate," I shout at her. "People are waiting to get their dose of radiation and we're arguing about philosophical issues."

"They're not philosophical, Jeremy. When you get older you'll understand that," says Mom, taking me on.

"Yes, it's true, Mr. Witherspoon. You'll understand better when you're older."

"What is this, two against one? C'mon."

"Okay. I'll do it," says Mom, finally relinquishing her position, giving up at least temporarily the fight. "I'm with Doc Goldman."

"That's the spirit, Mrs. Witherspoon."

"What do my children know, anyway?"

So they strap Mom onto the machine with a couple of belts to hold her in place. I hold her hand, as she's being prepared on the machine. She's still trembling. The Zapper fires up, this behemoth of modern technology, all white and gleaming, its nozzle pointed at Mom's breasts. I think to myself, Hey, I hope it works, I hope the cancer hasn't spread too far. Doc Goldman stands over her, while I'm about ten or fifteen feet away, and she looks at me rather sadly from a distance, over her shoulder. I can feel the currents, waves of sadness in the cold air, and I wonder in my gut if she'll be okay.

In a moment she's shot with a beam of radiation that makes a slight buzzing sound. I keep looking for some flicker of light or energy but can't see any. The stream's invisible, yes. She's not in pain, she is in pain. There's really no way to tell. It's supposed to last just a couple of minutes but it feels like an eternity. Slowly, the machine goes round, burning the cancer out of the body's cells, a death ray. She holds up pretty well, all things considered. The doctor comes over and says it'll be okay, she's doing fine. A nurse appears and escorts me back to the waiting room. I'm sitting there now with the other patients, a motley crew, pathetic creatures, sad, maimed and wounded from the cancer that's attacked them like the virulent disease it is. A man whose skin has turned dark, his hair fallen out sits right next to me.

"How long have you been undergoing treatments?" My voice sounds so rational when it's not.

"About six months, off and on."

"Is it painful? My mom's here for her first one."

"Hey, mister, it knocks the holy crap out of you. Mind if I smoke?"

He lights up a cigarette before the nurse rushes over to tell him to put it out, looking at him sternly, as if he's a disobedient child.

"They're giving me three months to live."

"I'm sorry."

"Not your fault."

He lights up another cigarette and crawls into a corner to hide the smoke. Soon Mom comes out of the radiation room, with Doc Goldman on her arm and she's smiling. I can tell that she loves the doctor. By the look on her face, I can also tell it wasn't so baddiwad. Meanwhile, I'm almost in tears. There's a slight release of tension on my face. I put my arm around her, wishing I could do something, but she's okay.

"It wasn't so bad."

"Thank you, Doc Goldman."

We walk slowly to the elevator, stand and wait before riding up from the bowels of the hospital to the main floor. She's by no means fragile; there's still a lot of life left in her, a thickness of skin, a toughness of spirit that she's built up over the years. She's a tough cookie indeed.

We leave the hospital ready to take on the world, or in Mom's case, whatever it is she's fighting, which is probably equally challenging. But soon, in the car on the way home, her toughness and stamina give way to another set of feelings. She starts to shiver uncontrollably in the car seat next to me. I'm getting worried, a little freaked out. "You want a blanket, Mom? C'mon, I've got one in the trunk."

"No, no. I don't want that."

"C'mon." I stop the car at the corner of El Camino and Embarcadero, get out, pop the trunk of the VW bug, which is in the front, reach in and skvat my red Scottish plaid picnic blanket.

We argue while I wrap the blanket around her, bundling her up like a newborn. At the house we sit and drink hot tea, which Dad has brewed in the kettle. The trembling's stopped, except for her hands, which quiver, then go steady, then quiver again. I'm fearful of terrible side effects. The tea warms her up.

"What can I get you, Mom?" I ask, trying to comfort her as best I can.

"Nothing. I'm finished."

"A bite to eat? That'll help."

"I'm not hungry.

"You have to eat something, Mom. You didn't have

breakfast."

"I can't. Listen, Jeremy, thanks for helping."

"No problem."

Two months later she's dead.

❦

THE SUNLIGHT DANCES ON THE WATER. Seagulls squawk. The sounds of the Marina, with wind chimes ringing, boats powering up, voices whispering, are pleasing to the ear. Looks like a perfect day for a sail, I say. Sure does, replies Dad. Brought some food for you. Thanks, Son. What happened last night? Nothing. Just had a run-in with a guy I used to knock gullivers with; we got into a fight.

Dad, you're always getting into fights, I tell him, not afraid to speak my rassoodock even though I'm just a kid, not even twelve years old, and he's much, much bigger than me, with powerful arms and shoulders from years of fishing for wild salmon with his crew out in the Pacific, casting nets and pulling ropes and reeling in the day's catch. When I look at his hands, which are now calloused and puffy, I can still feel their iron grip. You will too, kid, he says. Wait till you get older. Ha ha.

We climb inside the cockpit of Dad's boat, a forty-foot sloop, and I scurry down below. I hand the Old Man a bag of food and a sixpack of Coke. He opens the bag, spots the sandwiches and puts the soft drinks in a small refrigerator. He leaves out two cans and pops them open. He and I drink and toast. We climb up the stairs, outside, on the deck. We get the rigging set up. We put on life jackets.

The in-board fires up. Soon we motor out of the San

Francisco marina, out the harbor and into the Bay, until the flap of the first sail cuts into the wind. The boat moves fast; in the distance, I can see gusts of wind kicking up. Is there a storm brewing? You take over, Son. Set a course. Let's go to Angel Island, and anchor offshore. Sounds good. Oh, Dad, this is really a lot of fun, I tell the Old Man.

The sun is still really bright. Other boats are filling up the Bay. Dad scans the horizon all the way out to Alcatraz Island and beyond to the Golden Gate. Look at all those sailboats. A lot of *laundry* out there, he tells me. Let's tack, I say. I handle the rigging myself. We tack, and shift directions. Dad, I'm having a great time, I tell him. When we finally reach Angel Island, Dad pulls down the sails and anchors the boat. There's a quiet, still cove between Angel Island and Belvedere Cove. The water is absolutely smooth and calm. We skvat a sandwich and something to drink, another Coke from the refrigerator below.

The sky suddenly clouds up. There's a storm brewing, all right. We've got to get back. The weather looks like it's really starting to change on us. You take the rudder, Dad tells me. He goes down below. Incredibly, with the sky partly sunny, it starts to rain. I got it. Dad comes up, wearing a yellow rubber hat. The rain's coming down harder, the waves are kicking up. The boat rocks from side to side, bow to stern. My gulliver knocks on the boom, as Dad tries to tack. The waves pick up.

A blow from the boom stuns me and I suddenly fall into the icy Bay water. Immediately Dad dives in after me. After some frantic swimming, he rescues me. I'm shaken but okay as the boat still rocks on the stormy waters. Dad, you saved me! It's all right, kid, says Dad. Just some water splashing over. Let's get her back to shore, he says. You bet. He navigates the boat back to shore. I'm still wet and shaken from the accident.

❧

"DADDY DIDN'T GIVE AFFECTION," Eddie Vedder's singing on the radio in that deep, raspy voice of his. "Generally spoken."

There's a hard rain falling when I get to the curly lip of the Bay Bridge. I'm driving fast because I know I'm going to be late, we agreed to meet at five o'clock, and being on time is a big thing of his lately. Dad can help with this, see things that I don't want to see. I'm going to enlist, join the Marines, if they'll take me, if I've got what it takes, the few, the proud. There's some defending of democracy I've got to do, I'm going to tell him. Dad needs to understand that, even if he's a sailor and commercial fisherman, a hippie dad when it comes to fighting wars and defending the country. Pellets of rain blind my vision, as I navigate the turns that take me across the bridge down to the waterfront, along the Marina where Dad's got his boat.

He lives on that boat, the one we used to sail around the Bay.

I got to come forward, I got to hold back. Hey, why is it I feel Dad's opposed to me? What have I done wrong? Private thoughts, private dreams, I'm going to war even if he hates war; hates all it stands for. Rain hits me hard when I get out of the car, drenched to the bone in a cloudburst. I walk to the gate along the pier not far from where he's got his sailboat, this forty-footer on which he's been living, for God's sake, since Mom died. He steps out to greet me, coming toward the gate.

"Glad you could make it, Son."

I nod, then grimace. At any rate, we climb onto the boat, which rocks back and forth gently in the rain. What's a little rain, anyway, when he's taken his boat down the Kahleefornia coast all the way to Baja, when he's sailed the Pacific to Tonga and Fiji? This is how he lives.

Inside, he's got a little electric heater cranked up, going strong down below. I sit down and peel off my wet blue jacket. "A monster storm out there, Dad," I mumble.

"Want some tea, kid?"

"Okay." He disappears into the makeshift kitchen by one of the sleeping compartments and puts on a kettle of water. I rub my hands, trying to generate some heat of my own. In a minute or two I hear the kettle whistling. When he gets back I sip the hot tea he's made for me; tastes good, steam rising to the tip of my nose. For a moment, lifting my eyes, I'm fixated on the trim of his beard, which has grown substantially since the last time I saw him; it's getting all white and full, Papa Hemingway-style, I'm thinking.

A cold, icy wind suddenly kicks up in the late afternoon and the boat sways back and forth, rocking hard and bobbing with a fury on the water. The headwall in front of the Marina takes the biggest hits from the storm that's brewing. "Not too many boats out there," I say. "Not much laundry."

We used to laugh at the mention of the word *laundry*, as a way of describing all the weekend fleets and flutters of sailboats tacking on the Bay, but this time, Dad's gone stone silent.

My fear underneath it all is that he'll snap at me, berate me, humiliate me in some way. I'm guilty and ought to be punished, but for what I don't really know.

His face is cold as a whiff of Arctic air blowing in from the north. He looks stern, forbidding. There's no emotion, as if he won't yield an ounce of anything to me. I feel, for a moment, inadequate, weakened by the intensity of his look, not up to the task of meeting him and telling him I'm going to war. I'm going to enlist.

"What's on your mind, kid?"

"Lots of things, Dad."

"Well, like what?"

"Sure you don't mind if we talk about it?"

"Don't pussyfoot around with me, kid. You know I've got a low threshold of patience when it comes to family matters. Speak up or forever hold your peace."

"Dad, just for once try to be a little patient," I say, ready to burst into a fit of anger, of rage, like Eddie Vedder's been singing. "I know you hate me, you can't stand having me around after Mom's death because you think all I do is remind you of my mother."

"Hate you, kid? I don't hate you. No father hates his son. It's what the son's become that—"

"And what's that? Huh? What is it that you don't like that I've become. C'mon, Dad, let's have it out."

"You itchin' for a fight, kid? You came all the way from the South Bay on a day full of rain to stir up anger with the Old Man. I get the picture and I don't like it."

"Neither do I. So it's got to change. Listen, I'm joining up with the Marines. Don't need your permission. Just wanted to let you know, in case something happens, like my whereabouts and crap like that."

"I don't approve of your going off to some freaking war to

kill Iraqis, steal their oil and make them believe our form of government is better than theirs. What's got into your head, Jeremy? Where are you messed up like this?"

"Know what I have to do, that's all. Know what's right for me."

"Do it then, okay?"

"Okay, Dad, I will."

All of a sudden I feel as if I'm taller than Dad, even though I'm already physically taller than the Old Man by at least a couple of inches. But now I stand taller, my gulliver banging against the ceiling of the boat down below. I'm my dad, only I'm not my dad. I'm me. I've got his shoulders, his cheekbones, his eyes, his hair. We're the same but not the same.

On the floor I notice a box of tools; I figure he's been working on something, perhaps fixing the boat's small, inboard motor, which he needs when he pulls down the sails and scoots into his berth in the Marina. It's hard now, after what's been said, letting go, giving in, to pull his attention toward me; he looks distracted, maybe somewhat disoriented. I rattle off details of my plan to enlist in the Marines, when I'm going, how I'm preparing, what I'm doing to get in shape, like a sputtering fax machine on the fritz.

"How does that saying go? Those who don't learn from the past are doomed to repeat it," he says, getting philosophical on me. "Made a mistake when I dropped out of school and joined up, and landed there, a foot soldier, a grunt in the jungles of Cambodia on a secret mission that the government had lied to everybody about and came this close to getting my head blown off. That was my karma, so now you're repeating it. Nothing I can do to change your mind, is there? Okay. We'll have to live with it. Your choice, Jeremy."

His glances pull away from me; I try to stare directly at him—and I get a reflection of myself. He can mirror me with uncanny accuracy. I fidget in the chair next to him, clasp my hands, wringing them for a while, then lean back. I try to center myself. His gulliver turns from the view outside.

The experience leaves me feeling hurt and wounded, yet strangely happy with myself. I've gone as far as I want to go this time. I've tested the waters, as it were, and they're cold but not freezing. In a sense, there's no turning back now; I've already decided, made my choice. Then I get angry at Dad, the prick. He seems so mean-spirited, a tyrant, uncompromising, without sympathy, without compassion. If he only knew my angst, if he only listened to me.

A fierce wind has picked up. A bolt of lightning breaks fast across the sky, then disappears into the murky waters of the Bay. The horizon turns dark for a moment, then glimmers of light emerge through the inky clouds above the arches of the Golden Gate Bridge. I need the illumination and so does Dad, so we can see each other again in a different light, with a different kind of understanding.

He stands there, a large man, with a look of reassurance, as if he's saying, "You've done the right thing." An acknowledgment, grudging or otherwise, of courage, an act of courage.

In the summer, while I'm in Ramadi, the news comes of Dad's deteriorating condition. There's a letter I crack open with baddiwad news. I knew that he had been diagnosed with the prostate cancer but figured he'd beat it, and now we don't know how much longer he'll live.

AFTER THIRTEEN HOURS ON A BUS, I arrive early morning at Camp Tombo, the Marine Corps camp for infantry training, near the city of San Lucia in Southern Kahleefornia. There are two such camps in America, I learn: one here, the other, Camp Lejeune, on the east coast in North Carolina. Camp Tombo is huge, a sprawling compound of jagged rocks and sand, resting on the lip of the Pacific Ocean, complete with bunkers and barracks and camouflage-painted buildings. At the far end is a giant mess hall, where you can eat all you want, seconds, thirds, fourths, even fifths. To keep track of everybody stands a giant observation tower at the center, jutting upward to the sky, a frontier outpost of the proud and the few.

Getting off the bus, I catch the sounds of rapid gunfire, flashes of light, followed by surfer waves of explosions coming from the hillside behind the camp. I start to freak out, thinking we're under enemy attack. But the other recruits on the bus laugh at me: "It's practice, man," says one of the recruits, an African-American man with a cocky, devilish grin. "Get used to it." I am not sure if I can because my instincts are finely tuned to noises or disturbances of any kind, the slightest movement in the streets, any threat, whether real or imagined. My instinct tells me to pounce, defend myself and fight to the death, if necessary. "It's a fire zone," says another recruit, smoking a cigarette. "What the hell you think it was going to be, dude?" I have no idea.

As we walk in line, single file, toward the entrance of the induction center, I slowly begin to like and even appreciate the feel of Camp Tombo, everything moving smoothly, with great precision, like clockwork. There are platoons of soldiers marching in orderly fashion, lots of signs of discipline in the air and the natural sweat that comes from the rigors of training young men to be part of a well-oiled fighting machine. I am an entry-level recruit, and according to the terms of the agreement negotiated by my dad and the Marine recruiter, I am required to report at 09:00 hours right after getting off the bus from Los Angeles to headquarters at Camp Tombo for processing and formal induction into the Marines. They advise me not to take any personal belongings with me to camp, as they will be confiscated and replaced by all-Marine gear, right down to my shoes and socks and skivvies.

My papers read:

The Skolliwoll of Infantry (SOI) at Camp Tombo handles both entry-level and advanced infantry training for active duty and reserve Marines through its five subordinate units and two supporting Navy units. The mission includes fifteen different programs of instruction. Accordingly, and as agreed under California law, I am required to report to building number 520420, which is the Student Administration Center (SAC).

In a daze, I wander around for a few minutes looking for SAC before following my fellow recruits to the front entrance. There, they begin my processing into the skolliwoll. I have my orders tucked neatly under my arm and do my best to be a good soldier on the first day of arrival.

A tall, blue-eyed Marine in uniform, one of the few, one of the proud, I think to myself, shuffles through the folder containing my papers, smiles and winks, then takes a hard look at me, from gulliver to toe. "We've had other kids in Camp Tombo from your part of the state," he says, with a deep, almost hostile voice, "but none with your keen sense of hearing and seeing, soldier."

"Well, I'm born with those things, sir," I say, flexing my shoulder muscles and expanding my chest up against his. "And hope to put them to good use in Iraq."

"Move forward, son."

"Yes, sir."

I salute, rather awkwardly, then return to filling out more paperwork, at least one hundred questions, some of them asking if I am married and who my parents are and if I have any relatives in the United States Armed Forces. I answer no to the last question, and to the first. For a moment I am thinking of my girlfriend from high skolliwoll, of Brianna and the wild times we had together, and if we'll get married while I'm in the service. Brianna is something of an airhead and she lingers in my memory for a few moments, then disappears into the dust kicking up around camp. After finishing the questionnaire, I feel the impulse, now that I am officially in Camp Tombo, to write and tell my dad of my induction into the United States Marine Corps and how proud I am to be serving as a soldier. After processing with SAC I am assigned to the Infantry Training Battalion (ITBN).

Basic training for Marines, I am told along with my fellow recruits, involves a strenuous thirteen-week program. "Hell on earth," whispers one of my fellow recruits. "But it makes you a man, tough as steel, a killer." The thought of killing does not bother me, but then I realize, among the recruits, we'll be trained to kill other soldiers, young men, from other armies in other countries, men like ourselves, all in the name of protecting our families, our values, our country. The thirteen weeks will end, I am told, in the ultimate test, an event called "The Crucible." After graduation from the Skolliwoll of Infantry—and not everybody would graduate—I will move on to another skolliwoll for training in a specific job before being sent out in the field into combat. I figure I'll be sent to either Iraq or Afghanistan.

In boot camp, I must complete a series of drill, physical training, swim qualification and other training programs. I'm going to be assigned to one of three battalions, consisting of four companies. In the First Battalion are companies Alpha, Bravo, Charlie, and Echo. In the Second Battalion are companies Delta, Fox, Golf, and Hotel; in the Third Battalion India, Kilo, Lima, and Mike. Each company is broken down into platoons and each platoon given a number. Rivalries are established, I'm told, between each platoon, so I have to be prepared to do combat against my fellow Marines. At the end of it all is a grueling test of manhood, courage and endurance, a fifty-four-hour event, known as "The Crucible."

My assignment: First Battalion, Bravo company. I'm told to "kick the ass" of every other platoon recruit in my company. And I am assured they will do the same. All's fair in love and war.

On Day One I'm told to memorize the Eleven General Orders for a Sentry, along with the Marine Rifle Creed. I struggle to memorize the Marines' Hymn and am told to know by heart the first and second verses by the end of the week, or else. There is more to memorize: the *USMC Core Values* book, details from Marine Corps history and all facets of the M16A4 Rifle, as well as the Code of Conduct. I can do all that, I figure, but it'll take time. Then I am told I will be tested on my swimming ability. Swimming ability? Man, I never learned how to swim; Dad never taught me, even though he's a sailor and lives on a sailboat.

☙❧

DOGG IS A HOLY MAN, a holy warrior. He sees things coming, his vision apocalyptic. I ask him what he sees coming to Kahleefornia. That's what I'm writing, man, he says. Want to take a look? Sure, I reply. How much have you written? Just the first part, he says. You can imagine the rest until I write it, or until the real thing happens. Then you'll believe. Oh, I believe, I tell him. So this is what you're seeing on the outside, when we get out, if we ever do, but you're saying what? Don't understand. Nothing to understand, he comes back to me, his voice cool yet slightly on edge. Just a matter of black and white, cool or not so cool, whatever, like that, he says. Damn, if I can figure him out. Damn if I know what he's talking about. Okay, I'll take the manuscript with me, hide it under my bed away from the prying eyes of the docs and nurses, and give it a good read at night with the moonbeam I pinched from Supplies, I tell him. Thanks, Spoon. Fine with me. And he hurries down the hall, disappearing into the gloom.

"Unthinkable"
a novel
by C.J. 'Dogg' Williams

The boy's mother had arrived early to pick him up from soccer practice. He was not feeling particularly well, his face flushed red, his cheeks dripping with sweat. When she got out of the van she sensed immediately something was wrong. In the distance she spotted him easily, among a cluster of players, as all mothers can do. She feared he had been kicked in the shins again by one of the larger boys, or hurt himself going after the ball in a rush to score a goal. A look of worry came over her face. He was too young to play, not strong enough to compete with the other boys. All of her protective instincts came bubbling to the surface. With his father gone to war, she was all the boy had. She had become both the man and woman in the house, and she did not like it, not at all.

She said hello to the soccer coach, a stocky man with a big head of hair and jowly cheeks. He had a whistle hanging from his neck and seemed too preoccupied to give much time to any arriving parents.

Are you okay, son? she probed. No, Mom, I'm not if you really want to know. But I thought it was just practice, not a real game, she said. I'm tired, he said. Wait a minute, what happened to your face? What do you mean, Mom? He seemed anxious and she picked up on his fear. His skin had darkened, a sudden tanning from head to toe, as if he had been out in the sun too long, much too long for a boy of ten.

When she got home she stepped into the bathroom and soaked a washcloth in warm water and ran it across his forehead and cheeks.

His face continued to darken, red dissolving into shades of brown. I think we ought to see a doctor, she said. Why? I'm feeling okay, Mom. There's nothing wrong with me. But your face and arms and legs are turning darker and darker, I'm concerned, I really am. Listen, I'll feel better if we see a doctor. Come on, let's go. Vamos, as your coach says. Oh, he's just trying to get us to move faster. Honestly, Mom, I'm okay.

Driving to the hospital she noticed the fiery dome of the sun glaring through the windshield, its preternatual light almost blinding her. The ball of sun was burnt red, hanging low in her line of vision at sunset. Everything seemed darker, and when she got to the hospital she found other moms with their sons from the school and from the soccer team waiting to be examined by the hospital staff. This can't be natural, she thought. Can't be, she shook her head. Everybody's here, said her son with a kind of gleeful elation she found difficult to understand. I wish I could call your father while we wait. Yes, I'm here with him, we're waiting to be seen, she said. No, it's not some kind of emergency, far as I can tell. He says he's fine. But her husband was off to war, unreachable, even when it mattered. She had to live with it. In her mind, she said, I mean, it's odd to see all the kids from school waiting too. I'll call you as soon as we see the doctor. Love you, she added. She hoped her thoughts travelled across the ether to the other side of the planet or wherever he happened to be stationed.

By this time, her son's face had got even darker than she recalled from seeing it on the soccer field and later at the house. After an interminable wait, sitting on pins and needles, growing more and more anxious by the minute, the doctor appeared. A tall man with a pencil moustache and tiny, piercing eyes, he reached out to her, extended his hand and smiled. You're about the tenth parent I've seen whose son or daughter has come in this afternoon. Let me take a look and determine if it's the same as what I've seen before. In the examining room, he lifted the boy's chin upward, then fixed his gaze into the boy's eyes, which had swollen with large pupils. He felt the back of the boy's throat with the tips of his thumbs, then turned to the boy's mother. We don't really know what this is. It might be a skin rash of some kind, spread by contact on the soccer field with an irritating substance, but frankly, we've never seen anything like this before. Tell me, I said. I want to know. Are all the children turning black? she asked in a voice of deep concern. He hesitated, then replied, Well, not everyone. What can we do? I'm going to give you some ointment, in case he begins scratching his face. A quarantine of all those infected may be necessary, in case we determine it's a virus of some kind, capable of spreading from human to human. He says he's fine, she said, although he got a little banged up on the soccer field. Nothing too serious. One of the other boys kicked him in the groin by accident, he says, and the coach reprimanded the boy. What about the other children?

Are they also unaffected except for the darkening of skin color? I can't really say, said the doctor, shaking his head. We'll know more tomorrow; I've asked some of the darkest children to stay the night in the hospital. I don't want to, cried the boy. I'm okay, just a little hurt from the match. I kicked one ball into the goal before I got kicked myself in my privates. I understand, son, said the doctor, trying to keep things at an even keel. If you don't want to stay in the hospital tonight, I can't make you. But I'd recommend staying indoors, not going out or having contact with others. Is that okay? Yes, said the mother. That's fine with us.

The soccer coach had noticed the boys on the field, their faces turning bright red in the heat of the afternoon sun. He had made sure under the circumstances there was enough water to take care of any dehydration problems; bottles were in the big cooler he kept on the sidelines. He had run the boys hard but had also encouraged them to drink as much fluid as possible. When the boy who had got kicked in the privates complained of dizziness, he had pulled him off immediately and sat down with him to check on his condition. The sun was beating down brighter and more intensely than he could remember; the air was heavy, no wind, not the slightest hint of a breeze in the late spring.

The boy's mother had arrived a little early and she had fetched her son without saying much to him. It was not the coach's fault the young boy had been beat up on the field, yet the mother's look made it clear he was to blame. Her real concern was the coloration of his face, the reddening, the flush of redness, even though the boy said he was okay and wanted to continue with practice. She had dragged him away, as the other boys watched as if to say, Hey, what's the matter? Why can't he keep playing? He's no sissy but his mom makes him that way.

Soon the other boys were also beginning to redden, the coach noticed, their faces turning darker, hands and legs burning. He wanted to call the practice off and get everybody out of the sun. A nearby group of trees by the schoolyard had lots of shade. The coach hesitated, as nobody looked ill or affected by the heat and sunlight. The boys were playing better than he had ever seen them, stronger, with sharper reflexes to the ball, moving faster up and down the field, kicking with long strokes of the foot, even tackling with the precision of slide he had taught them. Better to err on the side of caution, he had told himself. Okay, let's call it. Blowing his whistle, he walked out to the field and waved to the boys, all twenty-two of them, to stop practice. Get some water! Let's cool off. The boys followed him to the grove of trees, drinking gulps from the bottles he had saved for them in the cooler chest.

The cars with moms at the wheel were arriving now one after the other. He told each boy what they had done well during the practice and what they needed to work on, as the moms approached areas by the shaded trees. No one wanted to linger, so he grabbed a couple of soccer balls and loaded them into a bag and headed to the school locker room. In the distance he could hear one of the moms berating her son for not drinking enough water and letting his face turn bright red. She demanded he use sunscreen next time and in a huff hauled off the boy to her van.

It was odd: nothing like he had ever seen before. All the boys somehow changed color. For a moment he choked on his own breath. The air was harder to take in and let out than earlier in the day. Looking at his own arms and legs, he also noticed a darkening of skin. Usually, he would grow darker by early or mid summer after spending long hours on the soccer field, teaching his boys the fundamentals and preparing them for the competition ahead. The first of the season's matches was coming up this Saturday, less than a week away. He worried that it might be an especially hot spring and early summer, so he reassured himself he had done the right thing by calling practice. In the locker room he inspected all six soccer balls he had brought out to the field that day. Perhaps the balls had picked up something on the field, a chemical or toxin of some kind, and infected the skins of all those who had come in contact. He rotated each ball and picked away with his fingernails at the grass stains and dark patches along the seams. Every ball looked okay. No problem, nothing out of the ordinary. He loaded the balls on the metal rack in the locker room and noticed a whole row of balls was missing. Damn, he shook his head. Somebody's stolen them again. Is there a black market in soccer balls, or what?

Driving home from school, he heard his cell phone ringing constantly. He was in no mood to talk to anybody and he hated anybody who spoke on his or her cell while driving. But the ringing would not stop, so he finally pulled over to the side of the road and checked his messages, figuring if the calls were important, somebody would care enough to leave their name and insist on his returning their call. As it happened, the principal of his school, a testy, white-haired woman with a demanding personality, had called three times. He listened for what she had to say, fearing he had lost his job. She had been trying to reach him, her voice insistent, aggrieved. What had he done wrong now? Parents had been calling the school, complaining of this strange, attacking virus that had altered the color of their children's skin, and all of it had occurred after practice on the soccer field. Each message was more distraught than the previous one. He thought of immediately returning the principal's phone calls, but then hesitated, trying to compose himself to deal with the situation. There was nothing out of the ordinary he could detect on the playing field; each kid he had coached seemed fine, without pain or injury except for the one boy who had got kicked accidentally in his privates. It was more a wound of dignity, rather than anything that had caused physical harm. He had examined each soccer ball for any signs of a fungus or growth; the field itself was unchanged. Yes, he had noticed a darkening of skin color, both on his boys and himself, but thought it nothing more than heavy-duty exposure to the sun. The day had been particularly hot and dry, yet not really any different from other days in late spring. What could he tell the principal? He had no good answers for her, he figured. So he would have to make one up. On the phone she breathed a sigh of relief when she heard his voice. I thought you'd never call, she said. What happened on the soccer field? Nothing I know of, he told her. But maybe the boys ate something bad in the cafeteria and it caused a chain reaction. That's what I'm thinking. Listen, it might be just a case of excessive sunburn. Ever think of that? The sun's brighter than I can remember. The principal was not buying any of it. She gasped, then raised her voice. I can't tell the parents who've been calling me nonstop since school let out it's a case of excessive sunburn. I'm concerned about our liability, the liability of the school, you understand? The last thing we need is some kind of medical lawsuit because we were irresponsible in caring for their needs. Do I make myself clear? Of course, he said, trying to calm her down, but without much luck.

He wanted to tell her about the missing soccer balls and the man he saw whose automobile was filled with them. The thief had got away, but maybe he had something to do with the spreading virus. He doubted the principal would listen to any of this; she was rattled. Come in early tomorrow morning to my office, she told him, finally, and we'll talk this over. Good-bye.

He started up the car and drove back to his apartment slowly and carefully, navigating all the turns with caution. Something strange was in the air.

At the young boy's house there was a sense of panic, as his skin had turned from red to dark red to brown to dark brown, every part of his body that had been exposed to the sun. You okay, honey? I'm worried about you. Hey, Mom, I'm fine, I don't mind being a little dark, nothing wrong with that. But you weren't that way when I picked you up at soccer practice. That was then. Well, the doctor said I should keep an eye on you, see if there are any other changes. I'll be okay.

She cooked up dinner for the boy, but grew fidgety in the kitchen. The boy's father was off to war in another country; she had not heard from him in four weeks, and that contributed to her anxiety. She dreaded the prospect of one day answering the front door and being greeted by two soldiers delivering bad news. Now the problems with her son: why had she allowed him to play soccer in the first place? It was that damned field, some chemical or toxin spread across the length of the field, something used to paint the lines, the boundaries, which her son had picked up. She wanted to call the other mothers from the school, the ones she had met at parents' nights, and ask if their boys were being affected the same way, but she tried to keep calm. The pot with boiling water spilled on the floor and food she was cooking had burned while she stood still, unable to move or take care of things. Mom, what's going on? Her son came in running. Well, I'm not okay, she said, I wish your father were here. I do too, said her son, hugging and tugging at her.

That night she had difficulty sleeping. She tossed and turned in bed, then got up several times to check in on her son. He had fallen asleep fast and was snoring softly on his left side, unaware of the changes to his skin color. She wanted to wake him up and drive back to the hospital for another examination. When she returned to bed she fell asleep from exhaustion and was tormented by one bad dream after another. There were explosions and gunfire, and she was running in the desert after her husband who had been wounded.

By the time she got up in the morning she could hardly move. She walked into the kitchen and saw her son sitting at the table drinking orange juice and filling a bowl with cereal from a box. He had turned completely black: his face and arms and legs dark as coal. The shock sent her reeling. She staggered on one foot, unable to say a word. In a split second she had tumbled to the floor, suffering a heart attack. Her son came rushing toward her, throwing his arms around her. The sight of his black arms embracing her seemed to aggravate the look of terror on her face. She had seized up and was not breathing. He was yelling, Mom, come on, come on, what's the matter? He tried pounding on her chest, but to no avail. Her breathing had stopped completely now. He got up and raced to the phone to call the emergency number she had pasted on the kitchen wall next to the phone cradle. His voice stuttered as he tried to explain to the operator what had happened: I'm, I'm calling because, because my mom's had an accident, she's not breathing, I'm here, here in the kitchen. The operator assured him to stay calm, an ambulance would be sent right away. Did he know CPR? No, he did not. Is, is she dead? The operator said there was no way to know, but to stay calm. Help was on the way.

At his apartment the soccer coach paced around the living room, then found himself in the bathroom. He looked at himself in the mirror; yes, he had darkened somewhat, owing to the intensity of the sunlight in the afternoon, but he had not burned. His skin was not peeling or damaged, as far as he could tell. I'm okay, he told himself. So these kids got a little too much sun while playing soccer, it's not my fault, he reassured himself. He decided to ring up the teacher who taught in the classroom next to his at school; she was a couple of years younger than him, very attractive, with auburn red hair and golden hazel eyes, a cheerful smile and an easygoing manner. While he taught soccer with great passion to his students, she taught science with equally great passion, as he had observed one day when he had sat in on one of her classes. They had gone out a few times, sharing dinner and a movie, but no romance had flourished. He liked her and, he hoped, she liked him. He was not sure if he wanted to get involved any further, complicating their mutual experiences teaching at school and making them the target of unwanted rumors.

When he spoke to her on the phone she sounded panicked. The principal had called repeatedly, also, and relayed the messages from concerned parents who had found their children, not simply boys playing soccer, but also girls in after school classes coming home with altered skin colors. Can you believe it? They're talking about quarantining the whole school, she said. I'm really worried. Is there anything wrong with us? I wouldn't worry, he tried to reassure her, it's just a heavy dose of sun, more than usual, and it's got all the moms in a tizzy, you know. Well, what can we do? Can you come over? I'm having trouble dealing with this. Sure, no problem, he said, I'll bring some pizza and soft drinks. You can handle that, can't you? Of course, she said. Of course I can.

The pizza shop was not far from his apartment, but when he got there it was nearly empty. People had retreated from the outside and were staying home. There was a television screen above the counter and the news was pouring forth: wildfires burning out of control, a spate of violence in the war, unseasonable climatic changes, extremely hot and dry weather, with many folks reporting excessive damage to their skin from the rays of the sun.

He waited for the pizzas to be cooked and paced around the shop, the only customer. His cell phone was ringing again but he decided not to answer it. Had enough for today, he told himself. By the time the pizza was ready and placed into a box the sun had faded into a dark red and was setting in the distance. Twilight shadows were falling across the parking lot where he had left his car. The air was gradually getting cooler. Things will be okay, he smiled, before heading out to his fellow teacher's apartment a few blocks away.

She greeted him at the door in jeans and white blouse, her auburn red hair curled and flowing to her neck. I'm glad you could make it, she said. I really need somebody to lean on. I'm your man, he said. Here, I got it with everything on it. He handed her the box of pizza. I think it's still hot. Inside, they sat down and ate pizza. I haven't eaten anything all day, she said. Don't mind me if I'm a little piggy. Okay by me, he said. Just save me a slice or two. I'm not that piggy. What do you think is happening? You mean, with the kids getting sunburned and all at school, he said. It's like some kind of virus, isn't it? We're all getting infected, she said. No, not at all, if you want my opinion, he said. There's a big hole in the ozone and we're being bombarded by heavy doses of ultraviolet radiation. It could burn us to death if we're not careful. But beyond that, I don't know. The kids have been hit first, lots of sensitive skin there, unprotected, but who knows why they're turning from red to brown to black. You been watching the news? Only a few minutes, and nothing's gone out of the city. I mean, no reports of this happening elsewhere. I'm scared, she told him.

That night he slept on the living room couch. In the morning he noticed a further darkening of his skin, although she was as milky white as ever. When she got up and dressed she found he had made breakfast for her. They sat down at the table and watched the news on television. Still no reports from anywhere of problems with the children whose bodies had darkened the day before. This will pass, won't it? she asked him. I hope so, he said.

When the ambulance arrived the medics rushed into the house where his mother was lying on the floor, her face having turned blue and pink and green. They tried every technique possible to revive her, then placed her on a stretcher and whisked her away, sirens blaring, red lights flashing. He had been left behind, alone in the house. The boy began to cry, but stopped himself after a few minutes, damping down the tears streaming down his cheeks. Why did this happen? Who was to blame? The medics had hardly noticed him and now they were gone, the house empty and cold, even though the sun was beginning to beat down again for the second day in a row. He felt ashamed, as if it were all his fault for frightening his mother to death. After a while, a faint glimmer of hope took hold and lifted his head, making his small body twitch and bend like a leaf in the wind with the possibility she was still alive, or could be brought back to life.

He had no idea what death was, why or how it happened. His father was off to war in a distant land, unreachable except on certain occasions when he happened to contact his mother. Death meant going to sleep for a long time, in the boy's mind. It never quite dawned on him that his mother, poor woman, might never wake up. Gone forever. He pondered what to do. Everything had happened so fast even the neighbors had not had time to react. The family next door never appeared, never showed their faces. Nor did the ones who lived across the street. An ambulance arriving at his house, an emergency crew rushing forth and taking his mother away had not aroused even the slightest curiosity, or if it had, nobody was forthcoming, nobody cared. He grabbed his backpack for school, stuffed his pockets with money he had saved in his piggybank and headed out of the house. As he was about to close the front door behind him, he pivoted on one heel and went back inside. He had forgotten something. There was his beloved soccer ball, the one his father had given him for his tenth birthday. He tucked it under his arm and disappeared outside.

Down the street several blocks he ran into one of his neighbors, an older man, now retired, who was watering his front lawn with a long green garden hose. The old man barked at him, Hey, kid, what are you doing in this neighborhood? I live down the street in the white house, said the boy. There are no colored children in our neighborhood, I don't know who you are. I'm your neighbor, I play on this street, I've never seen you before, go away. But I'm living here with my mom, she's hurt, she had an accident, they took her to the hospital, Hey, kid, where'd you get that soccer ball, better give it back or I'm going to call the police.

The boy fled. His feet were moving fast as he darted in and out of back streets until he got to a convenience store a few blocks away. He was hungry and thirsty and wanted to buy something. Out of breath, the soccer ball tucked under his arm, he walked up and down the aisles looking for a candy bar and a soda. When he found what he wanted he held the items, one in each hand. The man behind the counter started shouting at him. Hey, what are you doing? Give that stuff back. I'm going to pay for it, I've got money. Sure you have, right. Honestly, I've got money. And he reached into his pocket but by this time the man had moved toward him. I know what you're doing, kid. You're stealing in my store. Give it back or else I'm calling the police. The boy threw the money on the floor and ran out of the store.

Around the corner he stopped for a moment to catch his breath. From his pocket he grabbed the candy bar, peeled open the wrapper and sank his teeth into the meat of the chocolate. He was hungry, and after taking several big bites, he began slurping his soda drink. He was eating and gulping down the soda fast as he could, all the while looking behind him and over his shoulder to see if the man at the door was on his tail. Who else was chasing after him? he wondered.

The school was almost entirely empty when the two teachers arrived. Only a few children had come to class while a few others were milling around the hallways. Most of the children had darkened, now sporting brownish skin colors in varying shades. Parents, concerned as to what was going on, had jammed the principal's and the administrative offices. What was the explanation for this change? Had a virus broken out? Were there toxic chemicals on the school grounds? The soccer coach and his fellow teacher and companion overheard the principal telling the parents that a disease control team from the government was arriving soon and the grounds might have to be quarantined.

This looks bad, said the soccer coach. I don't like it at all, said the woman teacher, but what can we do? I don't want to be detained and quarantined, do you? No way.

A few minutes later the boy came sailing into the soccer coach's room, out of breath, his face darker than before. What's happened to you? My mom's in the hospital, she had a heart attack or something when she saw me this morning. I'm the cause. Is she okay? I don't know, I don't think so, they took her away in an ambulance, but they were all shaking their heads, the emergency people. The boy was frazzled, squeezing his soccer ball, bouncing it on the floor. The room was empty now. The woman teacher had come in and heard what he was saying. So you're left at home all by yourself? Yes, I was afraid, and then an old man on the street didn't recognize me, said I didn't belong, I was a colored person, what's that, anyway, and told me there were no colored people in the neighborhood. Same thing happened when I tried to buy a candy bar and some soda. I was thirsty, really thirsty, and the man thought I was trying to steal from his store. Slow down, this all happened. Yes, so I came to school, Can you help me? Of course we can.

The soccer coach and the woman teacher embraced the boy and tried to calm him down.

Meanwhile a voice came over the loudspeaker. Everybody stay put, this is an emergency, a government team is arriving shortly to deal with the situation, we think there's been some kind of natural disaster on the school grounds that's caused everybody's skin to change, don't panic, we have the situation under control.

Sure they do, said the coach. It looks like everybody's affected, said the woman, turning on the television. The news was reporting that the entire state was experiencing the same thing, any exposure to sunlight yesterday would result in a change in skin color, children were the first to be hit because of their natural sensitivity to light, doctors were looking into the matter, and special government teams in hazardous materials were investigating the spots most recently hit, and most dangerous. We urge you to stay put and let the government take care of everything.

No way, said the woman. We should get out of here as fast as possible.

The boy was starting to cry. We'll go to the hospital and see how your mother is doing. We'll slip out the back, Jack. I'm with you, she said. They gathered their things and left.

The streets were deserted, half empty. The light and heat from the sun was beating down. The day was hotter than the day before.

The woman science teacher was breaking down: I can't take this anymore. I'm not handling the crisis very well, I have poor survival skills. How do we get through this? She had to lean on the soccer coach, he was her protector. There's not much to do if you want to get through this.

I'm being peevish, she said.

Let's take the boy to the hospital. The soccer coach kept trying to get through to the hospital switchboard, but all lines were busy. She tried as well but to no avail.

They left the school and drove through town to the hospital. The streets were devoid of life, no cars, nobody out and about.

At the hospital he and the science teacher and the boy were met by security guards at the entrance. We're checking on the condition of the boy's mother, she suffered a heart attack. You have to let us through. I can't without authorization; the hospital isn't taking any new patients. We're not new patients, we just need to find out about the boy's mother. Who are you? We're his teachers. Is his mother white? Yes. Then why is the boy black? That's another story. C'mon, let us through. I'll have to check with my supervisor, we were told not to let anybody through unless they were authorized by the hospital staff. I can assure you, we're okay.

The guard went inside and came back out after ten minutes. It's okay, he said, waving them through.

When the soccer coach and the science teacher stepped inside they found the nurse at the front desk, overwhelmed with patients, many of whom were black, skin darkened, mothers with children, in a state of panic.

I know the doctor here, she said, we go back a long way, I think I can find him. Okay, let's go, this is a zoo, a mess. I'm getting hungry said the young boy. The coach embraced the boy while the science teacher made a call on her cell phone. Yes, it's me, long time. That's for sure. Listen, I'm really jammed. I know, I'm downstairs on the first floor. Everybody's here to deal with the panic about the overexposure to the sun. Well, you know I'm the only one who never tans, isn't that why you liked me? Hey, what can I do for you, babe? There's a boy from my school whose mother had a heart attack, apparently, and was taken here, and now we can't find her, the reception's jammed with people. Yes, we're overwhelmed. Can you help? Of course, what's her name?

The science teacher gave the doctor the name, and four or five minutes passed while she waited to hear on the phone. Sorry, the news is bad, she didn't make it, actually, we tried to resuscitate her but the shock apparently was so severe her heart simply stopped beating. Want me to tell the boy? No, I can do that. Where is she? Taken to the morgue already, earlier on.

The doctor gave the address of the morgue. Will I see you again, honey? Maybe, maybe not, what is this plague that's out there turning everybody dark? Wish I knew, we're thinking it's because of that hole in the ozone layer, and a flareup on the sun, new sunspots appearing and blasting all this radiation at us, but right now it's all just speculation, nobody knows for sure, and we're trying to stop the panic from setting in. More folks are dying from shock than anything else.

When she told the boy he broke into tears. With a father off in a distant land fighting some distant war and now his mother dead, he had no one to turn to. There were no aunts or uncles living nearby, and he had no brothers or sisters.

What do we do now?

The soccer coach said, Let's head out of the city, up to the mountains until this blows over, I have a cabin in the mountains and we can stay there.

We should stop at the boy's house and pack up. That's a good idea. There's no reason to stick around.

At the house the boy gathered some clothes while the soccer coach and the schoolteacher yanked items out of the refrigerator and found blankets and other supplies.

On television the voices of the government were urging calm, and a state of emergency had been declared. People were told to stay home and not risk any exposure to the sun; the rays were deemed deadly, even though there were only deaths reported from families whose members had died of shock. Doctors were saying there was no current damage to the skin, but all known sunscreens were deemed unsafe. The beaches were deserted, towns shuttered, and those venturing outside were wearing clothes that bound them completely, blocking out any sun. A report appeared about a school of elementary students, the one where the teachers taught, describing the catastrophic event of having half the children turn coal black after a soccer match. The school was now classified as a disaster area, and the streets were cordoned off, teams of hazardous materials crews had appeared and were detoxifying the entire school.

I'm glad we got out when we did. Me too. This is madness.

Meanwhile the boy had collected some items of clothing and stuffed them into his backpack.

There isn't anyone you can call? No? What about the neighbors? They don't know me. I don't belong here because I'm black.

The soccer coach noticed his arms and legs darkening if he had just a limited exposure to the sun, darkening even further than the day before. How do you explain this? But the science teacher's skin had not been affected at all. I'm a medical miracle, that's how I got to know the doctor. He wanted to know if I was just a freak or something, he ran some tests on me and concluded I had a special gene of some kind that prevented my skin from burning in the sun or getting a tan, so here I am. If this thing continues, they'll be coming after you, trying to find a remedy to this climatic disaster. That's what I'm thinking, are you ready?

The boy had packed his bags and was prepared to take off with the two teachers. They were going to drive to the mountains where the coach had a small cabin hidden away in a canyon.

The doctor at the hospital had been working for three days and two nights straight without going home. The hospital had been flooded with patients seeking treatment or some type of medication to deal with the pervasive transformations in skin color, especially among the young. He had found many of these kids to be healthy, without damage or deterioration in their bodies, aside from the simple darkening of skin. Mothers were hysterical, often in varying states of shock, upon seeing their children's altered skin color. What's causing this, he heard the urgent voices, demanding immediate answers. Is it temporary or permanent? The questions had been repeated ad infinitum, and he had no answers, at least he was sure about. There were no skin lesions, no abrasions, no burns except mild ones. The hysteria was simply about the change in color. In the meantime he had neglected his own family, calling in every few hours to check in on circumstances at home. His wife's voice was panicked: You've got to come home now. Okay, okay, I'll be there, I love you. I love you too. Stay calm. I can't. What is it? I don't want to say over the phone, I'm worried, really worried. This will pass. When? It's some kind of sunspot, or hole in the ozone, they're saying, and it's unleashed these rays, which aren't harmful, really, if you're careful. I can't go out. Okay, I'm on my way. Hurry.

When he got home he found his wife in tears, sobbing with her head in her hands. I can't bear to look at her. What is it? Tell me. See for yourself.

His twin daughters were sitting in the family room, watching TV. One had turned dark chocolate in color while the other was white. She got out in the sun, said the twins' mother. It's my fault, I should have never let her go outside. I kept the other inside. The doctor tried to comfort his wife as best he could.

The twins seemed quiet, eyes riveted to the tube. Each seemed to accept the other.

I've finished Dogg's book, the part he wanted me to see, but I still don't know what to make of it. Maybe it'll happen one day in Kahleefornia like he says it will, a gigantic hole in the ozone layer, a crater in the sky, opening wide and far, and swallowing up all those milky white bodies lying happily on the beach. There'll be a darkening of the skin, a mellowing of the spirit, as we all become more like each other, without difference in color, all races on Earth blending together into one, like mountain streams and rivers flowing into a sea of common humanity. Maybe that's good, maybe not. I can't get a fix on Dogg, what he's really thinking or saying. He's writing fiction, right? Or is it all *true*, all what's coming, and we've got to be prepared for it? He's pointing the way.

I do know when I was in Iraq, back then, back when I still had pieces of my body and gulliver still intact, I saw us as liberators, as white folks coming to change the ways and means of the Arab, which was wrong, seeing Arabs as darker than us, *lesser* folks, when the truth was, *we* were the lesser ones, the savage and primitive beasts of prey, the invaders with no business in that ancient Muslim land, no understanding of its culture and history. What we discovered over there blew us away too. Sure, some Arabs were darker than us, but many were fair skinned with blue eyes and brown or blonde hair. Go figure. So maybe Dogg, the holy warrior, man of God, is saying, Hey, the day of reckoning is coming, payback time for past sins and transgressions. Be prepared.

🍂

HEY, MATES, GOOD NEWS from Kamal!

Word comes that our wine, which got labeled "Kamal's Shiraz," harvested from the grapes in John Hart's field, scored big at a wine tasting, a whopping 93 points. "Can you believe it?" Kamal tells me in Reception and asks me to pass on the news.

"It was at that critics' tasting at the Sage Mill Winery I told you about. The owner calls me and says, 'You've got to come, Kamal. Your wine is ready for its first pouring from the barrel, and I've brought a crew of local wine critics in for the occasion. I've already had a taste of it myself, and I can tell you, hands down, this is one of the most extraordinary Shirazes I've ever had. How did you guys do it? How did you grow those grapes? One day you'll have to tell me your secret, no?'

"By the time I get there early Saturday afternoon, the tasting is already in progress. I'm late. Downstairs in the basement, I find the owner and his son doing the pouring. On the table are a dozen bottles of wine, all reds, I'm told, including the one you guys produced from your hard work. It's a blind tasting, with each bottle covered by a special silver wrapping to cover its maker and producer. This is amazing, truly amazing because the time for tasting has come so soon; your Shiraz grapes must have been hearty and bold, ripening early enough to pour.

"The owner and his son sit me down next to a couple of wine critics from the local newspaper; they've been tasting, all right, each getting a nose of the wine in a glass, then methodically letting it touch every nook and cranny of the palate, their heads pulled straight back, eyes rolling, then gargling and spitting out the contents into a bowl, and moving on to the next wine after rinsing their mouths clean with water. It's an ancient cleansing ritual performed with consummate skill and ease by this class of wine tasters. The critics grade each wine on a card, awarding points in different categories. The owner is beaming; he peeks over their shoulders and sees the high marks the critics are giving to his wines. At the end of the afternoon, the results are tallied up and we've won the highest scores for the Shiraz! I don't believe it myself, but then I do believe it. Why not?

"Next time, I promise to smuggle in for you guys a case or two of the Shiraz you made. It has healing properties, especially for wounded warriors from the war, I'm sure of that. Everybody who has tasted it has been saying it relieves the aches and pains of life itself."

ONE DAY JOHN HART WAVES to me and says, "Hey, Spoon, do me a favor, buddy. Open this manila envelope."

"Sure thing, boss."

He's got this big, fat envelope tucked under his arm and from the looks of the return address it's from Washington, from the big boys at the Pentagon.

"You have a problem with envelopes, Hart man?"

"Yep. After my ex-wife served me the divorce papers in a manila envelope, I've been real touchy about opening up such things," he says. "Maybe this time she's taken out a huge life insurance policy on me, and is looking to collect a bundle real soon."

"This one's got something inside," I tell him, rubbing the contents between my thumb and forefinger. "I can feel it."

When I pry open the envelope and reach inside, out pops a medal. It's the Purple Heart, along with a sheet of paper that appears to be a citation with John Hart's name on it. "Congrats, man!" I say. "You've been awarded the Purple Heart. Says so right here. 'For being wounded or killed in any action against an enemy of the United States or as a result of an act of any such enemy or opposing armed forces.' "

"For what? Don't remember."

"C'mon, Hart man, you *must* remember something. Want me to read it?"

"No, not now, I'm feeling dog-tired."

"At least let me pin the medal on your breast pocket. Okay? You can be cool with that, can't you?"

After I pin the medal on his chest, a couple of guys come

over to check out the scene and congratulate John Hart. He still doesn't want to talk about whatever he did over there in Iraq to win a Purple Heart, the most coveted award for a soldier to win in the call of duty and service. I slip the citation back into the envelope and for the next couple of days stay close to the man to see if he'll talk about his experiences, about what went down. As it turns out, Kamal gets him to do it for me.

Kamal shows up one day at the hospital, and he's also got a big, fat manila envelope for John Hart. I get close to both men in Reception and overhear bits of their conversation, which, given the snooping that's been going on in the hospital, no doubt everybody else is going to overhear as well.

"John, I have something that was sent to me from people you knew in Iraq," says Kamal. "People you were close to, people whose lives you saved."

"Don't believe it. How'd they find me?"

"They found you through me. You forget, I still have my connections," says Kamal, lifting an eyebrow. "Once they found out I knew where you were, in St. Richard's, they wanted me to bring this message and this photograph to you."

Now my curiosity is really aroused. John Hart saved people's lives, I'm thinking. It figures, but how did it happen?

All of a sudden, when Kamal shows him the photograph, this large panoramic shot with dozens of people crammed together in a village house with a garden behind them and a young couple with three kids standing in front of them, John Hart breaks down and weeps. Tears stream down his cheeks; he's really feeling it, all right. Then his head rears back, he calms down, and studies the details of the photograph.

"They attached a note," says Kamal, "the people in the

village. It's in Arabic. Want me to translate for you?"

"Okay, sure," says John Hart, his eyes still mesmerized by the images of the people in the photograph.

"The note says, 'This is from Hassan-Ali and Zahra. We want to thank you, Captain Hart, for saving our village and for saving our lives on the wedding day. If you had not done what you did, we would not be here today. Zahra gave birth to three boys, triplets, a year after our wedding. You can see them in the photograph. We're hoping you didn't mind that we have named our firstborn son after you. He is named John Hart. We wanted to name all three boys John Hart but we thought it might be confusing. We hope you are well and recovering from your wounds. We heard you were badly wounded in the war. We pray for you every day to get better and heal.

'With God's love, prayers, and great thanks for all that you've done for us and for those in our village. One day, we hope that you will come again to our village in a time of peace and be our guest for as long as you like. You are always welcome to our home, Captain Hart. Signed Hassan-Ali and Zahra, and our boys.' "

Kamal's reading of the letter rallies the whole crew from the hospital around John Hart. Nurse Mee, Nurse Judy, Ricki, Doc Shuffle, Chico, the Lone Ranger and Tonto, Major Pink, Dogg and others all appear in Reception, eager to hear more.

"We'll be very honored, Captain Hart," says Kamal in his most persuasive voice, "to hear from your own lips what happened in that village, even though I've heard first-hand from the family in the village about your act of heroism."

John Hart, looking a bit embarrassed, yet feeling the warmth and camaraderie of his mates, then speaks as he has never spoken before:

"I'm with my platoon near Naseriyeh in southern Iraq in one of the outlying villages. It's a Saturday, the weather's turned cool. For days, I've been huddling with the village elders, trying to convince them that we'll provide security for the villagers if there are any mortar attacks from al-Qaeda or other insurgents. We're here to help and we're committed to rebuilding the parts of the village that have been destroyed in the war. Trust us, I tell them. The elders sit with us, legs crossed, on the floor, covered with carpets, old men with flowing white hair and white beards. This is tribal culture, we must be savvy in its ways in order to win hearts and minds. I assure the elders we'll bring in trucks with food, with medical supplies, we'll treat the wounded, but you must trust us. I place my fist across my chest. The elders sit with AK-47s leaning against their shoulders, rounds of ammunition strapped across their chests. It's a war of attrition, of resolve, of slow and painful negotiation with all factions, all players at the table.

"I'm a firefighter by training in the National Guard and now I'm here fighting the biggest blaze of my life. How do you deal with that? Somehow, some way, I'm able to gain their trust; they keep looking me in the eye, probing my character, my integrity as a man worthy of their trust. These are all Shi'a and they've suffered in one way or another under Saddam, under the tyranny of his rule, and in some respects, they see us as no different. We've imposed our will on them, our brute force, our might; they want to know what they can get from us without giving up too much. I understand that, I'm cool with it, human nature and all.

"We reach a point in our negotiations where it suddenly

turns, turns for the better in my view. They tell me one of the village elders is having a wedding next Friday for his oldest son; hundreds of people will attend, a very special occasion. Can we provide security for that day? If so, if we can deliver, we'll have their trust from then on. Of course, I reply through my interpreter. You can count on us.

"So we have a deal; it appears workable. I contact my commanding officers and explain the situation: do I have buy-in? Will you go along with the necessary backup? They tell me I'll have to wait for approval. I need at least another platoon, maybe two or three, boots on the ground, plus aerial support. I keep having to justify my actions, the why and the wherefore of it. I'm told it's only a small village of farmers, goat herders, camel raisers, poor people. How do they fit in the overall scheme of things? What's their strategic importance? All this explaining I have to do. Until I get final approval.

"I should've known it wouldn't be this easy. On the day of the wedding, a week later, the villagers gather together in the public square. It's early morning and I've got my boys securing the perimeter of the village, lying on rooftops and squeezed into alleys between buildings. We're fearful of a Sunni reprisal, an attack on the Shi'a; it seems unlikely but since the events of Samarra, the torching of the golden dome and declaration of war against the Shi'a by certain elements of the Sunni population, we've got to be wary of any situation that might exacerbate the already delicate balance of power between both factions. I promised to secure the village during the wedding; the elders might have sensed imminent danger. There would be the firing of weapons, the discharge of guns in celebration of the young couple's tying the knot. There could be a disturbance, an infiltration of Sunni militants into the wedding party and an opening of fire in an act of defiance and tribal revenge for God only knew what injustice, perceived or otherwise, had occurred.

"My instincts tell me to hang tight, cover my ass, and trust no one. An hour before the wedding ceremony, I get the shock of my life. A couple of Shi'a guards, armed with AK-47s, have grabbed another man from the crowd and brought him to my attention. The man babbles incoherently. He has been beaten by his captors. The Shi'a guards had spotted him being paid by a known Sunni insurgent, and got him, with threats of execution, to cough up the truth. It's a plot, the guards tell me, and all hell is going to break loose. When the wedding couple say their vows and a hundred shots are fired in the air, our planes are going to swoop and rain the wedding party with an aerial assault the likes of which nobody had seen before because certain houses in the village are filled with armed al-Qaida militants, jihadis, insurgents of every stripe and color, and we, our coalition forces, are going to take them out.

"None of this is true, of course. The houses are all occupied by Shi'a, friendly to us, whose trust we have earned. The insurgent Sunni had got wind of the situation, and misinformed Command. An attack on this village by us will be seen as a monstrous betrayal, a lesson to all Shi'a never to trust the Americans. That's how I read the situation an hour before the wedding.

"They tell me, hey, they've already painted the target, and if it includes the boys in my platoon, so be it. *Death to all Americans by their own hand!*

"When I radio Command I get a runaround. I'm told to move

my troops out of the theater, and then reprimanded for not having done so earlier. But I was never informed. Never told. Events have changed on the ground, I say. We've got the Sunni spy in custody, the one who gave false information to fool us into believing al-Qaida and the insurgents have safe houses in the villages. Command says, I don't believe you. I say, but we've interrogated him. He says, interrogations don't work.

"Then I go ballistic, I threaten the commanding officer that if he does not stop the order to attack the village, I will personally come to his house and kill him with my bare hands. I will have no hesitation in doing do, I tell him. I have evidence that this is a Sunni plot to destroy all trust we have worked to build up with the Shi'a, that a village wedding is symbolic and could cause a dramatic change in our struggle to win hearts and minds. He listens but says nothing. I repeat again that if he does not stop the order, I will retreat my men and then I will personally slit his throat.

"He says, I'll see what I can do.

"That's not good enough, I tell him. I want you to take action now and stop any aerial assault.

"He does and the wedding goes on without a hitch. The villagers fire their weapons into the air, in a burst and rain of bullets that make me think of the Fourth of July. Afterward, the elders come and shake my hand, embrace me and my troops. We have earned their trust in a situation that easily could have been catastrophic."

Kamal and the rest of the crew fall silent; nobody knows what to say. Then Kamal steps forward and adds a philosophical touch: "Ironic, isn't it, Captain Hart? Thousands of miles away in a foreign land named Iraq, with an ancient culture so different from your own, with people speaking another language, a family unknown to you that you saved has honored you— honored you by naming their firstborn son after you, believing that you are worthy as a man and a hero forever in their eyes, while in your own land, here at home, your own wife and kids have chosen to discard and abandon you because they don't see you as a man anymore. You're disfigured for good now. You're just a metalhead!"

"Wise words, indeed," says Ricki. "I'm in *total* agreement."

Part V

I AM ONE LUCKY CAMPER. My new hand arrived this morning and the docs are working madly to get it attached properly to the stump of my left arm. I am feeling no pain, even though they've got some heavy duty needles stuck in my elbow. It's what they call an endoskeletal prosthetic hand, with batteries inside and sensors that detect when your arm muscles bend and move and contract. Amazing stuff. The sensors transform the signal into electric power and let you move a motor in your hand, so the docs tell me. My new fingers expand enough to give the illusion they're real, sort of. The hand itself is made of soft silicone, and it's almost lifelike in appearance, with fake hair and popping veins and nails that could pass for human. I like my new hand, like it a lot. Can I sleep with it on? I ask the docs. Take a shower? Yes, to both questions.

The doc is friendly, in a talkative mood. I've never seen him before; he must be a new arrival. Out of curiosity I ask about the lab experiments going on behind the scenes. He laughs at me, this tall, lean, geeky doc with beady eyes and a hooked nose. While he works on getting my hand attached properly, he buckles over with laughter. What's so funny?

"This is the sequel," he says.

"To what?"

"PROJECT BLUEBIRD. We've come a long way, kid. And it's only the beginning, from what I can see."

"Sorry. Don't know what you're talking about."

"You mean you don't know about PROJECT BLUEBIRD?" Says the doc, hooking up the wires in my hand. "Guess it was before your time, kid. They had it all figured out back then, the boys in the Company, right after the war, around nineteen fifty-one or fifty-two, according to classified reports I came across. They recruited a bunch of us docs, like my father, to make it work, mind control experiments, the stuff of fiction and wicked dreams. The real progress came when they began to perfect the methods for inducing false memories. You know how that can mess you up, kid? Amnesia, hypnosis, getting dosed on heavy quantities of LSD, even using electric shocks to alter personality—all of it went down without a peep from the Brass, all of it developed and nurtured by the boys in the Company. And the research's been going on ever since, one war after another, more soldiers coming home with mental disorders, prime candidates for more research. It's a wonder you have anything left in your head at all. False memories are the big thing, because it's like taking an eraser to your brain. You get scrubbed clean of things that might bother you, like committing crimes of war, torture, any kind of brutality you'd find uncomfortable telling your friends and family at home. Violence gets the job done, agreed? Who wants to remember what they've done?"

"But I remember," I tell him. "Not a day passes when I don't think about it. I did some pretty baddiwad things over there. Nothing to be proud of."

"That's your problem, Spoon, why you're here, right? Hey, don't worry, be happy. They'll have you wiped clean in no time. The tools are in place; we've got the procedures down to a science. You won't feel a thing. Trust me."

"That's what I'm afraid of."

"Hey, the Hendrix Treatment wasn't so bad now, was it? A little blast of rock music, good stuff from the sixties, our national anthem amped up, to keep you boys under control. Heh heh."

I didn't want to tell the doc about the earplugs Ricki had given me to block out the music and subvert the dominant control paradigm. I felt for them in my pocket with my right hand while he was still hooking up the wires in my artificial left. And once I found them, I rubbed the earplugs together. It was the best feeling I'd had in a long while.

"Have no fear, soldier," smiled the doc, finishing the job.

"Who said I did?"

"Look, you've already got a brand new hand, stronger, lighter, more powerful than the old one you had. And it feels no pain. The rest of you comes next. Ha ha."

And the man could not stop laughing, until he keeled over, cleared his throat, and abruptly left.

❧

Ricki IS TELLING ME, she won't stop talking. She's telling me about this thing called entropy and how everything in the universe moves from order to disorder, how it's increasing all the freaking time, this entropy thing. I'm beginning to grok it. The war's been going in that direction, coming apart, twisting and bending the lives of the soldiers on the ground, dislocating the locals, driving them crazy, making them fight each other. "Thing about entropy is," says Ricki, "you don't get it back.

The disintegration continues, non-stop, unabated, like a roller coaster ride in hell." She adds, "I'm a soldier of orange, and I'm trained to defend my country, but now, now, I'm a victim of entropy, like everybody else." Enough of Ricki's rant. Life is not better in orange. I need a cold shower, if I can get one, and a hot meal, if I can get one, and a visit from my dad.

❦

IT'S GONE BADDIWAD, worse than anybody expected, from what I'm picking up on the one-eyed glass monster in the Large Assembly. I mean, there are stories and images streaming by about torture and killing for its own sake among the Sunnis and Shi'a. We're hearing about ordinary people in Iraq getting their eyeballs gouged out, faces burned with acid, nails pounded into their chests, or drilled into their stomachs. Why? Hard to figure. There's been some kind of regression to barbarism, to the law of the jungle, savagery. They're coming after our soldiers, not just killing each other with death squads taking revenge or militias out of control. We're caught in the middle where nobody wants to be.

❦

GONE BADDIWAD IS RIGHT. I'm told I've got a letter waiting for me in Reception, hand-delivered, and I better come over and get it. Nobody writes to me, nobody bothers. Why should they? I'm thinking maybe it's from Leila: she's got news of a negative nature. She's heading back to Beirut at the end of the semester and never wants to see me again. Par for the course. I head for Reception and one of the nurses whom I don't recognize hands me an envelope, good-sized, chubby with papers and something else inside. I'm apprehensive. Maybe the Brass is delivering an arrest warrant, all formal and heavily documented, charging me with war crimes.

When I open the envelope I find a letter from Brianna's mother, plus a gold necklace. Shock me or what? Quickly I scan the contents of the letter, still puzzled by why Brianna's mother would be writing to me. Baddiwad news: Brianna died over the weekend in an automobile accident, my high skolliwoll sweetheart, the girl who came viddying for me one day. Now she's gone and her mother is writing to me that Brianna really liked me and wanted to viddy me again, even though she sensed we weren't quite made for each other. So her mother is giving me a gold necklace Brianna wore almost every day as a kind of remembrance. I'm balling up with tears as I read the letter. It's an omen, sure enough, of more baddiwad things to come.

🍃🍂

SHE'S RIGHT UP ON TOP of the building. How she got up there nobody knows. The sky's blue, cloudless. The air fresh and damp. Perfect. When I look up I see her there, perched on the edge, a bird out of her cage, flapping her wings. I can't make out what Ricki's saying but she's saying something, all right. Her wings are fluttering in the light breeze. A crowd has gathered below, heads arched back to witness the spectacle. It's too late, I'm telling myself.

In a moment she's soaring through the sky, her wings outstretched, a swan dive to the bottom. Never seen anything like it. I'm trying to stop it with all the psychic energy I've got. I'll push her back up, I'll catch her in my arms and cushion the blow of her landing, if it comes to that. But she hits the ground hard, falling six, seven, eight, ten stories to her death.

❦

I'M IN A BADDIWAD FUNK after Ricki's death. Everybody's got it, a wicked virus. I'm coughing and spitting up blood orange. The neurons that once told my left hand what to do are in a frenzy too, worked up by Ricki's death, knowing something's missing, somebody I love gone. I'll kill myself too. I can't go on under the circumstances.

After Ricki's death there's a deep sadness around camp. I'm feeling it among my colleagues. Am I to blame? Did she stop taking her meds because of me and my Shiraz? Nobody's pointing the finger at me, not yet at least, but I can see it coming. In camp the docs and nurses are whispering under their breath. There's all this talk about taking responsibility, about accountability, which is another way of saying they're looking for a fall guy. That'll be me, I figure.

In the afternoon one of the orderlies comes into my room carrying a big cardboard box about three feet long and half a foot wide. It's got my name on it, he says, handing it to me. Ricki left it for you. I hold it as best I can with one hand. It's got some weight. I'm looking at Ricki's scrawl on the front of the brown cardboard: *one day you'll need this. love, Ricki.*

"Aren't you going to open it?"

He looks at me with a curious smile, as if he's the one who wants to see what's inside.

"No."

"C'mon. You ain't curious, man?"

"Later."

"Whatever."

And he hops out of my room. Truth is, I am curious. But I'll open it like Ricki says when I need it. That day will come, sure enough, and I'll be ready. You can bet on it.

❦

NEXT THING I KNOW Major Pink isn't around. When I ask about him, Doc Queenie tells me, "Pink is in for repairs." He's in the Body and Repair Shop, I'm thinking, getting a lube job or a tuneup, or a fender bender fixed. Why else wouldn't we viddy him? Maybe I'm a little too naïve and trusting for my own good. Pink's on the mend: it's a good sign. And then I spot the clown with Pink. The two of them are walking into the Small Assembly and Pink looks different, somehow; he's moving stiffly, hardly bending his arms, and his face is frozen. Those cherubic cheeks, the wicked, devilish smile, the cocky attitude—all gone. He's like a windup doll of some kind, half man, half robot. What have they done to him? I run toward the two of them in the Small Assembly, but the clown motions to me to back off, move away. He's got a nasty look on his face, even though he's supposed to look happy and cheery, all bright-eyed and friendly, as if everything's just hunky-dory. Fascism comes with a big smile on its face, I remember John Hart telling me. And suddenly they're gone, disappearing down the hall to the elevator. I sneak behind them and catch a glimpse of the buttons the clown presses and the identity card he uses to gain access. When I reach the elevator, I viddy the lights but there are no floor numbers visible. Either they've gone to the top or the bottom of the compound. I'm thinking it's the bottom, down below, where all the trucks have been making deliveries of equipment, down to the Rat Labs, as Ricki called them. They're using Pink for some kind of physical or mental experiments. I go wild for a moment, pressing all the buttons on the elevator, one after another, trying to figure out what's going on.

❦

I'M RUNNING OUT THERE in the cold morning light. I had a hunch John Wu would try something; it was too good to last, his having awakened like that and having started to talk again. Which he did.

The tanks and bulldozers and monster earth-moving machines are roaring through the field, through St. Richard's Annex, chewing up everything in sight. John Wu is standing in front of the long row of Shiraz vines, motionless, his gulliver thrown back, his body erect. I viddy the same man who stood in front of the tanks in Tiananmen Square, defiantly refusing to move as the tanks lined up ready to run him down and tried to maneuver around him, but he kept moving in front of them. But John Wu doesn't move at all; he's like a statue, fixed in time. Somebody ran out in front of that lone Chinese dissenter and yanked him away from it all. I'm going to do the same thing for John Wu. I've got to run faster but my knees are wobbly, unstable. I'm not in good shape, slow as a snail. I yell at John Wu to get out of the way. The words burn in the pit of my lungs.

The machines keep coming at him.

I stumble and fall, pull myself up and look. John Wu is being crushed by the machines. They plow him into the ground as the vines are destroyed by the grinding wheels. I shout, "No! No! No!" But nobody's paying any attention. Nobody hears me.

The vineyard is gone and John Wu has been buried deep down in it.

❧

NOW WE'RE HEARING the hospital is under new management. What's going on? Nurse Mee has been fired; Doc Queenie, the best doc in the world, has been placed on administrative leave. They're doing some housecleaning, a reshuffling of the deck, and I don't like it. The big bronze statue of Chief Bromden out in the front lobby has been removed, hauled away in pieces, crushed to the ground, like Saddam's statue in Firdos Square. Doc Shuffle, the three-hundred-pound elephant, absent-minded, never around, a slacker if there ever was one, is in charge; he barks orders at everybody. Yes, I've got my new left hand and it's functioning well, enabling me to grip items like cups and glasses of water, even knives and forks at the dinner table, which I hadn't been able to do before. M'kay, I'm eternally grateful to the docs for that. How can I ever repay them? St. Richard's has been good to me, but things are spinning out of control. John Hart is next. I haven't seen him for three days; maybe he was crushed out in the field like John Wu, but I doubt it.

What do they want with John Hart?

HOW'D HE FIND ME? What does he want? My gulliver was spinning with questions when I was told that Peter Krill from the *Times* was waiting in Reception to talk to me. If there was ever a time to put up a smokescreen, to lie through my zoobies as necessary for my own self-preservation, it was now. He was coming to viddy me, he had an appointment; small matter. Peter Krill, the reporter embedded with us in Ramadi, was going to expose the hell out of me to the higher-ups. I'm finished, I kept thinking to myself. How do I get out of this?

Nurse Judy came to fetch me. "Can't you tell him I have no comment?" I tell her as she drags me out of the large assembly room and down the hall to Reception. "Tell him to go away. What part of no comment does he not understand?"

"Spoon, you're a crybaby. Grow up," she barks at me. "What have you got to be afraid of?"

"Everything."

"He's here to write an article for the *Times*, telling readers about all the good things we're doing here in the hospital. That's what you'll tell him, won't you?"

"Of course, you bet. I'll sing your praises, too. You're the best nurse on the planet. I'm comfortable with the party line. For sure."

"That's what I like to hear," she smiles at me, then winks.

Peter Krill is at Reception, reaching out to greet me and shake my right hand. I've wrapped the phantom left one behind my back; I'm embarrassed. He pats me on the back and says, "Good to see you, man. You remember me, don't you? I lived with you and your platoon, off and on, for weeks at a time.

Sorry to see what's happened. Are you in recovery?"

"Yes and no. I mean, am I getting better? Well, a little, though the ringing in my gulliver is worse than ever. They got me loaded up with medication, every painkiller in the book. Also, meds to prevent seizures, which could be fatal. It's going to be a long road to recovery."

"Any regrets?"

"Not a one. I served my country proud. What brings you here?"

We walk into the visitors' room, me and this tall, lanky reporter from the *Times*, who looks to be in his early thirties, with an aquiline nose and thin wire-rim glasses that droop down below the bridge. He's sporting a dark, three-day stubble, roguish in his swagger, confident, all the things I'd like to be but never will. The man has an air of righteousness about him and wears his conscience on his sleeve. When he turns and lifts his arm in the air, I can viddy that conscience chomping at the bit, ready to bite and take me down for all I've done wrong. We sit down on a couch at the far end, out of earshot, although I'm convinced we're being videotaped by the cameras lodged in the four corners of the room. I better watch what I say and try to fluff every answer.

"Let me get some things straight right up front, you dig?" he says in a gruff voice. "I'm not here to talk about what happened in Ramadi. You know what happened, and I'm piecing together the threads of the story. It's pretty grim, from what I can determine so far. I've got no bias. Trust me, man. I'm not out to get you, so don't be paranoid. The military's been pretty tight-lipped, as I figured they would be. You may have some testifying to do and I hope you come clean, for yourself and for your mates."

I breathe a little slower, trying to figure out Krill's game. He wants to win my trust; that much is obvious. There's something else on his mind. He's using Ramadi as a pretext. "So what else is it that you want, Krill?"

"You're not off the hook." He smiles at me. "Ramadi may come back to haunt you and the events that went down over there won't be forgotten."

"You've said your piece, man. Now what is it?"

At this point he scratches something in his reporter's notebook: I know we're being watched and recorded, he writes. Call me at this number and tell me what's really going on in this so-called hospital. I've heard of experiments. That's the story.

Meanwhile, Krill chats up a storm: "They're doing great things here, aren't they? Fixing up all you wounded soldiers, a lot of repair work on damaged body parts. True heroes of the war, all of you, and the nurses and doctors doing the healing. It's a terrific story, and my editor at the *Times* will want to know all the details, you dig?"

After a half hour of mindless chatter in which I sing a happy tune and do a dance at the charity ball, he gets up and shakes my hand. "Mr. Witherspoon, you've given me a lot of valuable insights into the workings of this great hospital, this outstanding compound. I thank you, sir. Don't hesitate to call. I'm on my way."

And soon enough, he's out the door. I've got the phone number on the piece of paper he gave me, out of view from the cameras. It's twisting in the palm of my hand, and it's soaked in sweat and blood and tears.

NEXT ONE TO GO IS CHICO. He's the one I least expected, but I viddy him in the morning coming towards me while I'm having breakfast in Mess. He looks disoriented, confused, wobbly, which is unusual because he's so tuned into the wiring of the compound; he's the keeper of the electrical circuits, the geek who knows how it's all hooked up. I'm munching on burnt toast and tasteless scrambled eggs, washing it down with a glass of cold milk. I've got a ring of milk around my mouth in the shape of a white, curly moustache, just like you viddy in those telly commercials and that makes him chuckle. "Spoon," he says, stuttering a bit, as if he's fighting some meds about to take hold of his nervous system. "Glad I found you. Listen, listen carefully. They're doing something to me, more mind control stuff. I may be finished, man, but here, here's the device. Use it if you want to get out. You know what it is and what it does."

"Sure, the remote control for the sound blaster."

I'm thinking about the earplugs Ricki gave me to stop the music from driving me bonkers.

"You got it, man. Flip this switch to turn it on and off, if you get into trouble. Take my security card too. You'll get entry to anywhere in the compound."

"What about you, Chico?"

Just at that moment the clown appears and drags Chico away. I've got the remote in my pocket and I fumble with the buttons. By accident, I press one and the music comes on. Quickly, I press another button and it shuts off.

FROM THE NIGHT BEFORE I've got my bag of surviving vines, which I've hidden under my bed. Time is short now, I can feel them getting ready to come for me at any moment. I rip open the box Ricki left for me, long strips of cardboard strewn across my room. Inside is a foldup bicycle, along with a little pump for the tires. The thing snaps into place and I adjust the seat and handlebars. The tires need air, so the pump is really handy. How did Ricki know? In a short while I'm sitting on it, balancing as best I can with my artificial left hand and missing right eye.

Can I ride out of here on a foldup bicycle? Have I lost my gulliver completely?

❧

NOW I'M ON THE CELL PHONE to Leila and she promises to help. She's setting it up for me, planning the details of my escape.

"You need to wear a disguise, Jeremy," she says. "So you won't be recognized."

"Like what?"

"I'm thinking, you could dress up like that clown I saw last time I visited."

"Bozo the Clown?"

"Why not?"

I could wear that clown costume, she tells me, apply a little clown makeup, some dabs of white cream on my face and attach a poppy-red ping-pong ball to my nose, and nobody would know it was me when I walked out the door, would they? Leila's got quite an imagination, all right, yet her plan is just crazy enough to work.

"Okay, look for a clown when you come to retrieve me from St. Richard's," I tell her, doubtful we'll ever get that far. "At least we'll get a laugh out of the whole thing."

"C'mon, get *serious*, Jeremy," she barks at me. "This isn't child's play. There's a lot at risk."

So I'm trying to remember: didn't Chico tell me the clown outfit was stored in a locker at the far end of the Body and Repair Shop? I'll have to sneak in there fast when Bozo's not around and grab it.

Leila promises to get Ricki's friend Masood to help as well. He'll pick me up in the van down the street, circumventing Security, playing a cool game with the boys who patrol the perimeter, the boys he knows well. Meanwhile, I've got to see what they've done in the Lab downstairs, many levels below.

My backpack is filled with the videotapes, tiny cartridges of digital images and movies Chico shot, along with a copy of Dogg's apocalyptic novel, some memorabilia from Ricki, and of course the rootstocks I managed to retrieve from the Shiraz vines before they were all crushed. Masood's agreed to pick me up at 19.33, as he's scouted the compound and knows when the security guards are on break and how to fool the others who are still working. My cheap analog watch, which I'd won in a card game, can't let me down; it has to be ticking out the right time, or else I'll be dead meat. That gives me about an hour to take care of business and set the stage for my escape.

I sneak out through the back room of the kitchen when the cooks are on break. Nobody's seen me and I follow the path down a long corridor to the elevator. When I get there I'm sweating like a pig, drenched to the bone. I must be dripping with cold sweat, trying to get the last round of drugs out of my system. The elevator door opens and I press the buttons that take me down three levels; it's Dante's inferno, all right. Welcome, my friends. Have we got some surprises for you. Be sure to stay a while.

Stepping out of the elevator, I viddy the Lab ahead and run Chico's security card through the reader at the door. For a moment, I almost panic because if the card doesn't work, I'm sure to get caught. The signals will be transmitted upstairs to Security and I'll be hosed. They'll send the bruisers down to catch me and haul my ass away. But amazingly enough, the door to the Lab swings right open.

I can't believe my eyes when I get inside. There's John Hart, hanging by a hook on the wall, his arms stretched wide, his legs pulled and tied together, crucified. I doubt he could still be alive, but I catch a faint hint of breathing. Am I hallucinating? They've changed his body into some unrecognizable shape, adding metal parts to his arms and legs, face and chest. He's half-man, half-machine. John Wu's lying on a table next to him, or at least what's left of the man after being crushed by the giant earthmover two days before. He too is half-man, half-machine. Behind them I catch sight of a dozen other metalheads who've disappeared, including the Lone Ranger and Tonto, Major Pink, and Dogg, whose muscled body and shining black dome has been chopped up into various pieces as if the docs are planning some kind of reassembly or twisted robotic creation. Ricki is untouched, as her body's been flattened already from the leap off the rooftop; somehow, her face glows angelically, and I realize if it weren't for her and her connection to Masood, I'd have no chance of ever getting out of here. I kiss her face, which has been bent way out of shape and close her eyes. The docs who work in the Lab, in the Body and Repair Shop, must be on some kind of vacation, because nobody's around.

Out of a darkened corner steps Skank.

❧

"I KILLED THEM ALL," SKANK says. "I pushed Ricki off the roof, I stabbed John Hart in the back a dozen times and watched him bleed to death, I electrocuted Pink and watched him twist in the wind until his body burned to a crisp. And that was only the beginning. I'm telling you I got my orders. I'm only doing my job. Dogg was a tough one, tougher than I expected. He fought me like a true soldier, he fought hard. We went at each other with samurai swords, and even though he got cut real baddiwad, as you'd say, and his blood splattered all over the lab—the docs were watching, cheering me on—he fought me to the bitter end. Chico was easy, I'm letting you know, because you're next, Spoon. You're easy. You stood there in Ramadi while I did my job on that Iraqi girl, you and your buddy, and you did nothing to stop me. That's how I know you're easy. Figures, doesn't it? Spoon, come closer and I'll make it fast. You'll die quick, I promise you. There's honor in death as a soldier. You've sacrificed for your country. You've done the right thing, haven't you?"

"Skank, you're a freak of nature." I circle around the table, never for a moment taking my eye off this monster I helped create.

"Said I'd make it quick."

Skank snarls and laughs and exhales fire. He breathes his own fumes, getting high on them. Behind him I viddy the collected bodies of Ricki, John Hart, Pink, Dogg, John Wu and now Chico, all of them objects of experimentation, in various stages of disassembly, ready to be moved into glass cases stacked against the lab walls. Skank twirls a samurai sword like a baton and now he moves in for the kill. He says something to me and I viddy his lips moving, but I can't hear a word because the earplugs Ricki gave me have blocked all sound. In my pocket I've got the switch Chico left and I flip it on. The music blasts away, Jimi Hendrix doing his heavy metal rendition of the "The Star-Spangled Banner," the one the docs have been using for crowd control with us metalheads. Skank feels the shock waves of the amplified music ripping through the lab. His body is jittery and he can't hold the sword in his hands. The decibel level climbs higher and higher, the glass cases behind my fallen comrades break open, and Skank writhes in pain, hands slammed against his gulliver and his ears. I stand there for the longest time until I take his samurai sword away from him and with a big swing, the biggest swing of my life, chop off his gulliver. It bounces on the floor and rolls down the aisle of the lab table like a bowling ball until it bumps into the wall and explodes into a thousand pieces, metal and neurons coming apart.

❦

I GO TO THE LOCKER at the far end of the Body and Repair Shop. The clown outfit is there. It's inflatable, so the arms and legs and chest will balloon up if I put it on. I also find a jar of whiteface and red paint and a good nose the size of a ping-pong ball. "You gotta work fast, man," I remember Chico telling me. "Security pops in and out at random, but they won't say nothing if you're dressed up as the Clown. They're in on it. What could be easier than having Bozo the Clown lead people to the lab? Who'd put up any resistance?"

He was right, of course. And that's what I'm counting on: a quick exit wearing the clown outfit and a face smeared with paint and a big red nose. So I slap on the paint and pull the clown outfit over my body. The thing is made of plastic, like an inflatable inner tube you'd viddy kids using in a swimming pool. I have to yank and pull and stretch the plastic to fit the contours of my body, and make sure my own plastic hand won't look too conspicuous. I mean, the clock is ticking. Once I get it on and make it fit and look in the mirror inside the locker, I break out for a moment in a shriek of laughter. This is what it takes to get out of here, I think to myself. Use the enemy's weapons of war against the enemy. In the locker I find a big white Macy's shopping bag, which the clown had probably filled with kids' toys and other goodies. That bag is a gift from heaven, as I am able to drop my backpack (with my own goodies) right into it and pull it up by the handles.

As I get ready to leave, I take one last look at John Hart. They kept him alive for their Project Bluebird experiments; he's still breathing somewhat, as if he's in a state of deep sleep. This is not right. John Hart is in pain from the look on his face; I know that look, know it well, know how much he'd suffered after losing his family and how much he'd given to the rest of us in the course of his days in the zone, in the ward, in the company. He deserves better. I have no idea what to do exactly. I can't do anything for him; his body almost half-made of some titanium-composite alloy, his eyes shut tight yet moving rapidly underneath, as if he's dreaming, dreaming of a time when he would be greeted with a hero's welcome from the war, wearing his Purple Heart, being driven through the streets along with the rest of his buddies while crowds cheer them on and shower them with confetti and fresh flowers. I decide to pull the plug.

Nearby I find the device that controls the electric currents flowing through his body and shut it down. I have a hunch they'll come after me for that, they'll know I've seen what was going on in the lab, they'll get rid of me like they got rid of Pink, Ricki, Chico and the others. On the outside, if I say anything, I'll be discredited and if they catch me, I'll be brought to trial in a military court and held in detention for years before I'm dumped in a trashcan somewhere by the side of an unknown road. Now I am messing with their instruments, and without doubt, John Hart is one of those instruments, a new breed of soldier and warrior, machinelike, robotic, like the Governor himself, and the price for exposure will be my life now, not later, not after I've gone public with my revelations. I'm sending a message by shutting down John Hart: I'm saying, "Hey, I'm a fighter, I've got your number. You did wrong and you'll pay a price."

I give John Hart a kiss on the forehead as I viddy his body come to a halt, the eyes stop flickering, the lips and mouth stop breathing. John Hart is gone. It's better this way, much better for him, for all of us.

When I check my watch I spot the hour as exactly 19.23. I've got time to get out in my Bozo the Clown uniform with my goods in a Macy's shopping bag. The elevator takes me upstairs to the kitchen and from there I stroll into my room and get the bicycle Ricki gave me. Nobody messes with a clown on a bicycle, do they? In the front lobby I wave to the staff at the front desk, manned at that hour by a woman substituting for the regular guard, and she waves back at me. Perhaps she knows what is going on, perhaps she doesn't. I am out the door and pedaling down the street to the entrance of St. Richard's. Security takes one look at me and smiles and waves me through. A clown on a bicycle, who could be more innocent? I wave back and do a little wheely, spinning in a figure eight for fun. Two streets away, I race the bike, pedaling like a madman until I catch up with Masood's van. There it is, waiting for me. I start to turn back and viddy over my shoulder, but Masood yells, "C'mon, dude. It's time."

The door slams and Masood speeds off. I'm in denial, I'm mumbling something like, "I made it. Can't believe it. I'm stoked."

"Hey, you did it, you did it," says Masood as he races the engine along the backstreets away from the hospital.

"Did I?"

"Ricki always said you would. Told me that a couple of times, she did, and hey, now you're here in my van, a hero of the war against the war. We know what's been going on at St. Richard's for a long time. You guys deserved better. I'm a soldier too."

"Ricki told me she was with you in Kabul."

"Bagram, actually," he says. "I'm going to miss her."

"I took care of some business with the soldier who pushed

her off the roof."

"Now you're talking."

"He's no more. And he had it coming."

"You look ridiculous in that clown outfit," Masood says, holding back a spit of laughter.

"Masood, listen up. This is serious. If anything happens to me, you've got to take these tapes in my Macy's bag to the *Times* reporter, Peter Krill, the guy I talked to. Got that? Krill. He's going to expose the whole mess in the labs at St. Richard's. Told me so, promised. And the vines from Shiraz, I've got those too, and if they're planted right again, they'll make you a rich man. Trust me, I tasted the results before they bulldozed the field. They've got healing powers."

"Understood," says Masood.

I let out a big sigh of relief, as my gulliver throbs with pain. "Where we going?"

"To the mountains, my friend. Afghans love the mountains and can hide in them forever. You need to cool out, man," he says with a wink and a smile, like my Dad. "Leila will meet us there, as will her father."

"Awesome."

"She likes you, Spoon."

"Hey, I'm getting hot in this clown suit. I got to take it off."

"Sit tight. Leave it to me," he says, grinning.

In the back of the van, Masood has a couple of giant spools of string and two big kites in the shape of a lion. He tells me about how he and his brother used to fly kites in Kabul when they were kids until the Taliban cracked down, and if there was one thing kids liked to do, as a show of freedom and independence, it was to fly kites. The cool drafts of mountain air allowed the kites to soar high as the moon.

After an hour of driving, winding our way above the jagged ridge behind the hospital along back roads without a single beam of headlights, bouncing up and down in the van, Masood finally pulls over and we get out. No idea where we are. The lights of the city flicker below. My clown outfit feels silly and I want nothing more than to strip it off my body and throw the dang thing away. Taking it off, I am ready to discard the pieces, but Masood has other plans. He feels the contours of the material, finding pockets where it can still be inflated like a balloon, and with a lungful of air blows hard on the tubes and bubble rings that make up the outfit. When he's inflated the Bozo the Clown outfit, Masood connects the kite string and the two lion-shaped kites to the clown and waits for a gust of wind. Sure enough, after a few minutes, a big gust appears along the hills above the city, and the creatures are airborne. I watch them climb higher and higher into the twilight sky, as Masood steers the kite string in the direction of a skolliwoll in the hillside below. "The kids should see this, even if it's still night," he says. "The neighbors around the school will see it first."

"Won't they know our position, then?"

"Hope they do, because we won't be here for long. Besides, when the clown and the lions descend from the heavens, they will hit the schoolyard and the kids will find them and reporters will come out and report the event on the morning news. Everybody will ask many questions of a philosophical nature, as we've asked in Afghanistan throughout our long history. Questions of meaning. Questions of justice. The truth will come out. It always does. You catch my drift, don't you?"

"Yes, I catch your drift."

About Tom Maremaa:

Tom Maremaa is a novelist, journalist and playwright whose works of fiction and non-fiction have dared to take on the most challenging themes of the times. His writing has appeared in a broad range of publications, including *The New York Times Magazine* and *Rolling Stone*. A graduate of Dartmouth College, he has studied at the University of Zurich, Switzerland, and worked on advanced degrees in literature at the University of California, Berkeley.